"I think you don't want to like me."

Cole stilled. His first impulse was to deny it. His second was to admire Taylor's instincts. His third was to back up fast. "I have nothing against you."

"But..."

"No 'but.'"

"Liar." She spoke softly, holding his gaze in a way that warned him not to underestimate her.

She could have easily moved away, but she didn't. Her expression shifted ever so slightly, then she reached up to touch his face as he'd touched hers in the SUV the day she'd taken him to the doctor.

She leaned closer. "If we kiss—"

He didn't wait for her to finish the sentence, didn't wait for her to set goals or outline parameters. He made the "if" a reality, sliding his hand around the back of her neck as he brought his mouth down to hers.

Taylor met him halfway.

She was dynamite in his hands.

Dear Reader,

There's nothing I love more than an opposites-attract story, so when I wrote *Wrangling the Rancher*, I decided to triple down. My hero and heroine, Cole and Taylor, have opposite temperaments, lifestyles and goals. He's an introvert; she's an extrovert. He wants to work alone; she wants to be part of a major business. He's a country guy; she's a city girl.

I had so much fun writing these two. After working on a guest ranch where he catered to the whims of the often-rich patrons, all Cole wants is to be left alone to farm. After being laid off from her firm, all Taylor wants is another high-powered job. Instead she ends up on her grandfather's Montana farm, which Cole is leasing. Cole has to deal with yet another privileged city girl and Taylor has to work on the farm to earn her keep. In the process, both Taylor and Cole learn a lot—about themselves.

I hope you enjoy *Wrangling the Rancher*. If so, please check out the other books in The Brodys of Lightning Creek miniseries, as well as *All for a Cowboy*, in which Cole is first introduced. I also hope you'll stop by my website, jeanniewatt.com.

Thank you, and happy reading!

Jeannie

JEANNIE WATT

Wrangling the Rancher

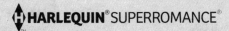

Recycling programs
for this product may
not exist in your area.

ISBN-13: 978-0-373-64041-6

Wrangling the Rancher

Copyright © 2017 by Jeannie Steinman

Printed in U.S.A.

www.Harlequin.com

Jeannie Watt lives on a small hay-and-cattle ranch in Montana's beautiful Madison Valley with her husband, dogs and cat, horses and ponies. When she's not writing or dealing with animal matters, Jeannie likes to work on her almost-finished house (is a house ever really done?), horseback ride, read and sew.

Books by Jeannie Watt

HARLEQUIN SUPERROMANCE

The Brodys of Lightning Creek

To Tempt a Cowgirl
To Kiss a Cowgirl
To Court a Cowgirl
Molly's Mr. Wrong

The Montana Way

Once a Champion
Cowgirl in High Heels
All for a Cowboy

HARLEQUIN WESTERN ROMANCE

Montana Bull Riders

The Bull Rider Meets His Match
The Bull Rider's Homecoming
A Bull Rider to Depend On

Visit the Author Profile page at Harlequin.com for more titles.

To Rachel, my new daughter.

CHAPTER ONE

FAILURE DID NOT sit well with Taylor Evans, which was why she did her best to never fail. And she hadn't...until exactly eight weeks ago today.

Taylor lifted her glass of chardonnay and sipped. It was her last bottle, and she needed to savor every drop. She also needed the false courage if she was going to call her grandfather and confess that she, who'd nailed down full-ride scholarships and been courted by three different companies upon graduating, had been a victim of downsizing—and no one else would hire her.

The truth hurt.

Okay, maybe she'd been a bit vain, thinking she was so integral to her organization that it couldn't function without her—but in defense of her vanity, how many eighty-hour weeks had she worked for the good of the company? Her cheeks grew warm as she recalled laughing when, after rumors of the reduction in force had started, a colleague stated that everyone was replaceable. She'd rather vehemently disagreed. There were several people in the company, including herself, who were so necessary to the operation that even in this economic climate, they *had* to be safe. It would be detrimental to the company to cut them loose.

She'd been the first person let go. When she'd been called into her supervisor's office, she'd assumed that it was to let her in on what was about to happen so that she could help shore things up once the layoffs were announced. Uh…no. Don Erickson had thanked her for her dedication to the company, for the extra time she'd spent working on projects, and then directed her to the next office to discuss severance and the fate of her excellent insurance plan.

Taylor never, ever wanted to experience that cold, numb feeling again. Or to do the walk of shame back to her office, where her belongings had already been packed into a cardboard box. The bus ride home had been hell—until the anger hit. She *would* get another job with a competing company, and then who would be sorry?

Those thoughts had sustained her for almost two weeks. But when the rent and utilities came due and she hadn't been called for even one interview, when the headhunters had remained frustratingly unhelpful, she'd known a moment of panic—very similar to what she was feeling now.

Call. Get it over with. Tell Grandpa the truth.

But since Taylor had rarely given her paternal grandfather anything but good news, this was not an easy call. She needed his help.

No. She needed to be bailed out.

Taylor's throat started to tighten up as she reached for her phone, which was wedged under sixteen pounds of sleeping cat. Max twitched an ear as she tugged the phone out from under him, and then he stretched out to his full length. Telling herself that Max was a big eater so she needed help as much for him as for herself, Taylor dialed her grandfather's number. It rang four times, which was the norm.

"Hello?"

Taylor froze at the unfamiliar voice, deep and somehow commanding, then held her phone out to check the number. The word *Grandpa* showed on her screen. Right number. Wrong voice. "Uh…hi. I'm trying to reach Karl Evans."

"He doesn't live here."

Taylor blinked. "What?"

"He's been gone for almost three weeks."

"Who are you?"

"I'm renting his place."

"Your name."

There was a brief pause, and then the man said, "What's *your* name?"

None of your business. Taylor bit her lip. In this day and age, how much information could she afford to give? "Could you please give me the number where I can reach Karl?"

"You don't have his cell number?"

"My g—Karl doesn't have a cell phone."

"He does now."

That was news. "Then give me the number."

"Tell me who you are—"

"I'm his granddaughter."

"Then why don't you know that your grandfather has a cell phone or that he moved?"

"I—"

"Tell you what…you leave your name and number, and I'll pass along the message."

Taylor pressed her lips together to keep from telling this guy what he could do with his suggestion. "Tell my grandfather to call me. I'm his only granddaughter, so there shouldn't be any mix-ups."

"That," the man said softly, "doesn't speak well for you."

Then, before she could suggest he take a flying leap, he ended the call, leaving Taylor staring at her phone.

What had just happened?

And more important, who was this guy and where was her grandfather?

KARL EVANS WAS not answering either his cell phone or his landline. Cole was just about to call his sister when his phone rang in his hand.

"Is everything okay?" Karl asked instead of saying hello. "You called three times."

"Everything is fine, except that I just talked to someone who is probably your granddaughter, but I didn't give her your phone number."

"Why not?"

"Because she didn't know you'd moved almost a month ago." In his mind, relatives should know that kind of thing. "Which made me wonder if she was who she said she was."

"You think young women are in the habit of stalking me?"

"In this day and age you can't be too careful. Anyway, I told her I'd give you the message."

"I've been meaning to call her. I figured

I had time because she hasn't been in touch since Christmas."

Five months. That was a while to go without contact.

"How's everything else?" Karl asked.

"I'm inspecting the equipment. So far, so good." If all went well, he'd be seeding the fields he'd leased from Karl along with the house.

"Keep me in the loop. I miss the place. And if Taylor calls again, give her my cell number."

"Are you going to call her?" Personal question, but Cole was curious.

"I'll try. A lot of the time she doesn't answer but gets back to me when she can. I've kind of given up on being the one to reach out."

That smacked of family drama, and Cole was not a fan. He'd had enough family drama, which was why he was no longer managing the family ranch turned guest ranch. Drama sucked. "Gotcha."

"She's a good kid, Cole. Just busy."

Too busy to answer her grandpa's calls? That kind of behavior was flat-out wrong, but again, family drama. Cole wasn't going to get sucked in.

"Any other relatives I should know about?"

"Taylor's the only one other than my sister, and you know her."

"That I do. Tell her hi for me." Cole hung up and then crossed the kitchen to the cast-iron pan he'd left heating on the stove. Karl had moved only a small amount of stuff to Dillon because he didn't believe the move was permanent. That meant the kitchen was still well stocked with pots and pans and cooking needs. As near as Cole could tell from what was left behind, Karl was probably closer to camping than actually occupying his new home next door to his sister while she dealt with her husband's death. Whatever, Cole had the farmhouse until Karl decided to move back to Gavin, which made life easier on him. When he'd left the family guest ranch after the last blowup with Miranda, his crazed step-aunt, he hadn't owned much in the way of house gear. He'd lived in what was essentially a larger guest cabin on the ranch property, ate most of his meals in the guest facility and cooked as little as possible. He planned to continue that trend, but he could handle steak and store-bought macaroni salad.

He'd just set his steak square in the middle of the cast-iron pans when he heard a knock on the door. Surprised, since the farm didn't get that many visitors, he crossed the kitchen, opened the door and found himself face-to-face with two deputy sheriffs.

"Hi. Can I help you?"

One of them met and held his gaze while the other looked past him into the room as if expecting to see a trail of blood or stacks of stolen cash.

"We're checking on the whereabouts of Karl Evans. Are you Mr. Evans?"

Karl's granddaughter had called the cops on him. Well, at least she cared enough to do that—or maybe she didn't take kindly to not getting what she wanted. Whatever the circumstances, Cole was fairly certain that the deputies knew that he wasn't Mr. Evans. "I'm Cole Bryan. I'm leasing the place from Mr. Evans."

"Do you know how to get in contact with Mr. Evans?"

"Just got off the phone with him, so I can give you his number and his sister's number in Dillon. Neither of them are any good at answering their phones, but you might get lucky."

Neither deputy smiled. "Do you have identification?"

Cole jerked his head toward his wallet that

sat next to his keys and sunglasses at the end of the counter. "I do."

"Get it, please."

Cole did as the other deputy dialed the number Cole had provided and stepped out onto the porch. The first deputy inspected Cole's driver's license.

"You're close to expiration."

"Yes."

He held the license out and waited for his partner to finish his call. Cole was thankful that the guy had gotten through on the first try.

"Do you have a copy of the lease agreement?"

Cole glanced over his shoulder at his steak that was starting to snap and pop in the hot skillet. "I do. Can I turn that down?" The deputy nodded and Cole stepped over to the stove and flipped the steak, the cop watching him as if he was going to use the piece of meat as a defensive weapon.

After he carefully put down the fork, he pulled the towel off his shoulder just as the second deputy came back into the kitchen and gave his partner a nod.

"Do you need to see a copy of the lease?" Cole asked.

The deputy who'd made the phone call shook

his head. "Mr. Evans established his identity as well as yours to my satisfaction."

"Good to know."

"Sorry to intrude on your evening."

"Not a problem," Cole said. "I, uh, assume that you got a call from Mr. Evans's granddaughter?"

"She requested a wellness check, yes."

"Sorry you guys had to come all this way."

"It's our job."

It was also a five-mile drive that could have been avoided if…whatever her name was…had called her grandfather every now and again. Cole went back to the steak. Hopefully the granddaughter was now satisfied that Karl was safe and sound. She'd call him more often after this scare, and all would be well.

TAYLOR WAS HOT—the angry kind. Nothing like driving through the night for eight hours, stewing, to get the blood up. By the time she hit the Montana border, she'd reached a decision. She was going to see her grandfather, but first she was stopping by his farm to meet the guy who'd somehow talked him into leasing not only the land, but his house. That didn't sit right with her.

In fact, there wasn't one thing about this situation that seemed right. Her grandfather had sworn he would never leave his farm. Taylor's aunt had tried to get him to Dillon more than once, but he always refused. He'd even gone so far as to say that he wanted to be buried on his property. Yet he had left.

Taylor yawned as she pulled off the freeway onto the state highway toward the Eagle Valley. Dawn was breaking. She'd driven all night, but all night was a way of life with her. It was how she'd become the most productive member of her team. And where had that gotten her?

Her throat started to tighten. Eight weeks in and she still felt hurt, betrayed—thoroughly screwed. The business part of her said that it wasn't personal.

That didn't change the fact that it felt personal.

Her job had been such a huge part of her life, her identity—it was impossible not to take the layoff personally…especially when they'd kept Kent McCoy on staff. The guy did half the work she did…

Stop.

Taylor did her best, although *stop* was not a well-used word in her vocabulary. If anything, she pressed on, but for the last eight weeks she'd been pressing against…nothing. It was exhausting having no goals other than getting a job. Not that she hadn't thrown herself into it—

Stop.

Think about something else…like where you're going to live once you give up your apartment.

Arrow to the heart, that. Her lease, which was up in three weeks, didn't allow subletting, and she certainly couldn't afford her rent without a job. The rock and the hard place were squeezing her hard, and the thing that most angered her was that for her entire life she'd plotted and planned so that these kinds of things would never happen.

Argh.

Taylor slapped a hand on the steering wheel. What she needed was someone to talk to. Most of her Seattle friends were work acquaintances who now seemed to feel totally awkward around her. Her real friends—Roselyn and Katherine—lived on the other side of the country, working in fields unrelated to her own. She hadn't talked to them since the layoff. It wasn't solely a case of not wanting to share her misery—Taylor didn't know how to share misery.

As she approached the Eagle Valley, nestled in the hollow of three mountain ranges, she felt a growing sense of relief. She was entering a world where no one knew that she'd failed, that her careful life plans had gone askew.

Sweet anonymity.

Even the guy she was stopping to see shouldn't know what was going on, since she'd only recently—as in nine short hours ago—confessed to her grandfather that for the past eight weeks she'd been unemployed and had no real prospects.

She needed to temporarily lower her standards, find a job—any job—so that she didn't have a big hole in her résumé. She could deal with a short-term cut in pay and fewer benefits, but if she did that, she had to come up with a way to cover expenses until she once again landed a job in her field. That was where Karl came in. She was going to have to ask her grandfather for a helping hand—no easy task when she'd been incommunicado for months. She'd been bad. And karma had bitten her on the ass.

COLE WAS DRINKING coffee when he heard the sound of an engine. He glanced at the clock and frowned. Five thirty seemed too early for a social call…maybe the granddaughter had once again called law enforcement?

He set down his cup and went to the door. The car that pulled up was low slung and sexy. A thin coat of dust covered the silver finish, but it was obviously a car that had been well cared for. The woman climbing out of the driver's side wasn't that tall, but she was fit and sexy, with long blond hair pulled into a low ponytail. She perfectly matched the vehicle. She shaded her eyes when she caught sight of him standing on the porch watching her, then squared her shoulders and marched toward him.

The granddaughter. This should prove interesting.

Cole leaned against the newel post and waited. A guy didn't spend eight years working on a guest ranch without learning to both read people and deal with them effectively. His read on this woman—simmering anger. Frustration. In need of a scapegoat for…something. No question as to whom that scapegoat might be.

"Hi," he said when she hit the end of the broken-up walkway. "Want some coffee?"

Her brisk steps slowed. "You don't know who I am."

"I'm guessing that you're Karl's granddaughter." He jerked his head toward the house. "I just made a fresh pot." He ran his gaze over her. "You look like you could use a cup."

Her bemused expression changed to something approaching a smirk. "Thanks."

With a casual shrug, he opened the door. The woman hesitated, then preceded him into the house.

"It hasn't changed much," she said.

"Why would I change it?"

She shot him a look. "I guess that depends on why you're here."

He went into the kitchen and pulled a second mug down from the cupboard near the sink. "I'm here to farm. Why are you here?"

"I'm here to check on the welfare of my grandfather."

"Then," he asked in a reasonable voice before handing her the steaming cup, "why aren't you in Dillon, where your grandfather is?"

Her eyes narrowed ever so slightly. A woman used to playing her hand carefully. "That is where I'm going."

"Just thought you'd stop by? Introduce yourself?" He set down his own coffee and held out a hand. "Cole Bryan."

She returned his handshake. "Taylor Evans."

"Nice to meet you, Taylor. And thanks for calling the deputies on me."

"I didn't have a lot of choice. My aunt wouldn't answer her phone, you answered my grandfather's phone and I was concerned."

"Yet not concerned enough to keep closer tabs on your grandfather over the past several months."

Her expression iced over. "There were circumstances at play there." He lifted his eyebrows politely. "*Private* circumstances," she said in a tone indicating that if he had any manners at all, he would stop the questions now.

He took a sip of coffee. If she thought cool superiority was going to make him remember his place, she had another think coming. Having worked with a master of the freeze strategy—his step-aunt and former boss, Miranda Bryan—she was going to have to do better than this.

"Are you satisfied now that all is well?"

He could tell the word *no* teetered on the edge of her lips, but she caught it before it fell. "I guess I don't understand why you're here in the house. My grandfather said he doesn't think he'll be in Dillon for all that long."

"Maybe your grandfather is lonely and would like a roommate."

"My grandfather is not the roommate kind."

"You sound certain."

"I know him."

"Yet you didn't know he moved."

Irritation flashed across her features. "Would you stop bringing that up?"

"Sorry." He set down his cup and gripped the counter on each side of his hips. "Maybe if you told me why you're here, I can help you out, and then you can continue on to Dillon."

She smiled tightly. "Yes. What a great idea. I wanted to meet you."

"Make sure I was on the up-and-up?"

"My grandfather always leased his land to the neighbor to farm. I understand the neighbor is still farming."

"Are you suggesting that I might have persuaded him to lease to me instead?"

She gave a small shrug. "The thought crossed my mind."

"I did."

Her eyes widened, and it took her a few seconds to say, "How long have you known my grandfather?"

"He used to cowboy with my grandfather a long time ago."

"Karl never was a cowboy."

Cole said nothing. He wasn't going to argue the point.

Her eyebrows drew together. "Not that I knew of anyway."

A slight step back, which gave her a couple of points in his book. "I didn't use any kind of coercion. I just…talked to him."

"And ended up living in his house. Using his stuff."

"I'm a smooth talker." And since her suspicions—her attitude, really—was starting to piss him off, he saw no reason to mention that Karl had been concerned about the place being broken into during his absence. Having Cole living there solved a problem for both of them, but too much explaining was only going to give her more to latch onto. He glanced past Taylor to the teapot-shaped clock on the wall. "I also have to get to work."

"You have a job?"

"Yes," he said in his patient guest-ranch-manager voice. "I'm a farmer."

CHAPTER TWO

TAYLOR DIDN'T KNOW what to think when she got back into her car. The guy didn't seem like a criminal, but he also wasn't giving her much to work with as far as making judgments about him. Even though he was a self-proclaimed farmer, she'd bet money that he'd worked in a people-related field in the past. And he was ridiculously good-looking. His face was all angles and hollows, and she was fairly certain if he smiled, he'd have some decent creases down his cheeks. Dark hair, light green eyes…a lot to like there. Physically. Having worked with her fair share of attractive guys who turned out to be control freaks and douchebags, she no longer judged the book by the cover. A pretty face didn't mean the guy wasn't taking advantage of Karl. She'd ask her grandfather a few more questions once she got to Dillon.

And then she'd sleep. Night was her time, but it had been a long, rainy drive and she was exhausted. She hoped Karl had a spare room so she could crash.

As it turned out, there was no spare room in either place. Her grandfather and great-aunt shared a small duplex—two one bedroom apartments separated by a garage. Elise's side was crammed with bric-a-brac, pillows, afghans and all manner of comfortable, cushy things, while on Karl's side furniture was scarce, consisting of a secondhand dinette set, one leather recliner and a hundred-year-old sofa that he proclaimed to be "just fine." And it was, if you didn't mind sinking to the floor when you sat down. Taylor had a feeling that her grandfather didn't much care—he had his recliner and very few visitors, since his friends all lived in the Eagle Valley.

After visiting with Elise, Taylor and her grandfather went through the connecting garage to his side of the duplex. Taylor took the cup of tea he brewed, then made the mistake of sitting on the sofa. She sank low and her knees felt like they were close to her chin. There was no end table to put her cup on, so she was stuck sitting there until she either finished her tea or asked her grandfather for help. She decided to finish her tea. Karl settled in his recliner, and if he noticed her discomfort, he said nothing.

"I'm sorry I didn't call," she said. "I was in a work frenzy from Christmas until two months ago—"

"And then you got fired."

"Laid off, Grandpa." She stared down into her tea. Laid off. Let go. It was the same as being terminated but didn't carry quite as much stigma. "I didn't see it coming."

"After working those crazy hours, I imagine not."

"Yeah."

"So now what, Tay?"

"I've been looking for work in Seattle, and it seems that everyone is tightening their belts."

"Have you looked elsewhere?"

"The Bay Area, Portland. Spokane." But it was going to be expensive to relocate.

"Nothing?" He gave her a look that made her feel as if she needed to say something to convince him that she wasn't slacking. Or maybe to convince herself she wasn't slacking.

"Not even an interview. The most I've gotten is 'we'll keep your name on file.'" She took a sip of tea and managed not to choke. Her grandfather made tea the way other people made coffee. "I just need to be patient. Times are tough, but I know if I persevere, I'll nail something down." Another small sip, because small was all she could handle. "Something even better than what I had."

"And for now?" Her grandfather gave her a shrewd look. "Because it appears that this might take some time."

Taylor balanced her cup on her knee. "Yes. About that…if I don't get an infusion of cash soon, I'll lose my apartment."

"I can see that happening," Karl agreed, which was *not* the response she'd expected.

"I was on a waiting list for almost two years to get into that building." Downtown, close to the Wharf. She loved it so much—she felt a rush of gratefulness every time she looked out over the city and the Sound from her bedroom window—and since there was only one bedroom, a roommate wasn't possible.

"Things change, Tay."

Things change? Yes, they did, but if one was resourceful, they didn't have to change too much.

"I don't want to lose my apartment, and I don't want to drain my savings keeping it."

"What about your car?"

"I can't get out of it what I put into it, but yes, I will sell it…if I have to."

Karl leaned forward in his chair. "What do you want, Taylor? From me, I mean."

She felt her cheeks go warm. He was gently chiding her. They'd been super close at one time, and he'd always been her biggest cheerleader. But when she went to work for Stratford, she'd started logging the crazy hours, living a crazy life. When she wasn't working or trying to cram some relaxation in—which was almost as exhausting as working—she was sleeping. She'd meant to call, truly she had.

But she hadn't.

"The money you lent me to go to school?" Which she'd paid back in full over a year ago. "Could I borrow it again?"

Her grandfather's mouth tightened, and the fact that he didn't instantly say yes made her stomach knot up. "I put it into some long-term funds. If I pull it out now, I'm going to lose money."

Taylor's heart sank. It was his money, of course, but…honestly? She'd figured borrowing the money back would be a slam dunk and mutually beneficial. Karl would get interest. She'd get a safety net, which, properly managed, would help her if she took one of many much-lower-paying jobs she'd been looking at to tide her over.

Damn, damn, damn.

She tried to work up a smile but had a feeling it looked kind of sick, because she felt kind of sick. "I understand. And…this isn't the only reason I'm here."

"I know."

"I didn't want to tell you that I was a loser."

"Everyone loses, Tay."

Not her. Not often, at least, and never in such a huge way.

"I guess." She pressed her lips together. She couldn't stomach any more of the strong tea, which meant she was stuck on the sofa forever or until Karl relieved her of the cup.

She looked at her grandfather then and wondered, judging from the way he was looking at her, if he wanted her trapped there.

"You know," he said slowly, "you're welcome to live on the farm if you want and look for a job locally to tide you over. I'd invite you to live here, but I don't have much room."

That was an understatement. His house had one bedroom, one bath, a tiny kitchen and a living room. It was truly a single-person house.

"I…uh…" *Would hate so much to lose my place.* The apartment was even more of a symbol of what she'd accomplished than her car. And her mother was so ridiculously proud of her. "I appreciate it, Grandpa. But what about that guy living there?"

"There's always the bunkhouse."

"It needs work."

"You're resourceful."

"Me?" Taylor almost spilled her tea. And she felt ridiculously betrayed. "But—"

"He's paid a month's rent on the house. It wouldn't be right to ask him to move mid-month."

"Just one month?"

"I'm keeping my options open, so we have a month-to-month deal." He glanced through the window at his sister's place next door. "I don't know how long I'll be here. Elise is doing better, but she hates being alone."

"How long has he been on the farm?"

Her grandfather did a mental calculation. "Two weeks yesterday."

Which meant his month in the house was already halfway over. That made Taylor feel better. To a degree.

Move to the farm…? As much as she appreciated the offer, it was a crazy idea. More than that, it was demoralizing.

"The thing is…if I move to the Eagle Valley—" and somehow keep it quiet from her mother "—it feels like I'm giving up."

"Why? Aren't there jobs in your field in Missoula or Bozeman?"

"I'm sure there are." In her field, but probably not at her level.

"They may not be as prestigious," her grandfather said, reading her thoughts, "but they'd pay the bills."

"Yes." Hard to argue with that. Taylor took a drink of tea, trying to tamp down the feeling that she was being sucked into a farm vortex. She'd never once considered moving two states away from her beloved Seattle, or settling in a rural area, but the idea made an awful kind of sense. Her living expenses would be slashed to next to nothing. She was having no luck in her job search, and each day brought with it a deeper sense of desperation and depression. If something didn't change soon, she'd have to sell her car, find a new living situation—one that involved roommates—and she'd have to pass a credit check to join a lease and...

"The farm would be a stopgap, until you get back on your feet."

When had she become so transparent?

Taylor moistened her lips. "How would your tenant take the news if I decided to move in?"

"Cole's a decent guy."

If you say so... "What made you decide to

rent the house to him instead of just leaving it closed up?"

"I didn't want it broken into while I'm gone, and with him living there, he can farm more easily."

He could also farm easily from the bunkhouse. He was a farm guy. Probably used to roughing it.

"How well do you know him?"

"Not all that well personally. His grandfather and I were friends."

"Did you…cowboy together?"

Karl gave her a surprised look. "I wasn't much of a cowboy, but I worked for two summers on the Bryan family ranch near Missoula. It's a guest ranch now. Cole used to manage it until he got his fill."

So he had indeed worked in a people-related field. Her radar was working.

"And did you approach him, or did he approach you?"

"He approached me." One corner of Karl's mouth quirked up. "Are you concerned about him taking advantage of me?"

"It happens."

"Yes. But not in this case."

"You're sure? You said you didn't know him well, yet you let him live there with all your stuff."

"Yep. Because you know what? I'm a grown-up and I can make those kinds of decisions for myself."

"I didn't mean…" Taylor stopped. Regrouped. "I apologize, Grandpa. It startled me when he answered the phone yesterday. We got off on the wrong foot."

"He's a good kid."

Kid. Ha. He was a grown man. Good-looking. Sexy. But an interloper all the same.

"Do you want to move onto the farm?"

Did she? Was she that desperate? Totally, or she wouldn't be here right now. She'd started the drive because she was concerned about her grandfather and felt guilty for not being in closer contact, but she'd also needed to talk to him about a way out. The way she'd thought was so reasonable—the loan—wasn't going to work, so that meant she needed to get tough and try something new.

And lose her beautiful apartment.

"I might. If things don't change fast."

"How soon would they have to change?"

Considering what she was paying for rent and utilities…?

"Yesterday."

"I'll call Cole."

COLE CAME IN from the machine shed, wiping his hands on his bandanna for want of anything better. He was going to have to buy some shop towels. Karl had the equipment he needed to farm the place, but it could all use some work. This first part of the season, he was going to have to rely on baling wire and his wits to get things done on schedule, but after that he'd have time to fix things right.

He found himself smiling as he mounted the porch steps. Broken-down equipment? Not a problem. Not enough time to do what he needed to do? He could deal. Not having to saddle yet another horse for yet another clueless individual who wanted to know whether they provided spurs for the mounts? Priceless.

Cole didn't hate people, but he was damned tired of dealing with them. Smiling and pretending all was well when it wasn't. And dealing with Miranda…if he never saw the woman again, it would be too soon. His cousin Jordan had managed to get the better of her a few years ago, wrestling his small mountain ranch out of her grasp. Cole wished he could do the same with his family ranch, but his dad and his late uncle—Miranda's husband—had gone into business together and Miranda had slowly but surely taken over both properties. Cole had worked for her until he couldn't handle it one second longer.

Still, even though he'd wanted to tell the wicked witch exactly what he thought of her, he'd parted on relatively good terms. He still had stock in the family ranch and didn't want to make things any more impossible than they already were.

But he never wanted to saddle anyone's horse again—ever.

The landline rang as he walked in the door, and he couldn't help but flash on the last call he'd taken on that phone. Karl's granddaughter was a piece of work. Kick-ass gorgeous, but as far as attitude went…well, *princess* wasn't the right word. *Privileged.* Yes. She was privileged and obviously not all that good at hearing the word *no*.

Cole pulled the phone off the hook on the fifth ring. "Hello."

"Shouldn't you be making hay when the sun shines?"

Cole grinned at Karl's dry tone. "Trying. I have some work to do on the equipment, but everything should be up and running—" for a while anyway "—in short order."

"Good to hear. Hey…my granddaughter stopped by the farm, right?"

"On her way down to see you. She sure didn't waste any time getting over here after I answered your phone."

"Yeah. She's going through a rough patch. I, uh, told her she could move onto the ranch. I know you're renting the house, but the bunkhouse is there, and I figured you guys wouldn't be falling all over each other, in the different buildings, so…"

"Hey. You're doing me a favor letting me rent the house." The bunkhouse was in pretty good shape. It wasn't that different from the bunkhouses on the guest ranch, minus all the cutesy cowboy shit. "I don't mind moving."

"That makes no sense. You already have your stuff in the house. Taylor's happy to stay in the bunkhouse."

Cole scratched his head. "Are you sure about this?" Maybe he was talking about a different granddaughter. One who didn't have "pampered princess" written all over her.

"Yeah."

The sheer innocence in the guy's tone convinced him. "I don't care if she stays." Much.

"She's looking at getting work in Missoula or Bozeman, so it may not actually be that long."

"It's your place, Karl. I'm good with it."

"Thanks."

Cole hung up the phone and stood for a moment contemplating the floor. Had he been that wrong about Taylor Evans? She'd happily move into the bunkhouse?

Well, every now and again he'd read a guest wrong...but it didn't happen often—and he wasn't all that certain it had happened yesterday. Time, obviously, would tell.

He'd just started for the door when his cell phone rang. So popular today...

"Hello."

"Stop me before I kill Miranda."

He put a hand on the doorjamb and rested his forehead against his hand. "What happened, Jance?" His younger sister, Jancey, let out a long-suffering sigh.

"Just the usual bullshit. Passive-aggressive sweet stuff, followed by threatening me later."

"What happened?"

Another sigh. "She was embarrassed today because of a mishap in scheduling with some rich guests she wanted to impress, was all nicey-nice about it while the guests were there then pretty much told me that if it happened again, I was going to be demoted to kitchen work. But it wasn't my fault, it was hers."

"Quit."

"And then you'll pay for my living expenses at college, right?" Jancey had taken a year off after graduating from high school to save money for college. Cole would bet that she was counting the days until she could escape the ranch.

"I would if I could."

"I know. But beyond needing this job, I don't want to let her win."

"Are you insinuating I did?"

"No. Even if that had been your intention, it didn't work. She is still doing a slow burn over you quitting, and the beautiful part is that she can't find anyone competent to replace you."

Because no one else had enough emotional ties to the place to put up with her poor management style. Cole knew she'd already hired and fired a replacement and had tried out another, only to decide he didn't fit the bill either.

"I bet she'd make some concessions if you came back…"

"Would you wish that on me?"

"No. But I hate losing the last family on the family ranch."

"Things change, Jancey. All we can do is forge on ahead, make a new path."

"You're very philosophical today."

"I'm trying to distract you so that you don't do Miranda bodily harm. School is what? A short four months away?"

"Yeah. Something like that."

"Call anytime you need talking down," Cole said. "And if things get to the point that you can't take it anymore, this place has two bedrooms."

"If you get a knock on your door late at night, it'll be me."

"It'll be open. Just make yourself at home."

Cole hung up and slipped his phone back in his pocket. The only bad thing about leaving the guest ranch was that he was no longer there to put out the fires Miranda caused. He was so totally ready to be a farmer, ride in his tractor and ignore the world.

That might be a little harder to do if Karl's granddaughter moved into the bunkhouse, but even if she did, he didn't see her lasting too long. Women who drove classic 240Zs didn't live in old bunkhouses. She'd find another place to live, and if she didn't, well, at least he had years of experience dealing with the privileged.

CHAPTER THREE

TAYLOR WASN'T A CRIER, but her throat felt ridiculously tight as she drove across the Floating Bridge on I-90. Her cat, Max, was staying with her friend Carolyn until she could send for him, and she already missed him. Her furniture was in storage, and she'd temporarily given up the Z for a former coworker's SUV. *Temporarily* being the keyword there. She didn't like her baby being in someone else's hands, but the car didn't work in her new environment. The SUV could tow a small rental trailer with most of her essentials, and it could navigate snow if needed, but it ate gas like nobody's business. And it felt crazy to sit up so high when she was used to hugging the road. But at least she still owned her car.

Not so her beautiful apartment.

So hard to handle…

Taylor swallowed again.

She had put herself back on the building waiting list, telling herself that if she wasn't ready to rent when her name came to the top of the list again, then she was well and truly a failure. Which she wasn't. A few months—maybe a year or two—living and working in the wilds of Montana would do her good. Broaden her horizons.

Her ex-supervisor had said it would humble her, but Taylor had paid no attention. Madison said things without thinking. The woman had no filter, yet she still had a job with Stratford. She was like Kent—neither had put in as much voluntary overtime as she had.

Taylor wasn't going to think about that.

Nope. She was going to think positive thoughts—like how she was going to work her way into a position of power in a competing company and wreak some havoc on Stratford. Those were good thoughts. Satisfying thoughts.

She finally came clean with her mother, Cecilia, who hated Montana with a passion. Cecilia had moved to the farm shortly after she and Taylor's father, Tom, were married, but after the romance of rural life had worn off, she'd yearned for her old life in the city. Unfortunately, Taylor's father was as rural as her mother was urban and the two never found a middle ground. Taylor had been only five when her mother filed for divorce, packed Taylor up and moved back to Seattle. After that, it was vacations on the farm until her father passed away from a heart attack too young.

"I hope you know what you're doing," was all Cecilia had said after the confession.

"It's temporary, Mom." But even though she believed what she said, she still felt like a loser. Her mother had hammered into her over the years what a hellhole the ranch was. Yes, it was a nice place to visit, but if you tried to live there, it would eat your soul.

"I'm so sorry you've been driven to this. I'd help you out if I could, but—"

"I know." And she did. Her mother kept to a stringent budget with her artist husband of ten years in order to live in a tidy two-bedroom apartment in the heart of San Francisco's North Beach. Taylor had never once considered asking her mother for money, because she knew there wasn't any to spare.

The little trailer Taylor towed behind the SUV wobbled every now and again as the wind hit it, reminding her that she wasn't driving the Z, and then she'd slow down. There was really no hurry. She planned to spend the night in a motel in the Eagle Valley in order to avoid dealing with Cole Bryan after a long drive. She wanted to be fresh for that. They had a few issues to iron out, and she wasn't looking forward to sharing her environment with a stranger. But, as her grandfather had said, she was living rent-free and was within driving distance of job markets. Well worth having to share three hundred acres. As to who ended up in the house…well, her money was on herself.

It was almost nine o'clock when she pulled into the Eagle Valley. She debated about the mom-and-pop motel closest to the farm, then chose to drive through town to stay at the Manor Suites—a business hotel that made her feel more at home. She could grab coffee and breakfast in the lobby the next morning before heading out to the farm. It was good to be properly rested and nourished before tackling a potentially touchy situation. Cole Bryan likely wouldn't relish her being there, keeping an eye on him. But she'd be a good farm-mate to him, as long as he didn't cross her. Or try to keep her out of the house.

Taylor checked in and rolled her suitcase along the carpeted hallway to her first-floor room. Her last night of privacy. She'd assumed that she'd spend it stretched out on the bed watching bad television—which had become something of a habit since she'd been laid off—but instead she fell asleep almost instantly. She woke up a few hours later, disoriented. The lights were on and an infomercial blared away on the television. Instead of learning how a Wonder Blend could change her life, she snapped off the TV and peeled out of her clothes, crawling under the covers in her underwear. So very tired…

A car alarm outside her window brought Taylor fully upright in bed. She heard the sound of a kid's laughter, followed by a man's warning voice, and then the alarm shut off. Taylor lay back against the pillows, noting that it was daylight before snagging her phone off the nightstand and checking the time.

Eight thirty!

She practically sprang out of bed.

She never slept that late—not even when she stayed up until the early hours. Maybe it was the altitude or something. She headed to the bathroom, showered and dressed. What if that guy was out doing farm stuff by the time she arrived? She'd have to hunt him down or spend the day cooling her heels and waiting. Not acceptable.

By nine o'clock she was checked out of the hotel, her laptop case slung over her shoulder, rolling her luggage with one hand and hanging on to a much-needed cup of coffee with the other. The door had just closed behind her when she stopped dead.

Oh, no.

Taylor dropped the cup, only vaguely aware of the hot coffee splashing on her leg before she started jogging across the parking lot, her laptop beating on her hip and her suitcase bouncing wildly behind her. She skidded to a stop next to the partially open trailer door. Barely able to breathe, she pulled the heavy metal door the rest of the way open and peered inside, her stomach going tight when she saw the ransacked mess inside. Taylor blinked at the clothing carnage, then noted the neatly cut padlock lying on the ground next to her feet.

The bastards!

The trailer wasn't as full as it had been, but she had no idea what had been stolen. Everything was jumbled up, messed up, screwed up...just like her life.

"Are you okay?"

She gave a small start, then turned to see a man with a small child in his arms standing behind her. "No. I've been robbed." In Eagle Valley, Montana. It just wasn't right.

"That stinks. I'll go get the manager."

"Thank you." Taylor went to the SUV and peered in through the window, her heart pounding so hard she was having a hard time taking a full breath. Her small jewelry armoire was still in the back seat of the SUV, covered by an old blanket, along with her desktop computer and monitor, which sat on the floorboards, covered with a couple of old towels. Unfortunately, she'd put everything else—her cookware, her bedding, her clothing—in the trailer, and probably half the stuff was gone.

Welcome to Montana, Taylor.

WHAT WAS IT about balers that made them break down whenever they were most needed? In the case of Karl's old baler, it was probably a matter of the thing being almost twice as old as Cole was. He'd had the option of leasing Karl's equipment—some new, some old—or coming up with his own. He'd decided to lease, and still thought it was the best option, if he could get the baler back into commission.

After an hour-long wrestling match, he decided to break for a quick lunch, maybe with a beer chaser, then go back to it. He was on his way into the house when an SUV pulling a trailer slowed and then turned into the driveway.

His stomach tightened. She was here. His

space was officially invaded. But, as Karl said, the likelihood of her staying long was nil. How often would he see her anyway? She didn't seem to be the type to hang around when there were things to accomplish elsewhere. Bottom line, Karl was playing hardball with his granddaughter, but he loved her, and Cole was going to do whatever he could to help Karl out. He owed the guy for letting him escape from the guest ranch. Bottom line, he was going to make the best of a bad situation and hope against hope that she got a job and moved ASAP.

Taylor pulled the SUV to a stop directly in front of the barn door, thereby making access impossible, but one look at her face when she got out of the vehicle made the request to park elsewhere die on his lips.

"Are you okay?"

Her gaze snapped up to his. "No." The word dropped like a rock. A big, heavy one.

Years of working with guests had taught Cole that sometimes it was best to simply wait. Most people eventually let fly with whatever was bothering them.

"I got robbed."

His jaw dropped. "What?"

"I spent the night in a hotel in the Eagle Valley, and when I got up this morning, someone had cut the lock and gone through my stuff."

"Did they take anything?"

"I don't know. I have to go through my belongings and send a list to the sheriff's office."

"Well, that sucks." Because whoever had robbed her was probably someone passing through and she'd never get anything back. There wasn't a lot of crime in the Eagle Valley.

"Yeah, it does."

So much for climbing on his tractor and disappearing into the fields.

"Do you want some coffee or something?" She looked as if she could use a strong belt of whiskey—or, in her case, perhaps flavored vodka—and he didn't blame her.

"No. I want to unload what's left of my stuff and go through it." She gestured toward the house with her chin. "Would it be possible to just move it into the house now?"

"Why would we do that?"

"Because it makes no sense to move my stuff to the bunkhouse, then back to the house after your month of rent elapses—you only paid for one month, right?"

"Right," Cole said noncommittally. Did she really think that he was going to move to accommodate her?

"The first of the month is only a week away."

"And…?"

"Instead of moving my stuff twice and yours once, we could move mine once and yours once."

Really? For a moment, Cole considered it. A very brief moment. Whether she'd just been robbed or not, this woman needed to be taken down a peg. Or two. She was so obviously used to getting her way and telling other people how it was going to be that for once in his life, Cole wasn't going to do the good-guy thing.

"I'm not moving into the bunkhouse," he said.

"You're renting the house from month to month. After this month is over, we're switching."

He folded his arms over his chest. "No."

"My grandfather made it clear—"

"I don't think he did. Not to you anyway. He told me that his granddaughter would be in the bunkhouse until she got a job. Those exact words. *Granddaughter. Bunkhouse. Until she got a job.* Not until the month is over."

"I don't believe you."

"Call him." She reached into her pocket and pulled out her phone. "Add a little more stress to his life instead of just doing the right thing."

Her blue eyes grew fiery. Oh, yeah. Not too many people had stood up to the princess. And after years of smiling and taking guest abuse, Cole had to admit to feeling a certain amount of satisfaction at not taking it anymore.

"This is ridiculous."

"I agree. The bunkhouse is totally habitable. You'll be gone before long and I'll still be here."

Her chest rose and fell, and Cole could see that a mighty battle was waging.

He hooked a thumb in his belt loop. "I'm not leaving the house."

"Fine." She almost spat the word out. "For now." She jerked open the back door of the SUV and hauled out a suitcase, her eyes narrowing as she turned back to him. "You may not be correct when you say that you'll be here for longer than me."

As if this woman was going to stay on this farm a moment longer than she had to. But even though he believed that her threat was as empty as the silos on Karl's farm, it annoyed him. Again, he was no longer in a position where he had to put up with bullshit just because.

"You're threatening me?" he asked in a low voice. "Because I am within my rights to kick you off this property."

She stepped up to him and gave him a maddeningly innocent look. "And add stress to Karl's life? Are you sure you want to do that?"

It sucked to have his own words thrown back at him.

He leaned toward her so that they were essentially chest to chest, or chest to upper abdomen since she was about six inches shorter than him. But she spoke first. "I am not threatening you. I am grateful that you are letting me stay." *Even though it was her right.* She didn't say it, but it was written all over her face.

"Grateful in your own way."

"However," she said as if he hadn't spoken, "be clear on this...if things don't go smoothly, then we will get my grandfather involved, and I promise you I will come out on top."

He almost laughed. She didn't realize that she was currently on the receiving end of some tough love. Fine. He'd allow her the fantasy.

"All I ask is mutual respect," Cole said. He was done being treated like the help.

"Agreed." She held out a hand. Her nails were perfectly manicured. Apparently being out of work for two months didn't affect the beauty budget.

Cole took her hand and shook. "Agreed."

TAYLOR WATCHED COLE Bryan head toward the machine shed through narrowed eyes. He was more of an adversary than she'd anticipated. And he had a ridiculously nice ass. All in all, a great physical package coupled with a maddeningly stubborn personality. Well, she wasn't done yet, but she recognized when it was time to stop and regroup. Plot her strategy.

He hadn't offered to help her move her stuff into the bunkhouse, which was just as well. She needed time. Getting robbed was bad enough, but finding out that she was going to live in what was basically a primitive motel room while she conducted her job search… well, on the bright side, the circumstances would motivate her to nail something down as soon as possible.

On that positive note, she walked over to the bunkhouse and opened the door. Stale air enveloped her as she stepped inside, and she instantly crossed to the nearest window and attempted to heave it open. No luck. She went to the next. Again, nothing. Finally, the last window screeched open a crack. It would have to do.

Taylor turned to survey her new surroundings, fighting the sinking feeling in her gut.

The bunkhouse was just as she remembered it from her childhood visits, except that it seemed smaller. The single room was long and narrow, with beat-up vinyl flooring and dingy tan paint on the walls. In the corner was a bank of cupboards and a cast-iron sink that was worth a small fortune on the renovation market. She crossed the room to run a finger over the cast iron. She had a primo sink in a very sad environment. The only furniture consisted of two old bed frames, neither with mattresses, a chrome-and-enamel kitchen set that had seen better days—but would also bring decent money if Karl chose to sell it—and a single ratty, overstuffed chair that she wouldn't touch with a ten-foot pole. Who knew how many rodents were familiar with the piece?

Temporary environment. Remember that.

At the other end of the room was a small bathroom with a shower and an old toilet, plus a sink with a cheap replacement single-handle faucet that seemed out of place on the antique basin. The flooring was clean but disintegrating.

Taylor sighed as she stood in the doorway and surveyed the shower with the sorry curtain hanging limply from the cockeyed rod. She was so very much a soak-in-the-tub person.

Temporary.

Sucking in a fortifying breath, Taylor turned and headed out to the trailer to start schlepping boxes inside. It appeared she'd have to buy a mattress for the old bed frame. Or better yet...

She pulled the cell out of her pocket and dialed her grandfather's number.

"You made it okay?"

"I did. I hit a small bump at the motel I stayed at last night, but I'll fill you in on that later." Because Karl was protective and, despite what Cole might think of her, she didn't want to upset him unnecessarily. "I'm calling to ask if there's an extra mattress in your house that I could borrow while I'm in the bunkhouse."

"There's a bed in the spare room with a decent mattress, but you should clear it with Cole."

"I will. But if he has no issues, then I can tell him you have no issues either, right?"

"Right."

"Thanks, Grandpa. I'll settle in today and then start the job search tomorrow." She smiled a little. "I'll keep you posted this time. Sorry about before."

"Not a problem. Don't wear yourself out moving in."

"No worries. Thanks, Grandpa. Talk to you soon."

Her smile faded as she pocketed the phone. Twenty-four hours ago she'd said goodbye to her real life, and now she needed to adapt to her new, temporary life. She'd make the best of it, come hell, high water or a good-looking, stubborn farm-mate.

She turned toward the door, going over her schedule in her head. She'd unload the trailer, take inventory and try to figure out what was missing, make a shopping list, return the rental trailer to the local dealer, nicely ask farm guy to help her with the mattress—

The scream ripped out of her throat as a huge rodent appeared out of nowhere, almost running over her feet as it scurried toward the bathroom.

She was barely aware she was moving, but somehow she ended up outside where there were likely many more of the killer rodents. Wasting no time and barely allowing her feet to touch the ground, she made a dash for the SUV and leaped into the driver's seat, slamming the door behind her.

Her heart was hitting her ribs so hard that she couldn't catch her breath, and that was when she felt dampness on her cheeks. What had she done? What horrible thing had she done to deserve losing her apartment, being robbed and getting attacked by a rodent in less than one day's time?

A tap on the window made her jump a mile. Farm guy was there, peering into her window with a scowl on his handsome face. She took a chance and turned on the ignition so that she could roll down the window a crack.

"What?" The single word irritated her beyond belief, even as she told herself that this wasn't his fault.

"There's a rat in the bunkhouse."

"Really?"

The words that jumped to her lips at his disbelieving tone were not pretty, but Taylor managed to swallow them. "It ran in from outside."

"I'll take a look."

"Thank you," she said stiffly. He shook his head and stalked away toward the bunkhouse. Taylor rolled the window back up, leaned her head against the backrest and closed her eyes. Her lashes were wet as they hit her cheeks.

Damn.

Her new temporary life sucked.

CHAPTER FOUR

COLE WAS NOT a fan of rodents. Mice destroyed equipment, gnawed on saddles, and made their way into pantries and car engines. Pack rats did even more damage to vehicles, and heaven help you if you cornered one. Ground squirrels destroyed fields, gophers destroyed gardens. If there'd been a rodent in Taylor's bathroom, things wouldn't have ended well for Mr. Rat, but Taylor didn't have a rodent in her house. She had a young cottontail rabbit cowering behind the toilet, staring up at Cole with wide brown eyes. Cole's lips curled a little as he regarded the young bunny.

How in the hell was Karl, the most down-to-earth guy on the planet, related to a woman who mistook a rabbit for a rat? And how was he supposed to share his farm with her? Because legally it was his farm until the lease expired, which wasn't for another three years. Karl had the option of living there, but the land and the outbuildings were his.

Was the bunkhouse one of the outbuildings? That hadn't been spelled out in the agreement, but he assumed that since it could be used for grain or tool storage, yeah, it was.

Cole pulled his gloves out of his back pocket and slipped them on before slowly approaching the frightened baby, just in case Junior decided to bite out of fear.

"How'd you get in here, buddy?"

The petrified bunny rolled into a ball as he took hold of its nape and scooped it up, cradling its furry bottom in one hand. Holding his captive, he toed the door open and then kicked it shut again, in case the little guy had brothers and sisters lurking nearby, then crossed over to Taylor's car. He motioned with his head for her to roll down the window, and she did—about two inches. He held up the baby, and Taylor gave him a deeply skeptical look.

"This is your rat."

She gave her head an adamant shake. "No."

He lifted a skeptical eyebrow as he raised the bunny a little higher in front of her window. "You're saying that there's a rat *and* a rabbit in the bunkhouse?"

"The rat could have gotten in the same way the bunny got in."

She had a point, but since the bunkhouse

didn't smell of rat, he didn't think that was the case. "Have you ever gotten a whiff of *eau de* pack rat?"

Her mouth flattened. Judging from her silence, it appeared that Taylor did not like to be wrong or admit to being wrong. Well, in this case she was. "Trust me. You don't have a rat."

Color had crept up her neck and across her fair cheeks. Her mouth worked for a moment, then she reached for the door handle and got out of the car.

"I swear it looked like a rat when it raced in front of me."

"The dreaded hopping rat?"

She gave a brave attempt at a smirk, but her cheeks were still pink. "He wasn't hopping. He was running." She tilted her head to get a better angle, apparently falling victim to the rabbit's soul-melting brown eyes. "What will you do with him?"

"Let him go."

Her gaze snapped up to his in an almost accusatory way. "What if he's an orphan?"

"It doesn't matter. He's old enough to get his own food. He'll probably be raiding the garden within the hour."

"So he'll be okay?" She cautiously reached out to stroke the bunny's head with two fingers, and he couldn't help but notice again that the nails on those fingers were perfectly polished. Maybe if Karl had had more of a down-to-earth, get-her-hands-dirty kind of granddaughter, Cole would have been on board with this whole plan of her living in the bunkhouse and sharing his space. But this woman… The muscles in his jaw tightened as her fingers brushed against his as she stroked the rabbit again, then she looked up at him with a faint frown. "I asked if he would be okay."

"As okay as any wild creature will be." Her hand stilled, and he stifled a sigh. "Nature's a bitch, Taylor. There aren't any guarantees."

He could see that she didn't like his answer, but he wasn't going to tiptoe around facts.

"I wonder how he got into the bunkhouse."

"I have an idea." Cole crossed the drive to the thick juniper hedge and gently set the rabbit on the ground. The little guy sat stock-still for a few seconds, then gave a mighty hop and plunged into the shrubbery. Cole looked up to see Taylor studying him. "Let's go check out your place."

It was obvious from the way her mouth tightened that she didn't think of the run-down bunkhouse as her place, but that was tough. It was hers for as long as she was there.

He led the way down the dirt path to the bunkhouse. Before Karl's grandfather had broken up the original sprawling ranch into three smaller hay operations and sold them, the ranch's workers had lived in this building. When Karl returned from the service fifty years ago, he'd been fortunate enough to buy the parcel with the original houses and barns.

Taylor followed him into the dingy interior, and Cole allowed that she might have a legitimate gripe about her living quarters, if it wasn't for the fact she was getting them for free. Taylor headed toward the bathroom, which must have been where she'd encountered the bunny, but Cole crossed to the opposite side of the common area and pulled open the cupboard under the old iron sink. Sure enough, the floorboards there were rotted and broken from decades of water damage, and there was a hole large enough for a rabbit to squeeze through.

He looked over his shoulder at Taylor. "You're lucky this place isn't overrun with mice." Her expression was so comical that he had to clear his throat to keep from laughing. "Karl has some gnarly cats. They do a decent job of keeping the place clear of mice."

She wrapped her arms around her midsection. "I have a cat, too. I didn't want to bring him until I was sure of where I'd be living."

Cole looked over his shoulder at her. "I guess you know now."

The look she gave him was more of a "We'll see…" than a "Yes, I do." She set her keys on the counter and pushed her hair back over her shoulder. "Let me see the problem."

Cole gestured at the dark space in front of him. Was it just him, or did everything that came out of her mouth sound like a freaking order?

She crouched down beside him and peered under the sink, frowning as she took in the damage. Then she sat back on her heels. "Will you have time to fix this soon?"

"No." He pushed himself to his feet without looking at her. "You'll have to hire someone."

"This doesn't appear to be a big job," she murmured in a reasonable voice.

"Then do it yourself."

That was when he had the satisfaction of seeing a flash of annoyance cross her face. "I don't have tools."

"And I don't have the time." He might have had the time if she'd asked, but to simply assume that he would take care of things for her…wasn't going to happen. "Karl has lots of tools in the shed next to the barn."

"What's the problem here?"

"The problem is that I have the lease on this place and you're not going to come in here and direct my life."

"Direct your life?"

"I am not at your beck and call, sweetheart. If you have a problem, then you need to handle it. Because you were not part of my lease agreement."

"I'm out of work, I've just been robbed and—"

"Assaulted by a bunny."

Color flooded her cheeks again. "That's not funny."

"Not meant to be." Much. He took a step closer, halfway wishing that her perfume didn't smell so damned good. It was a light, teasing scent that irritated him because it made his thoughts drift in directions he'd rather not have them drift. He yanked his thoughts back into line. "Maybe if you'd asked instead of assuming…"

Her chin rose a fraction of an inch. "I don't think it would have made a difference if I'd asked or told. You've decided you're not going to do one thing to make life easy for me while I'm here."

"I'm allowing you to stay."

"So as not to upset Karl."

"The result is the same. You're here."

"Are you always this unpleasant?"

The laugh escaped before he could stop it. "No. Prior to the first of this year, I was a professional pleasant person." He smiled in a way that felt satisfyingly dark. "But now I'm a farmer and I no longer have to suffer fools gladly."

"Are you calling me a fool?" She spoke in a slow, measured tone.

"I'm calling you entitled."

Her eyes flashed, but her expression barely shifted. She, too, was skilled at hiding her true feelings. He wondered briefly what it would take, short of a marauding rabbit, to make her lose her cool—which was not the direction his thoughts should be taking. He was on the farm to enjoy some solitude. Live on his terms, not on the whims of others. And he certainly wasn't there to cause his unwanted tenant to lose it.

"I have things to do," she said coolly.

"Me, too." He headed to the door, stopping at the threshold. "The tools are in the building—"

"I know where the tools are," she snapped.

"Just making sure." With that he stepped outside, leaving Ms. Taylor Evans to soak up the ambiance of her new home.

TWO HOURS LATER Taylor was still stewing about her encounter with Cole. Entitled? No. It'd made sense for him to do the repairs. Yes, she could have asked rather than assumed, but in her world, the landlord took care of things like holes in the floor.

She rolled her neck, trying to ease the stiffness out of it. She'd unpacked the trailer and discovered that the losses were less than she'd anticipated. As near as she could tell, the thieves had blindly grabbed boxes, because if they'd looked inside, they wouldn't have bothered with some of the things they'd taken. She'd lost her flatware, some serving dishes, her lingerie and a box of miscellaneous electronics. The loss of the flatware and dishes she took in stride, but the lingerie…that pissed her off. Bras were expensive, and finding ones that fit properly—that approached nightmare territory, which was why she bought her underwear from a boutique that specialized in bra fitting.

Five hundred bucks of silk, lace and underwire. Gone. Like that.

Let it go. Move on. She could practically hear Karl saying the same words he'd said over the phone whenever she'd failed to ace a test or hadn't run her best during a cross-country meet. She wouldn't be sharing this particular loss with him.

Tucking her hair behind her ears, Taylor folded the list she'd made and slipped it into her purse. She'd get a copy to the sheriff's office and another to the insurance company. One more task tacked onto an already full agenda. She still had to return the trailer, buy flatware of some kind—and at the moment she was leaning toward plastic—and hire someone to fix the floor with money she couldn't spare.

It had to be done. She wouldn't have minded coming home to bunnies hopping around her house, but mice…she didn't do mice. The floor needed to be fixed.

So what now? Pick the name of a handyman at random? The way her luck was running, she'd hire a scam artist.

She needed advice in the worst way, and even though she hated to call her grandfather with a sad story again, she pulled her phone out of her pocket and dialed his number. Miraculously, he answered, so after making certain that all was well on his end, she launched into a description of what Cole had called the bunny attack, leaving out the part where she'd mistaken Thumper for a rat, as well as the part where she'd locked herself in her car. She had to hold on to some small shred of dignity. It was bad enough that her farm-mate had seen her. She ended her story with a description of the damaged boards under the sink.

"So what do I need? A plumber or a carpenter?"

"Why don't you ask Cole to fix it?"

Because she'd had it up to there with tall, dark and irritating. "He's pretty busy with farm stuff. I thought I could hire someone to do it."

"Yeah, you could."

"It'd be pricey, right?" She was guessing based on his tone of voice.

"I'll call Cole."

"No." The word popped out in a way that made it necessary to do damage control immediately afterward. She forced an easy smile into her voice. "I can handle things. I was just looking for a little guidance."

"You're sure?"

"Yes. Don't worry about it. I'll let you know when it's done."

Half an hour later she realized just how long

her grandfather was going to have to wait to hear that all was well. All the carpenters and plumbers were booked out for many weeks due to new construction in the area. The two local handymen were also seriously booked up.

"I'll tell you what," the last guy said, perhaps hearing the distress and desperation in her voice, "if you can cover the area with thick plastic and duct tape, that *might* keep the mice from coming in. If they're not hungry enough to chew. Don't keep food in the house."

Taylor rolled her eyes. No food. Right. "And you'll put me on the schedule?"

"Three weeks out."

"If there's a cancellation?"

She heard him suck a breath in between his teeth. "Five people ahead of you, but I'll slot you into the waiting list."

"Thank you." It was kind of hard to say the words in a meaningful way, but she knew better than to annoy a handyman.

Taylor didn't allow herself any breathing room between ending the call and heading for her car. She had to keep moving because if she stopped to consider her reality—no bras, possible mice, sleeping in a place in which she didn't yet have a mattress—then she might not move forward at all.

Temporary. Remember?

Maybe she needed to write the word on the back of her hand in indelible ink.

She carefully closed the bunkhouse door as she left so as not to let in more rabbits, and then headed for her car, only to stop when she caught sight of Cole in the big shed where the baler and swather were parked. Abruptly she shifted course. Why? She hadn't a clue. Maybe because she was still steamed about him calling her entitled. Taylor had never been good about leaving a fight alone. The same obsessive tendencies that had made her a great student also made it hard for her to handle unfinished business. He was bent over the baler, denim hugging the back of his thighs. Yeah, the guy was built. And yeah, he wasn't getting any points for that. She was more about attitude, and his sucked where she was concerned.

"Hey," she said. His head jerked up and he turned, the pained expression on his face clearly asking "What now, lady?" He was as ready for a fight as she was…so she wasn't going to.

"I'm heading to town. Want anything?"

He blinked at her as a suspicious frown formed. "No."

"Just checking," she said smoothly.

"Right." He turned back to the baler.

Dismissed. She didn't think so. She ambled closer, saw the muscles of his shoulders bunch just a bit. He glared at her again, and she wondered if he knew that scowling only made him look hotter—in the sensual sense, rather than the angry sense.

"I need access to the house this afternoon."

"Why?"

"Karl said I could have the mattress in the guest room." And rather than ask him to help her move it, she figured she could back her SUV to the side door, lay the seat down and shove it in. Awkward, yes, but she wasn't going to ask this guy for help.

"Fine."

She waited. He waited. Taylor was used to charged atmosphere—and there was a definite edgy vibe developing between them as each waited for the other to make a move—but apparently Cole also seemed to be comfortable with tense silences. Neither of them blinked, but Taylor was the one who had to get the rental trailer back within the hour or pay for another day. She'd certainly rather spend her money on new bras than a now-useless trailer.

Finally, she gave in—but only because of extenuating circumstances. With a curt nod she started to turn, but not before she saw the glimmer of victory light his eyes.

Walk away. Return the trailer. This is just one battle, not the war.

Taylor didn't let battles go lightly, but this time she would.

For now anyway.

AFTER WINNING THE FACE-OFF, Cole watched Taylor march out of the machine shop to her SUV, wondering what had happened to her Z. Had she done the sane thing and sold it to help make ends meet? Or hung on to it as she waited for some kind of miracle rescue for the situation she'd gotten herself into? A few seconds later he cringed as she peeled out of the driveway. Cool. She could pay to have it regraveled.

Cole stepped back into the machine shop. He could dig into the scrap lumber and fix the floor while she was gone, but he was still pissed about her assumption that he would fix things ASAP for her. More than that, he was irritated that she was there at all. He'd leased the place, and therefore it should be his…but Karl was a longtime friend of his grandfather's, and had given Cole a healthy break on the farm's lease. The least he could do was play ball for the undoubtedly short period that Ms. Taylor Evans would be in residence. Which was another good reason why he wouldn't fix the floor. The more uncomfortable she was, the quicker she'd be out of here. But if Karl asked him to fix it, he would.

Hell, if she asked him to fix it again, he probably would.

The wrench slipped and he banged his knuckles. Shaking his hand and cursing, he then braced his hands on the edge of the baler and let out a breath. It sucked being a decent guy sometimes. Decent guys tended to get taken advantage of. Miranda had taken advantage of him whenever she could, and since he had a conscience as well as a younger sister to protect, he stuck things out on the ranch until Jancey finished high school. Then he told Miranda he was through. The look on her face had been rather satisfying. And even though he no longer managed the ranch, he still had a stake in the place. A stake that Miranda would dearly love to relieve him of.

"Good luck with that," he muttered.

Once upon a time, the Bryan Ranch had been a joint venture between his father and his uncle. They hadn't made a lot of money, but they'd eked out a living—and then his uncle married his second wife, Miranda, who proceeded to talk the brothers into increasing their profits by turning one ranch into a guest ranch and leaving the other as a small working ranch for the entertainment of their guests…and to keep Cole's father happy.

The plan worked. Miranda turned the guest ranch into a popular vacation and retreat destination, making most of the family miserable in the process—everyone except for her husband, who loved her blindly until the day he died. Cole's father had immersed himself in the working ranch and ignored the guests and everything associated with them, so after graduating from college, Cole had become responsible for the trail rides, the outfitting, the cattle drives—anything that involved animals and guests. He was good at his job, and enjoyed it until his father died and Miranda went power mad. Everything had to be cleared through her and everything had to be perfect. Not just regular perfect, but exceptionally perfect—which was a direct quote from his step-aunt.

After their father died, Jancey had stayed in the family home while Cole had spent most of his time at the main guest ranch, a half mile away so that he could be on call—Miranda's idea, even though Jancey had been only a junior in high school at the time. The arrangement worked for the most part, if one didn't mind the animal-population explosion that had occurred once Jancey had the working ranch to herself. Whenever possible, Cole had escaped to his family home to spend time with his sister. Jancey was better at looking after guests than he was, which was why she had continued working at the ranch, saving money for college, after he quit.

Bottom line, the ranch made money and he and Jancey got a cut. But the price they'd paid in emotional turmoil was ridiculous.

Which was why he wanted to be alone, and the fact that he wasn't ate at him.

Maybe Jancey was right—maybe he was suffering from post-Miranda stress disorder.

TAYLOR DROVE PAST the hotel parking lot where she'd been robbed, then made her way to the sheriff's office. After dropping off her list of stolen items, and knowing full well that she needn't have bothered because she was never seeing any of that stuff again, she returned the trailer, then headed to the building supply store two blocks away.

Taylor pushed an oversize cart along the aisles, feeling remarkably out of place. She'd never been in a building supply store—not one that didn't also sell appliances and curtains and flowers in addition to lumber and hardware. She cruised the aisles, though since there weren't many, it didn't take that long. She bought thick plastic and duct tape, then, since she was in no hurry to get back, she stopped at the coffee shop on the other side of the parking lot and took her time sipping a chai latte.

Chai was her go-to calmer-downer, but instead of relaxing as she sipped the hot, sweet tea mixture, she found herself drumming her fingers. Abruptly, she closed her hand and dropped it into her lap, where it clenched into a fist.

Plastic and duct tape and a couple of gnarly cats were all that would stand between her and the rodent population of the Eagle Valley.

How was she supposed to sleep with that kind of a threat hanging over her head? Meanwhile the guy who probably didn't care about rodents slept in the mouse-proof house.

Her fist clenched even tighter, and Taylor made a conscious effort to unclench.

It was clear that her grandfather wasn't going to suggest to Cole that he trade places with her, even after the month was up. Which meant that she was probably stuck in the bunkhouse hellhole until she got back on her feet.

Taylor started drumming her fingers again, then she picked up her phone and went to YouTube, searching for videos on repairing rotten floorboards. She scrolled through videos, watching pieces here and there, before concluding that her repair didn't have to be pretty. It had to be mouse-proof. Who was going to see under the sink except for her?

And if things played out well, she wouldn't be there for that long. The obsessive part of her brain wouldn't have to grapple with the fact that there were messy boards under the sink. She'd spent the better part of the evening reading through job listings within driving distance of the Eagle Valley, so she had hope.

She felt better as she finished her tea. First she'd conquer home repair, then she'd find a job. Ever upward and all that.

Taylor got to her feet, shouldered her purse, tossed the cup into the trash and left the shop with a sense of purpose.

Forty-five minutes later she had short boards that the woman in the lumber department had cut for her, a box of wood screws, a cordless drill that made her feel kind of powerful and macho—and which had cost less than one of her bras—a hammer, just because, and steel wool for plugging extra space around the incoming pipe. She also had two mousetraps, just in case. Taylor smiled grimly as she pushed the cart through the automatic doors.

It was good to take control.

THE SOUND OF a drill brought Cole's head up as he walked by the bunkhouse on his way to the barn, where he planned to start fixing the corrals for the three orphan calves he was taking off his sister's hands. The drilling stopped, followed by a clatter and a muttered curse. When they'd spoken earlier about the hole under the sink, Taylor had seemed clueless about repairs, but judging from where the noise was coming from, she appeared to be tackling them herself.

None of your business.

Actually, in a way, it was his business. If it turned out that Taylor was handy with tools, then her assumption that he would fix her problem was going to irk him that much more. In fact, it had already irked him to the point that he single-handedly moved a mattress and box spring out of Karl's basement and hauled them over to the bunkhouse so that he didn't have to have any more contact with her than necessary. And if that mattress and box spring happened to be twin-size instead of the queen-size bed in the guest room, so what? A twin bed would fit her just fine, and maybe some-day he'd have guests.

Cole forced himself to ignore the bang that erupted from inside the bunkhouse and walk on.

He'd spent too much time on the guest ranch. Too much time smiling when he wanted to walk away from some self-important douche-bag with a snotty attitude. Granted, for every douche, there were at least ten people he en-joyed helping, but the jerks did tend to stick out. And then there were the ladies who seemed to think that he was fair game. He was game for quite a bit, but not with clients. Something like that was not only wildly unpro-fessional, it would have given Miranda an ad-vantage over him—and that was the last thing he'd have let happen.

He didn't have to worry about that anymore. It felt so damned good working alone, not worrying about politely dealing with the public, or what part of his life Miranda was going to try to control just to prove to him that she could.

Now if he only had his farm to himself…

In good time. After all, how long was Taylor Evans going to be able to stand living in a bunkhouse?

That was the exact question his cousin Jordan put forth to him when they met for beer and burgers at McElroy's Bar early that evening.

"Not long. I hope." Cole took a drink and set his beer back on the table. "But here's the thing—she must be desperate to be there at all, so maybe how long she stays is out of her control. The fact that she's there means that she's in a rough place."

"Good point."

"You should see her. Not exactly farm material. She drives a freaking classic Z."

"What year?"

"Looks like a '72."

"No." There was an envious note in Jordan's voice.

"Yep." Cole let his chin drop. "She can't stay

there forever." He realized that he sounded as if he was trying to convince himself.

"You hope."

"Thanks, Mary Sunshine."

Jordan laughed, and despite his dark mood, Cole grudgingly smiled. It was good to see his cousin so relaxed and happy. Jordan hadn't had an easy life. He'd been injured and disfigured during his time in the military, and while he was recovering, Miranda had done her best to steal his inheritance on a technicality. He'd been in a bad place for a long time, but now he had his mountain ranch, a wife he adored and a baby on the way. Cole's problems were trivial in comparison. He had a woman on his ranch when he wanted to live alone.

In all honesty, how bad was that? Cole let out a sigh. "Sorry to unload. It's not that big of a deal."

"I get what the deal is," Jordan said simply. "You've been working with the kind of people I avoid at all costs for years, and now, after you escaped, you have one of those same people invading your space for an indefinite amount of time."

"Pretty much."

"You have a right to be pissed off, but I'll tell you what I think is going to happen."

"Yeah?"

Jordan leaned his forearm on the table. "You're going to go about your business as if she isn't there. She'll do the same once she realizes that you aren't going to put out her fires for her. The two of you will live parallel lives until she moves on."

"If I have anything to say about it, we will." But she was still going to be there and he was still going to be acutely aware of the fact.

"You know she's still looking for jobs in urban areas," Jordan pointed out.

"I'd say that's a given."

"And if she gets a job locally, she'll probably rent one of those apartments on the lake."

"Good point." The lake near the center of the Eagle Valley had seen a lot of development, and there were several new apartment buildings and condo complexes. The little town was growing, and he couldn't see Taylor hanging out on the farm for a moment longer than she had to.

"Something will come through and she'll leave." Jordan spoke as if Taylor's departure was a done deal before reaching for the pitcher with his good hand. He topped off both of their glasses, then lifted his. "Here's to all this going down sooner rather than later."

Cole nodded and then drank deeply.

Let it be so.

CHAPTER FIVE

TAYLOR LAY IN her narrow bed, wide awake, listening to wind blowing through the pine trees next to the bunkhouse and missing traffic noises. This was her reality—a run-down one-room building with an ancient plug-in electric heater to ward off the night's chill. If that didn't spur her on to find meaningful employment, nothing would. Meanwhile, Cole Bryan slept comfortably in a house fifty yards away, quite possibly in the bed she'd slept in as a kid, unless he'd taken over Karl's room. Definitely in a bed that was a lot bigger than the one she was currently lying in. It ticked her off that he'd brought her the mattress from the cellar, but he had brought it and she decided that complaining would make it seem as if he'd won a round. He might have, but she wasn't going to acknowledge it. She had a mattress, and that was the important thing.

You also have a roof over your head. And

the hole under the sink is patched. No mice. Or bunnies.

It was amazing to think that these were things she was now grateful for. A roof. Patched flooring. So many things that she'd taken for granted as she was attempting to climb the corporate ranks.

Was she supposed to be learning some cosmic lesson from this?

What had she done to be put in a position where she had to learn a cosmic lesson? She'd donated to charity, volunteered, ran 5Ks for good causes. She'd never judged people... much. Okay, she'd judged a few of her colleagues, but that was from a purely professional standpoint.

Taylor rolled over and punched her pillow, trying to make it comfortable. She'd been surprised to find the mattress on her bed frame when she'd come home, but when she'd looked for Cole to thank him, he'd been elusive. Almost as if he were avoiding her. He hadn't answered her knock on his door, and then, just when she was about to try again a half hour later, his truck had roared to life and he'd left the property.

Avoid away, farm guy. If she wanted him, she'd find him. Right now she couldn't see any reason she *would* want him. She was here for only a short time, right? Somewhere out there was a job for her. It might not be as high-powered as the one she'd left, but she'd accept almost anything within reason to keep from blowing a hole in her résumé.

If you take a lower-paying job, then you'll have to stay here until you catch up financially.

Taylor let out a breath at the very logical thought. How temporary was her temporary? Was she going to have to give up and paint, rather than move, to escape tan walls? And what about a bathtub? At the moment she'd consider giving up her Z for a long soak.

Okay, so maybe she wouldn't go that far, but she wanted a tub, and amenities, and a fridge that wasn't from the 1970s. Who knew fridges even lasted that long?

Flopping over on her back, Taylor stared up at the moonlit ceiling. There were stains there that she needed to take care of if she was going to stay in this place. She closed her eyes. Beneath the floorboards, she heard the occasional rustling and thumping. After a particularly loud bump, she pushed back the sheets and crept across the floor, cautiously opening the cupboard to check her repair by the light of her phone. Nothing jumped at her, and she sat back on her heels, admiring her work. Pretty darned good, if she did say so herself. The boards tightly screwed into the nonrotten floorboards and the steel wool would keep the critters at bay, so let them thump and rustle all they wanted.

Besides, it was possible that the gnarly cats that she'd yet to see were responsible for the odd noises under the floor. In a day or two, she probably wouldn't even notice.

Or so she hoped.

Taylor got back into bed and pulled the blankets up under her chin.

So things had taken an unexpected turn. She could deal. Live her life as she had in Seattle. Reestablish the routines she'd let slide over the past months as she focused on her job hunt. Tomorrow she would take a short run to ease back into her neglected exercise program, make a tea latte on her ridiculously old stove, read the news. Then she'd attack the local— or relatively local—job market. Get something to tide her over while she shopped around for a real job in a company that competed with Stratford.

And then there was Cole. Great-looking guy, until he opened his mouth. Taylor had a feeling that he would, for the most part, continue to avoid her. And if he didn't, she could deal.

IT WAS A go-to-town day—for groceries, to be exact—so when the sun peeked over the top of the mountains on the other side of the valley, Cole was at his kitchen table dressed in clean jeans and sipping coffee out of a mug, instead of sucking it out of the beat-up metal thermal cup he used when he farmed or worked on equipment. The lights were on in the bunkhouse, and every now and again he caught sight of a shadow moving purposefully past the curtained window. The window hadn't been curtained the day before, so Taylor must have nailed something up.

Cool. This way they didn't need to look at one another. In fact, after talking with Jordan the night before, he was starting to believe they could lead parallel lives and not run into each other that often. He'd overreacted because of the way she'd sailed in and expected him to move into the bunkhouse and fix the hole in the floor. Yeah—it was the expecting part that got to him. But now that they'd hashed things out…what could go wrong?

He started to get up from the table, then sat down again as the bunkhouse door opened and Taylor came out, dressed in shorts and a hoodie, which she zipped up over a cropped top as she headed toward the driveway. She pushed her hands down into her pockets and walked, chin down, to the county road, where she broke into an easy jog. A moment later she disappeared around a gentle bend in the road.

Well, that explained why she was in such good shape. Not that he'd wanted to notice, but it wasn't all that easy to ignore toned legs and a nice ass.

Cole drained his cup and rinsed it in the sink before heading to the door and slapping on his hat. Thankful that Taylor had run in the opposite direction from town, he glanced that way before pulling out, surprised to see Taylor coming back. Had she spooked herself running along a country road in the early morning hours? But it wasn't like she was a total urbanite. She'd spent summers on Karl's place.

She lifted an arm and hailed him before he could turn to town, so he cranked the steering wheel the opposite direction and drove toward her. She stepped to the side of the road, propping her hands on her hips as she waited for him to come to a stop beside her.

"There are a bunch of cows out on the road ahead."

"Are they Angus?" Then, realizing that she

might not know an Angus from a Hereford, he added, "Black cows?"

She gave him a withering look. "I know what Angus look like. Both red and black."

"Yeah?" That surprised him. Karl had never owned livestock as far as he knew. He was all about the crops.

"I have a good base of general knowledge," she said blandly. "And yes. Angus. Black ones."

"Eric Pollson. He lives about a mile away and his pastures border the road."

"Thank you."

She started toward the farm, looking back when he leaned out the window and called her name. "You want me to give him a ring?"

"I didn't want to make assumptions about what you will and will not do."

"Hey," he said without pausing to think, "just because I didn't ask 'how high' when you told me to jump yesterday, it doesn't mean I'm unreasonable."

Taylor stopped in her tracks. "How high?" she echoed as she spun around and started back toward him, her running shoes crunching purposefully in the gravel as she strode toward him. She stopped in front of his window and squared her shoulders. "I merely assumed that, *because* you're leasing the place, *because* you allege yourself to be Karl's friend, *because* you probably *own* tools, that you would fix the bunny hole."

"But you didn't ask me *if* I would fix it. You asked *when* I would fix it. As if it were a done deal. Like I'm yours to order around. Guess what? I'm not."

"Sorry," she said with a small sniff. "We, the entitled, usually focus only on ourselves. Any perceived slight was unintended."

She was baiting him.

It was working.

Drive away.

He didn't.

"But you're trying to do something about that, right? The me-first attitude?" Snide felt good.

"Maybe I am," she agreed, her mild tone belying the smoldering look in her eyes. "I'm certain you'll give me updates on how I'm doing."

"Oh, I will—unless, of course, you manage to get a job and move on."

"That's the plan."

"Hasn't worked so far, has it? What's it been? Three, four months since you got fired?"

She started to speak, then closed her mouth. Tight. Really tight. White-lipped tight. A second later she opened it again. "Those cattle are a hazard. Is this Pollson guy in the phone book, or do I need to drive to his place?"

"I'll go," Cole said. Enough was enough. He wasn't generally one for cheap shots, but hey, everyone had their weak moments. He gave her a curt nod and put his truck in gear, easing back onto the road. In his rearview mirror, he saw Taylor standing right where he left her, staring after him and looking very much as if she wanted to flip him off.

So much for peacefully living parallel lives.

"HOW'S THE JOB search going?" Her grandfather asked the question cautiously, as if afraid of treading on dangerous ground. He was, but after the confrontation with Cole yesterday, Taylor was once again in full job-search mode. That guy was going to eat crow, even though she'd concluded that he'd made his snide comments to fire her up and get her off the farm. Since the result was the same—gainful employment—she decided to let him win this round. Let him think he lit a fire under her—what did it hurt?

Her pride. A little. But she'd taken so many knocks lately that her pride was starting to grow calluses.

"There's not a lot out there, but I've submitted two applications. I should hear soon. Both jobs close in three days."

The positions were several rungs down the ladder from where she'd been but still respectable, and she would be able to explain to future employers that she'd taken the job when the market had tightened. No shame there.

"Local?"

"Missoula."

"I wouldn't mind having you closer on a more permanent basis, you know."

She knew. Missoula was about seven hours closer to him than she'd been before. And she also knew that her mom was probably going to send her a calendar to mark the days until she could leave Montana.

"How's Aunt Elise?"

Her grandfather sighed. "Better. Looks like I might be here for the better part of the year, though. Until I convince her to move to the Eagle Valley anyway. So far she's not real receptive to the idea."

"Do you hate living there?" She was used to living in a small space, but she wondered how her grandfather was dealing with the confines of the tiny duplex.

After a silence, he said, "Not really. There

are things to do. I have new poker buddies, a couple of guys I knew a long time ago."

"I'll drive down to see you one of these weekends."

"You'd better be mindful of the gas."

"You're worth a tank of gas."

"Wait until after you get the job. You can call until then."

"Thanks, Grandpa. I'll talk to you soon."

"Keep me posted."

"Will do."

They said their goodbyes and Taylor hung up, then settled back in her overstuffed chair—the one she'd taken from Karl's basement, with his permission, while Cole was out doing something in the fields the day before. She'd climbed down the stone steps at the back of the house and unlocked the cellar door with the key from under the flowerpot. It'd been no easy task manhandling the chair up the steps by herself, but she wasn't in the mood to do battle with Cole—especially when she'd lost the last battle. And she knew better than to think they could do something as easy as moving a chair without snapping at one another. She preferred to do it herself, even if the chair almost did her in when she'd lost her grip and it pushed her back down the steps. She'd been pinned against the cellar door, the wind knocked out of her. Thankfully she was able to push the chair off her, get a better grip and wrestle it back up the stairs. The only damage had been a couple of bruises on her thighs, and now the bunkhouse was a bit more comfortable. Emphasis on "a bit." It was a dreary place, and what bothered her most was that it represented failure. Living in the bunkhouse was the culmination of a steady downward slide, and even now she wasn't certain that she was at the end of the ride. If she were in the main house, she could sleep in her old bed. Feel as if she were just visiting. She would have a bathtub, a real kitchen. And she wouldn't be brought upright in bed by noisy thumps beneath the floorboards.

If she was in the house, maybe she could pretend that she wasn't so close to the very end of her rope.

Taylor sighed and laid her head back against the soft, crushed velvet cushion.

In five years, this experience will be an interesting anecdote.

But the problem was that, for an experience

to become an interesting anecdote, one had to successfully survive it.

A knock on the door startled her, and she scrambled to her feet. There was no question who her visitor was. All the same, Taylor pushed the sheet she'd tacked over the window aside. Safety first and all that.

It was Cole. And while he didn't look cheerful, he didn't look angry either.

A neutral visit?

Could be the start of something good. Taylor pulled the door open and she was struck—again—by just how ridiculously good-looking he was. High cheekbones, crazy-hot mouth, blue eyes. Dark lashes.

Touchy temperament.

Taylor smiled coolly. "Hello."

"Hi. I was wondering if you would mind parking your rig on the other side of the building. I'm having trouble getting my equipment through." He looked as if he'd like to be anywhere but her tiny porch.

"Sure. I can move my…rig." If he was going to be polite and nonconfrontational, then so was she. She'd even call her vehicle a rig. "That side?" She pointed at the wall opposite from where Cole stood. Cole who was now frowning at her overstuffed chair.

"Where did you get that?"

Taylor glanced at the chair. "The cellar. Karl said I could get some furniture."

She knew the instant she looked back at him what was coming next, so she launched into her defense. "I had permission. You were out in the field, and I didn't know when you were coming back."

"You shouldn't enter people's houses without asking."

"It was only the cellar, and I entered from the outside. I didn't set foot in your part of the house."

He did not appear to be mollified by her reasonable explanation. If anything, his expression hardened even more. Taylor pressed her lips together as she dropped her gaze to study the floorboards. Then she drew in a breath and met his eyes dead-on. "Are you looking for a fight?"

His eyebrows jerked up. "No."

"I think you are. I think you're looking for reasons to engage me, because getting this chair out of the cellar didn't impact you one bit."

He gave a short, humorless laugh. "Why would I engage you?"

"Maybe you get off on it."

His mouth curled at one corner, but she could see she'd surprised him with her answer.

"Trust me, that isn't what I get off on."

"Yeah?" she asked in a low voice as she raised her eyebrows. "What do you get off on?"

Instead of giving her a sarcastic reply as she'd expected, Cole came a step closer, looking down at her with a considering gaze, and for one heart-stopping moment, she thought he was going to show her. Instead, his rather incredible mouth quirked up at one corner. "That's none of your business, and I can't ever see that changing."

"Ouch," she said softly, thankful that he had no way of knowing that her heart was beating harder than it should.

He was too close. Or maybe she was. Whatever, the pull of gut-level physical attraction was there, making her wonder what would happen if she took another step forward, settled her palms on his very solid chest, tilted her chin up…

That was nothing short of crazy.

"Wasn't meant as an ouch." His voice was a little lower than before.

"Gee. I wonder why I took it that way."

Cole casually eased back a little and, even

though Taylor told herself to hold her ground, she did the same, folding her arms over her middle.

"How's the job hunt coming?" A small twist of the knife, but one she welcomed because it eased her toward safer ground, away from thoughts of touching him to see what would happen.

"I've applied here and there. I'm hopeful of landing something soon." Even though she was overqualified for the positions she'd applied for, and that was almost as deadly as being underqualified. Maybe more, since businesses didn't want to hire people who were probably still looking for a job more closely suited to their abilities.

"How soon is soon?"

Taylor shrugged and then leaned over to grab her keys off the bookcase, feeling the strong need to both end this conversation and put some distance between them. He needed to go back to his fields, and she needed to get back to her battle plans. "You want me to park on the north side of the building?"

"Yeah. I'd appreciate that."

She jingled the keys before palming them and moving past him. She heard him start after her, but instead of veering away, he followed her to the SUV. She opened the door, creating a nice barrier between them, before glancing up at him with a question in her eyes. "Yes?"

"I need a time line. If you get a job, how long do you think you'll be here?"

He settled a hand on the door frame, and while Taylor's gaze drifted down to his very strong, very tan fingers, she didn't allow herself to move. "Can't wait to get rid of me?"

"I want to store grain in the bunkhouse. I'm getting some calves."

Not the answer she expected, but an easy one to reply to. "Then how about I'll move into the house and you can stay in the bunkhouse with your grain?"

"I don't think so."

"I don't have a time line, but when I do, you'll be the first to know."

"Thanks."

Taylor smiled—kind of—then slipped into the driver's seat as Cole turned and started walking toward the machine shop, leaving her to wonder which of them had won that round.

CHAPTER SIX

TAYLOR TWISTED AROUND, doing her best to see her reflection in the small bathroom mirror, but short of jumping up and down, there was no way to see if her hem was hanging properly in the back. She'd have to assume it was.

Something thumped on the floorboards beneath her feet, but she no longer startled at the sound. Instead she leaned in over the sink, did a last-minute makeup check, then smoothed her hands over the light gray tailored dress. Simple, but not plain. Applying for a midlevel job in a smaller community was new to her, so she'd done her research. The last thing she wanted was to come off as overdressed for the position—not when she was overqualified for the job. Kiss of death.

After the interview request, she'd made calls to people she'd meant to contact before but hadn't because she was embarrassed about not instantly landing a job. Funny how being out of work for several months took some of the edge off her professional pride. She hadn't rebounded immediately, but she wasn't the only one. A few of her peers had landed primo jobs, but she was among those who hadn't. She wasn't alone—but it kind of stung that she'd twice thought she'd be the exception, as she'd invariably been during her educational career, and she wasn't. Sailing through life during high school and college hadn't prepared her for this, and she was starting to see that encountering the occasional obstacle might have done her some good.

She grabbed her leather carryall and headed out the door to the SUV. Again, probably a good thing she wasn't driving the Z. And maybe it was a good thing that Max wasn't yet with her, because she'd been unable to find her lint roller. The trailer thieves were probably having a fine time with it, or it was in the trash somewhere, along with her much-missed bras.

As she drove to Missoula, Taylor practiced answers to the usual interview questions, focusing on sounding efficient but not coming off as a know-it-all. Again—overqualification. That was a tough one to get past. Would it be wrong to pretend that she was willing to live on less because she loved living in Montana so much?

She was starting to feel desperate enough to lie.

Taylor parked in the lot behind the brick building that housed the bank and the financial services offices on the floors above and sat for a few minutes, getting into battle mode. She was competent, a good team player with strong leadership qualities. She was hardworking, willing to go the extra mile, put in the extra time. She was someone they'd be foolish not to snap up.

Drawing in a breath, she opened the SUV door, got out and caught her heel in a crack in the sidewalk, twisting her ankle hard. She stopped before she fell and yanked her heel free.

Not an omen. She'd recovered her balance without breaking an ankle, and that was an analogy for what was going to happen next. She was going to recover.

As it turned out, catching her heel hadn't been a harbinger of things to come. The interview went well. Really well. Almost-too-good-to-believe well after months of nothing.

The committee of four were positive throughout the interview and seemed pleased to have someone of her qualifications interested in joining their team. There was no mention of being overqualified, and as the interview wound down, the committee members were nodding and smiling as she spoke. They liked her. She liked them. But more than that, she could do something for their company. They would benefit from her expertise, and eventually she could apply for transfer to the corporate office in Seattle. She had nodded matter-of-factly when they'd mentioned that possibility while answering her questions about advancement within the company, but inwardly she was doing a happy dance. That was why they hadn't been put off by her résumé—they were looking to grow people. Perfect.

The salary was exactly half what she made in her former job, but the cost of living in Montana was lower. The cost of maintaining her professional wardrobe would be lower. She wouldn't be paying an exorbitant sum to her landlord to park the Z under cover to keep the sea air from corroding it. There were a lot of positives.

Just getting a job would be a positive.

You are getting this job.

It had taken a while to get the first interview, but she was moving forward in a positive way. It would be days before she heard anything, but she felt good. Hopeful. Positive.

Finally.

Taylor stopped at the coffee shop near the building supply center where she'd bought her new macho drill and again treated herself to a chai latte. She settled at a table in the corner and texted Carolyn, telling her that she'd interviewed and felt good about it, but that was as far as she could go before her jinx factor kicked in.

Regardless of what happens, I'll be getting Max soon.

She missed her cat.

The reply came back quicker than she'd expected, since Carolyn's phone was always lost somewhere in her humungous purse.

Can we meet in Spokane this weekend?

Taylor frowned before writing: Sure.

Her phone rang a split second later. Carolyn must have been on break. "Is Max being bad?" she asked.

"Oh, no, no," Carolyn said with a laugh. "Nothing like that—well, no more than usual anyway. It's just that I have an opportunity to take the Alaska cruise with my new guy and I'd hate to put Max in kitty day care."

"He'd hate that, too. So yes, I can drive to Spokane on, what? Saturday?"

"That would be great. And you said the interview went well?"

"I think so. I'll tell you about it when I see you."

"Can't wait."

They figured out a time and place for the cat-and-gossip swap, and then Taylor drained her latte. She had to buy cat food and kitty litter and maybe a nice bottle of wine to be opened upon the occasion of her employment.

Her jinx voice whispered again as she debated about the celebratory wine, and she told it to be quiet. If she didn't get the job, then she could drown her sorrows before continuing the search.

TAYLOR HAD JUST been to an interview. Either that or she'd dressed to the nines to go grocery shopping. Cole stopped sweeping out the barn storage room where he planned to store his grain and watched as Taylor slid the rest of the way out of the SUV and then reached in to grab a leather carryall, showing about a mile of leg in the process. No grocery bags. Interview for sure.

He swept a couple of decades' worth of dirt

into a broad flat shovel and then dumped it into the small barrel he'd brought into the room to collect debris. A cloud of dust went up, and he grimaced as he bent to load another shovelful of barn dirt. The bunkhouse would be better, since it was already clean, and it had been used to store grain in the past. But Cole wasn't going to push things. Every time he came in contact with Taylor, some sort of small explosion seemed to occur. It was as if they somehow sparked one another—and not in a good way.

In fact, he resented the number of times she'd shoved her way into his head while he was trying to work. This was not the solitary farmwork he'd envisioned. He shouldn't be wondering how the person who lived across the drive was going to aggravate him next.

On top of that, he'd broken his promise to himself and searched her name on the internet, finding pretty much what he'd expected via online news articles and professional profiles. Valedictorian of her graduating class. Magna cum laude in college. MBA from an impressive university. She'd been part of a state champion cross-country team, held a state record for the 800 in track for a couple of years. Life had gone well for Ms. Evans.

It showed.

He wasn't saying she hadn't worked for what she got, but he had a feeling that being at the top of the heap kind of skewed her view. And kept her from calling her grandfather as often as she should have. It also had her making assumptions about who would do what for her and the legality of breaking into people's cellars.

A few minutes after Taylor had gone into the bunkhouse, she came back out dressed in running gear. She didn't so much as look his way as she started down the driveway at a brisk walk that turned into a jog. Her movements were fluid and unconsciously graceful, as if running were second nature to her, which he assumed it was, given her background.

Could he still run a mile?

Probably.

Did he want to? No. Not one bit.

TAYLOR HAD PURPOSELY left her phone behind when she went on her run. It was too soon to hear anything from the interview—they'd said she would hear on Friday at the soonest—and she wanted to focus on the moment, something that did not come easily to her. When she got back and saw two missed calls, she kicked herself for indulging in phone freedom. The first was a robocall, but the second came from Stratford. No hope that they were offering her a job, since they'd gone through another wave of layoffs, but...

She called them back.

"Paul Medford."

"Hi, Paul." Taylor's shortness of breath had more to do with nerves than just finishing a punishing run. Paul had been her first supervisor at Stratford before moving to a different department. "Just returning your call."

"Hey, Taylor." He sounded so much more relaxed than he had during the week preceding her layoff. "I was contacted by US West Bank less than an hour ago."

"And...?"

"I gave you a glowing recommendation. Told them it would be difficult for them to do better." She could hear him switch the phone to his opposite hand as he did when he relaxed during a call. "I assume you want the job."

Even though it was many rungs down the ladder from where she'd been previously.

"Their main office is in Seattle."

"I know." There was a smile in his voice.

"Do you have yourself back on the apartment lists?"

"Just the one. Until I get back in, I'll make do."

"Just so you know… I'll only be with Stratford for another week. I'm making a move to Whitcote Management."

"Congratulations." She meant it with all of her heart, even though her application to the same company hadn't even garnered a response.

She heard a faint buzz and then he said, "I have another call, so let's talk later. I just wanted to let you know."

"I appreciate it, Paul. Thanks." She put down the phone and spun on her heel, hugging herself. The first good thing to happen in a long time had just happened.

Take that, Jinx Voice.

COLE HAD OPENED an account at Culver Ranch and Feed shortly after moving onto the farm, and since that time he'd been a weekly visitor. At first, since Karl was such good friends with the owner, Mike Culver, Cole felt as if he had to do all his farm business there. And after a few weeks, he found that he *wanted* to. And a week ago he'd been invited to take Karl's place at poker night.

Cole was a decent poker player, but the way Cal Sawyer, one of Karl's oldest friends, and Mike had exchanged looks when he'd agreed to play made him think that he was a bird about to be plucked. At least it would get him out of the house and off the farm for a while. He followed the directions to Mike's house and Mike's wife, Elaine, greeted him at the door, obviously going out as he was coming in.

"I just get in the way," she said with an amused smile.

"Meaning that she's heard our stories so many times, she prefers to take refuge elsewhere," Cal said.

"So it's just the three of us?"

"Dylan's supposed to stop by, but he got held up," Mike said, referring to his nephew. "He'll be here within the hour."

Cole hoped he still had some money within an hour. Cal shuffled the cards as if he was about to do an elaborate magic trick. Cole half expected him to fan them across the table and then flip them over in one smooth move.

"Beer?" Mike asked.

"You bet." Cole took his seat, glad that he'd brought only twenty dollars to lose.

"I saw that you bought grain yesterday,"

Mike said as he handed Cole a longneck. "Are you getting livestock?"

"Bringing some calves in from the ranch. Two leppies and one rejected twin that Jancey hasn't been able to graft onto another cow."

Cal gave a shudder. "Better you than me." He began firing the cards around the table with deadly accuracy.

"My sister has a soft spot for orphans." And usually that wasn't a problem, but without Cole there to intercede, Miranda was keeping Jancey busy to the point that she was having trouble keeping up with the feedings.

"Karl's not really set up for livestock, is he?" Mike asked, picking up the cards as they landed in front of him.

"His fences are all falling apart and his corrals are little more than a memory, if that's what you mean."

"Yeah. Pretty much. When I moved to town and had to find homes for my livestock, he wasn't a lot of help."

Cal smiled at Cole. "It's because of Marlene, you know."

"Marlene?" A woman had soured Karl on cattle?

Mike nodded. "His ma's milk cow. I guess she kicked him whenever she got a chance, slapped him in the face with her tail if he didn't have it properly pinned to the side. She hated him—"

"And he hated her," Cal added. "But his mother kept him milking until he left home. Even the nicer cow after Marlene hated him. Maybe it's a chemical thing. Maybe he has a scent...or something...that cows instinctively dislike."

Mike looked as if he wanted to roll his eyes at the theory. "Whatever the reason, he doesn't keep livestock. He drew the line at goats, too."

Cole glanced at his cards and managed not to frown. "But he cowboyed on our ranch when he was a young guy."

"He was in charge of the remuda. The horses. He likes horses but never had a mind to own one."

"Except for Taylor's horse," Mike murmured as he stared at his hand. Carefully he set one card on the table in front of him. Cole looked at his single pair of sevens and debated.

"That's right," Cal said, slapping four cards down. "Paid through the nose for a horse she rode for two months a year."

"Sounds like he indulged her," Cole said. She certainly showed signs of being well indulged. He laid down all but the pair, then picked up the hodgepodge of useless cards Cal dealt him. *Okay. Pair of sevens it is*.

"Let's just say that if Taylor wanted it, and Karl and Becky could afford it, Taylor got it," Mike murmured, his focus on his cards.

"But look at her now—living in the bunkhouse until she gets back on her feet," Cal said brightly as he tossed five chips onto the table. "She's scrappy, that one."

Scrappy wasn't a word Cole would use to describe Taylor, but he kept his opinion to himself. He pushed forward a stack of chips. "Raise." He figured with these guys, he'd literally better go big or go home. So he had a pair of wimpy sevens. Bluffing was part of the game.

Mike tossed some chips onto the table, and then Cal leaned toward Cole, who instantly wondered if the old cardsharp was trying to see his hand. "What will *you* do if Karl comes back to the ranch? Raise." He matched the raise and added another five chips. Mike laid down his cards.

"Keep him away from the cows, I guess." Cole studied his cards. This didn't feel right.

Cal shook his head. "I mean with Taylor in the bunkhouse and all?"

Cole shrugged carelessly and matched Cal's

bet. "I think she'll get a job and move before too long. I call."

There was a knock on the front door, and before anyone could move, Mike's nephew, Dylan Culver, came in. "Started without me, I see." He took off his coat and then grinned at Cole. "Got any money left?"

"He has plenty of money...for now," Cal said, slapping down three kings and pulling in the pot.

Dylan gave a snort as he grabbed a beer out of the fridge, then sat. He rubbed his hands together and cracked his knuckles. "I'm ready to be fleeced."

Cal rolled his eyes and passed the deck to Mike. "Hey...you said you were going to have to get someone new to help out at the store. Maybe Taylor, if she can't find anything else."

Dylan and Cole instantly looked at one another, and Cole saw that Dylan's thoughts were the same as his own. Fat freaking chance.

Mike coughed. "Uh, yeah." He stretched his mouth into a tactful smile and started dealing.

"Taylor never really fit in with the locals," Dylan said when Cal gave him a "what?" look. "She had bigger and better things planned than a life in the Eagle Valley." He picked up his cards before saying under his breath, in a voice that only Cole could hear, "And she wasn't shy about sharing that sentiment."

"THEY'LL LET ME know on Tuesday." Taylor handed Carolyn her drink. "It's a big step down, but I can work my way back up. It sounded as if that's what they expect me to do."

Carolyn gave a smile that didn't reach her eyes as she picked up her espresso. "If you were going to settle, I wish you'd done it in Seattle."

Taylor didn't agree. What would it be like not to head out with Carolyn on their famous shopping expeditions? Or meet for drinks or dinner once a week? If she had to take a step down in pay, she was glad she wasn't in the city she loved. This way she could pay her penance, then return to Seattle and resume her former existence—only this time with more savings and the sad knowledge that no one was irreplaceable, not even those who worked eighty-hour weeks.

"Where would I have lived?"

"It wouldn't have been in a farm barn thing."

"Bunkhouse." Taylor sipped her tea latte. "But it would have been something equivalent in Seattle, in neighborhoods I'd be afraid to live in."

"Roomies?"

"Who?" Where would she find someone compatible to live with? It was such a crapshoot.

She'd move in with Carolyn in a heartbeat, but her friend was locked into a lease on her studio for the next seven months.

"Sell the Z?"

Taylor sighed and set down her cup. "I've been so close…but…" It was stupid to be emotionally attached to a piece of metal. "I think it'll be good for me to work my way up again. Gain new experiences."

"Live in the sticks."

"Missoula isn't exactly the sticks. It's got a lot to offer." More than the Eagle Valley, even if it did have its share of the rich and famous. Most of the people of means who moved there did it to escape city life rather than bring it with them.

"Will you move to Missoula?"

"Just as soon as I get a nest egg built up. I figure six months of commuting and then I'll get an apartment. Right now driving is cheaper than renting." By a large margin, or she wouldn't have considered commuting.

They finished their drinks while chatting about people they both knew. Most of the staff who had been downsized with Taylor had also left Seattle for other cities, other jobs. Some had done what Taylor was about to do, accepting jobs at a lower level or in a different field entirely. One of their mutual friends had decided that this was the nudge she needed to head to LA and try her luck at acting.

Taylor paid the tab, over Carolyn's protests, saying it was only coffee and she wasn't destitute. Max complained loudly from inside the SUV and scraped his claws down the side of the plastic cat carrier as they approached the vehicle. Taylor made a face.

"His Majesty is about to take the kennel apart from the inside out." She pushed her windblown hair back. "I can't thank you enough for keeping him and bringing him to me."

"Least I could do." Carolyn's smile faded. "I miss you."

"I'll keep you posted," Taylor promised, "and I'll be back home before you know it."

Max let out a plaintive yowl. Taylor hugged her friend, then opened the car.

"Tay…" Taylor looked back at Carolyn. "Call anytime. No matter what."

"You know I will."

TAYLOR HAD DRIVEN away late Saturday morning as Cole headed out to the fields and returned to the farm midafternoon, parking the SUV closer to the bunkhouse door than usual. Cole stood at his kitchen window, eating a sandwich and watching as she opened the rear door and pulled out a large animal crate. It toppled awkwardly in her arms, and she struggled to lower it to the ground without dropping it.

Taylor half carried, half dragged the crate to her door and disappeared inside. A moment later she came back and collected a box and then closed the hatch door.

Taylor had a pet. Cat? Dog? Dragon?

Cat. He vaguely recalled her mentioning a cat.

He finished his sandwich then went to the slow cooker, where his dinner was simmering, and took off the lid. The one perk of the guest ranch was that he rarely had to cook for himself during the guest season, and during the slack times, he threw whatever was available into a slow cooker and let it do its thing. Tonight it was doing frozen meatballs in sauce. Pasta, lettuce, Italian dressing and a loaf of bread, and he was set. Not bad for a non-cook.

He'd just put the lid back on the cooker when

a knock sounded on the door. He set down the spoon he'd used to stir the sauce and headed across the kitchen, wondering what Taylor needed now.

After he and Dylan had lost all their money to Mike and Cal, they'd shared one last beer in Mike's living room while the old guys settled in for the news, and he'd been tempted to turn the conversation back to Taylor. But Taylor's past was none of his business, and he had no reason to be curious. Still, he kept flashing on Mike mentioning that if Taylor wanted something, her grandparents made certain she got it. If Cole read things right, Karl now regretted overindulging Taylor. Cole certainly regretted it, but that didn't stop him from being struck by just how good she looked standing there on his doorstep, her long blond hair falling around her shoulders instead of being caught back in an elastic or swept up in a bun-thing.

"Hi," she said in a voice that made him think that she was taking pains not to engage him in any way. "I'd like to go into the cellar via the back door, if that's all right."

"Sure."

She was three steps back down the walk before he could say anything else, which was probably a good thing, so he closed the door.

Leaned against the counter. Stroked his chin, then headed back to the door and followed Taylor around the house and down the cellar steps. She already had the key in the lock.

He stopped at the top step as she fumbled with the key. "How'd your interview go?"

She continued jingling the stubborn lock until it finally popped free. "Good," she said without looking up at him. "I hadn't realized anyone knew about the interview."

"I guessed," he said. "From the dress you wore."

"Ah. And have you guessed where I was today?" There was a note in her voice that put his back up.

"I'm not spying on you. We live together, remember?"

One corner of her mouth tightened before she pushed the door open and stepped into the dark cellar. A light snapped on, and after some scraping and general banging around, she reappeared with a largish empty wooden box. "Bed for my cat," she explained. After setting the box down beside her, she relocked the door and slid the key under the flowerpot next to the step.

"If you ever lock yourself out, now you

know how to get back in—unless you pushed the slide lock at the top of the stairs."

Cole shifted his weight, and she let out a small snort.

"You did, didn't you? Well, you never know when someone's going to sneak into your house, steal a chair and go through your things."

"It was locked when I moved in."

"Ah." He stood back as she wrestled the box up the steep stairs, but couldn't keep himself from reaching out to take it as she got close to the top. Taylor's hands dropped to her sides. "I'd appreciate it if you didn't tell people that I interviewed."

"Why? You're here to get a job, right?"

She shrugged carelessly, but Cole wasn't getting a careless vibe from her. "I like to keep things to myself until they're a done deal."

"It isn't like people are going to make fun of you if you don't get the job."

"I don't like to advertise failure."

"You haven't had a lot of failures in your life, have you?"

She narrowed her eyes. "Did you look me up?"

Caught. He'd been…curious. It was good to know one's adversary.

"Didn't you do the same with me?" he asked, feeling certain she had.

Her mouth twisted a little. "If I say no?"

"You've got more willpower than I do. I like to know who I'm dealing with."

"What did you find out?"

"You don't fail. Or rather you didn't, until recently." Mainly because she got a lot of help along the way. "What did you find out?"

"That you are pretty much off the radar."

He liked things that way. "Yup. No news-worthy successes or failures. No arrests or convictions either."

"So I assumed, or Karl wouldn't have let you on the place while I was here."

"Thereby saving you nineteen ninety-nine for the whole people-finder report?"

"Maybe."

"Where'd you interview?"

She shook her head and started walking again, leaving Cole to carry the box.

"You don't think you'll get the job?" he guessed.

She stopped and looked over her shoulder at him. "Oh, I'm going to get the job." He tilted his head in a questioning way, and she drew in a breath. "I don't talk about things until they're settled. Good business practice."

"Or you're afraid of jinxing yourself."

"I'm not afraid of jinxing myself," she snapped just a little too quickly. "And just so you're mentally prepared, I'm not moving immediately."

"Why not?"

She turned back toward him. "I have some catching up to do financially."

His eyes narrowed. "I assumed—"

"Incorrectly, it seems." She gave him a cool smile.

"This wasn't what we agreed on," he said in a low voice.

"How so?"

"Karl told me you could stay here until you got a job. You just said you were going to get this job, therefore, you're going to leave once you do."

She blinked at him. "That wasn't the deal."

"It was. Trust me." He leaned closer. "Better yet, call your grandfather. Ask him."

He watched her jaw set as she considered his words.

"I leased a farm because I wanted to get away from people, not so that I could share my life with them. I entered into the agreement in good faith. I let you stay here temporarily for Karl's sake. But what I really want is for you to make your own way in the world. Like everyone else."

"I don't have the resources to move again immediately."

"How long do you need? After you land this job?"

She quickly jerked her head to one side, giving him a perfect profile. "I'd planned to stay for six months."

He let out a disbelieving snort. "You need to alter your plan."

"You have no idea how costly it was staying in Seattle while I looked for work. I need those six months."

"And you have no idea how long it took me to save up to afford this lease."

"It wouldn't kill you to let me stay."

"And it wouldn't kill you to stand on your own two feet."

The corner of her mouth twitched, but that was the only way he knew that the arrow had hit home. "I have always stood on my own two feet." She pressed her lips together and swallowed. "You know nothing about me," she said in a low voice.

Not exactly true.

"Kind of the way I want things to stay. I like your grandfather and wouldn't hurt him for the world, but I'm not letting you take advantage of that fact."

She reached out and snatched the wooden box from him. He let go a little too soon and she almost lost her balance, so he reached out to take her arm. Her muscles tightened beneath his grip, but he didn't let go. "I know you feel like you're the one getting the shaft here, but Taylor, you're not. This is business. I won't be taken advantage of."

"I don't understand how my being here results in you losing any kind of advantage."

"Imagine if you rented an apartment and the landlord told you that he'd arranged to have someone living in your closet. You could try to ignore them, but they'd still be there, encroaching on the property you'd paid for."

"I can't afford to leave until I get a job."

"I know. That was the agreement. You stay until you get a job."

"I'll need at least four weeks after that to get a paycheck and rent a place."

"Four weeks is agreeable." It was a pay period. And giving her that was generous of him.

She lifted her chin, and he couldn't tell if she was angry or on the verge of tears. Maybe both. Maybe because she wasn't getting her own way.

"I'm not the bad guy here."

"Do you really believe that?" she muttered. She gave a small snort and then continued on past him, across the driveway to the door of the bunkhouse. She yanked it open with one hand, then shut it almost too carefully, as if doing her best to keep from slamming it.

Cole shook his head and followed the walk around his house. He wasn't the bad guy. He just wanted what he'd bought and paid for— privacy. And damned if he was going to let Taylor's needs supersede his own.

CHAPTER SEVEN

TAYLOR'S JAW MUSCLES were aching by the time she closed the bunkhouse door and set down the box. Max peeked out from under the chair where he'd taken sanctuary, then trotted across the floor to jump into the box, crouching so that only his ears showed above the edge.

"Wait for the pad, okay?" She bent to pick him up, noting that he must have gained at least a pound while in Carolyn's care, and heaved him against her chest. He pushed his head against the underside of her chin, and she automatically sat so as not to have to keep supporting his weight.

"Damn it, Max, we're in trouble again." Almost, because she wasn't about to allow herself to get into trouble again. Yes, she would stand on her own feet, and damn Cole Bryan for telling her she wasn't. He knew nothing about her, except for what he'd gleaned from the internet, and nothing there would bring one to draw the conclusion that she didn't stand on her own.

Which meant that he'd drawn the conclusion from other evidence.

What evidence?

That she'd assumed he'd fix the freaking hole?

She didn't think so.

He'd come here for privacy, which made her wonder what he had against people. Nothing in her online search had clued her in to his past profession. Karl would know, but she wasn't going to ask.

Max started to purr, but it didn't have its usual calming effect. Taylor closed her eyes and tried to take a deep breath. Yes, he'd definitely gained weight. Big cat. Big problems.

Think positively. You'll get the job, move out. Never have to see this guy again.

She'd also have to scrimp and make do, and you know what? She could do that. It made more sense to stay where she was, do battle with tan walls and judgmental farm-mates, but she would survive if she moved out in four weeks. She was lucky to have this place when she needed it.

Taylor wrapped her arms around her cat, and he pushed his head against her neck as if to say, "Yeah. We've got this. We'll be fine."

But where the hell did this guy get off judging her?

"That's his problem, not ours," Taylor murmured. That didn't mean she had to like it. She didn't mind being judged as a professional, but to have someone take a dislike to you simply because you existed…

Not acceptable.

Not one blinking thing you can do about it.

"Wine, Max. We need wine." Taylor eased the cat onto the seat cushion as she got up, and he curled into a giant ball, settling his tail over his nose and watching her through round green eyes. It felt good not to be alone.

It would feel better when they got their own place. Even though, deep in her gut, Taylor hated giving up and walking away without telling this guy a few home truths.

TAYLOR AWOKE EARLY on Monday morning, wishing that she could go back to sleep. The longer she stayed in bed, the more she tossed around. Finally she got up, leaving Max snuggled deep in the covers. She made coffee, tried to read the news on her phone, then finally, as the first bit of light showed over the horizon, got into her running gear. She didn't know if her general sense of being unsettled came from the fact that she'd hear about the job this week, or because of her face-off with Cole.

You need to stand on your own two feet.

Where did he come off saying stuff like that?

She had to stop thinking about it or she was going to march across the driveway and demand answers.

She ran longer than usual, doing her best to exhaust herself and thinking that maybe she could catch up on her sleep later that day. After all, if things went the way she hoped, she wouldn't have the luxury of midweek naps. She was just approaching the bunkhouse when her phone rang. Quickly, she unzipped her jacket pocket and answered without looking at the number.

"Miss Evans. Mark Roberts, US West Bank."

"Good morning." Taylor's heart was beating faster. His voice did not hold even a hint of "I'm sorry, but…"

"I know this is short notice, but are you available for another meeting tomorrow afternoon?"

"I'm free all day."

"Excellent. If we could meet at three o'clock, that would fit everyone's schedule."

"I'll be there."

"Thank you. See you then."

Somehow Taylor kept her feet firmly on the ground—probably because Cole was heading in from the fields and she didn't want to be caught doing a happy dance. But she did a quick twirl after shutting the door behind her. Max raised his head from the bed, then stretched and went back to sleep.

Second meeting…it had to be that they were offering her the job. Worst-case scenario, round two of the interview process. She reached for the phone to call Carolyn, then remembered that her friend was at work, so she fired off a text instead.

Taylor started pacing the rustic floorboards. If she got this job, then that would be the start of her upward climb. Her journey back to her old life. Proof to everyone that when Taylor Evans was faced with failure, she didn't break—she bounced. It had been a long, slow bounce, but a bounce all the same.

Taylor brewed a pot of tea, settled in her chair and started perusing rentals in the Eagle Valley. The problem with living in an area that was rapidly gaining in popularity was that housing was tight. New apartments and condos were being built along the lake at the center of the valley, but those prices were too rich for Taylor's new budget, and the moderately priced housing was at a minimum.

No. It was close to nonexistent, unless she wanted to rent a single-wide trailer on a small lot on the outskirts of town. If she did that, she may as well stay on the farm...for longer than four weeks, that is.

Taylor set her tablet aside and got to her feet, feeling as if she needed another long run. But running wasn't the answer. She had to come up with a way to convince Cole to let her stay on the farm without involving her grandfather. Definitely without involving her grandfather. In addition to not wanting to add to his stress, that remark about standing on her own two feet still stung.

She'd made mistakes in her attitude toward Cole. No doubt about that. And now she needed to fix things. Mend fences.

Start fresh.

The big question was how.

COLE HAD JUST gotten out of the shower when a knock sounded at his door. He glanced at the watch he'd left on the counter beside the sink. Seven o'clock. What did Taylor need at this hour?

He thought about ignoring the knock, but it came again as he struggled to pull his jeans up over damp skin. Best to deal with her and get it over with.

When he got to the kitchen door, still buttoning his shirt, he found Taylor waiting on the porch with a small cake pan in one hand and a notebook in the other.

Had he missed a memo?

Taylor held up the pan, which smelled heavenly. "Peace offering," she said simply. "My grandmother's recipe."

He almost said that he didn't know they were at war, then rethought his words. "Why?"

"I'd like to talk to you."

He gestured for her to come into the kitchen, and she did, walking past him to set the pan on the table.

"What do you want, Taylor?"

"I want to renegotiate."

"Renegotiate what?" As far as he knew they'd yet to negotiate at all.

She pushed aside his stack of mail and spread the notebook on the kitchen table. "Look at this."

He looked, and all he saw were columns of figures. "Okay..."

She rubbed the back of her neck as if it were

stiff from a night of heavy mathematics, then gestured at the book. "Last night I crunched numbers. Based on the salary mentioned during the interview—"

"Did you get the job?" If so, he was buying a celebratory bottle of whiskey.

"I have reason to be optimistic."

Good reason, he hoped.

"If I stay here for six months, I'll be in a better position to resume my life."

"Let me see if I understand this...you want to stay for free in the buildings I'm renting."

"You aren't using the bunkhouse."

"I could be."

She let out a breath, and he could almost see her counting to ten. "Why," she asked slowly, "can't you give me a break?"

"Because you expect it."

"No," she said carefully, "I don't."

"Yeah. I think you do. I think you've spent so much time focused on *your* needs and *your* achievements that you expect everyone else to be, too."

"And you came to this conclusion because of the rotten-floorboard incident?"

"I guess it started when you tried to bully me out of the house I rented."

"You *are* more suited for the bunkhouse."

Her voice began to tighten, but she seemed to catch herself. "You grew up on a ranch."

"And I'm renting this ranch…farm. You invaded it. I let you. But only while you were out of work. That was the deal, and I don't want to renegotiate."

"This is a big farm. Do you have some kind of complex about being alone?"

"Yeah. I do. I'm still recovering from my last job, dealing with the rich and famous."

She gave him a long, slow look. "By rich and famous I assume you mean spoiled and entitled."

"Yeah. Pretty much."

"And you also mean me." He didn't respond. Taylor was nothing if not sharp, and now she was sharp and angry. Blue fire sparked in her eyes.

"You judgmental prick." She jabbed a finger at his chest as she spoke, and he automatically caught her hand and held on, stopping her in the middle of the second jab. Taylor yanked her hand free and took a step back. Just one, probably so it didn't appear to be a full-fledged retreat. "You've given as good as you've got, Cole. It's like you're taking out all your previous job frustrations on me."

"Maybe so. But if you weren't here, I wouldn't be able to do that."

She smiled up at him. "I can take it if you can."

"You won't have a chance. You stay longer than four weeks, I'll charge you rent."

She picked up her notebook and the pan. "We'll see about that."

A moment later she was gone, leaving only the delicious aroma of the coffee cake she'd brought to bribe him with.

He should have eaten first and argued later.

COLE HAD DECIDEDLY mixed feelings as he pulled off the highway onto the road leading to the Bryan Guest Ranch, which had simply been the Bryan Ranch until Miranda gained control of the outfit.

The operation would have scraped by, as older ranches do, having good years and bad, but Miranda had wanted more, and by converting one of the ranches into a ritzy guest ranch and leaving the smaller sister ranch as a pseudo-working ranch where guests could enjoy "authentic" ranch life, she'd essentially tripled their incomes.

Cole didn't have a problem with that. He had a problem with the way Miranda had set herself up as queen, and after her husband died, she became unbearable. The guests loved her because she catered to them. The workers, those that weren't in her pocket anyway, despised and distrusted her. If not one of the chosen few, she could draw you into her inner circle one day, then viciously attack you the next. You never knew which Miranda you were getting, but odds were if you were on salary, you were going to see her scary side.

Her relationship with Cole had been different from the rest of the staff, since he was family and she needed him. That didn't slow down her passive-aggressive attacks, but she didn't hit him with them full on as she did the other employees. Jancey was another matter. Yes, she was family, but Miranda didn't need her in the same way she needed Cole. After she started college in the fall, Jancey would work only summers and that was mainly because of her stubborn determination to stay on the family ranch. "I won't let her chase me away from home," she'd muttered the last time they'd discussed the matter. Cole wished her well, because Miranda had succeeded in chasing him away from home. For now anyway.

When he hit the fork in the road with the expensive carved wood signs, one pointing to the

Bryan Guest Ranch and the other to the Bryan Working Ranch, he took the right, heading for what would never feel like home again.

Jancey came out of the house wearing her canvas coat and worn jeans that were at least two sizes too big. Raiding what was left of his closet, as she'd done since she was in junior high. She pushed her thick blond braid over her shoulder and leaned against the newel post, waiting for him to park.

"Nice jeans," he said as he got out of the truck. "And they seem so familiar."

She looked down at the washed-out denim, then back up at him, a smile lighting her eyes. "If you can't keep track of your stuff, then it's fair game."

"I think you hide my stuff."

"Only when I need a comfy pair of work jeans." She came down the steps, and they walked together toward a corral where several calves were milling around. "Sure you're up for this?"

"Yeah. Not a problem. I can work in the feedings around my other chores."

"Good, because my duty schedule has become so unpredictable, it's hard to get here when I need to be here."

"How many days until you go back to school?"

"One hundred and twenty-two."

"You'll make it."

"I know. I know, but I'm getting a little sick of being on call after hours. Miranda keeps sending people to get me for horse emergencies. Want to know how many of them are real?"

"She's trying to show you who's boss."

"Or just being herself." Cole put a hand on the back of her neck, and she leaned her head into his arm. "You left the ranch because of her, right?"

He frowned down at her. "I have to earn a living, and I couldn't work for her anymore." Their ranch was the working ranch, but the operation was so small now that it couldn't support them, and their cut of the guest ranch wasn't enough to see them through rough times. They'd both had to work for the family business and draw a paycheck.

"But you didn't leave because you hated the ranch."

Cole took hold of his sister's shoulders and turned her so he could see her face. "Are you starting to hate the ranch?"

First she looked surprised, then adamant as she said, "No. I don't."

They loaded the calves in the trailer, as well

as a yearling heifer that would be delivered to a couple in the Eagle Valley later in the week. After having a sandwich together, Cole headed back to the farm still thinking about his conversation with his sister.

He had a feeling that she was one short step from telling Miranda to shove it, as he had, and she couldn't do that while three calves had counted on her for sustenance. He hoped she did it now. They'd still have their ranch, but since it was part of the guest ranch structure— the working ranch where guests participated in cattle drives and brandings and soaked up ranch ambiance—Miranda would have to send crew members from the guest ranch to do the chores and such.

The setup of the family operation was convoluted, having started as a handshake deal between two brothers trying to increase cash flow. As the business grew, things were put in writing, made official. Cole's uncle had owned his physical ranch, and Cole's dad had owned his, but the operations were combined into one entity, and decisions were made by agreement between owners. Fortunately for Miranda, operations were in place and smoothly running by the time her husband died, because Cole wasn't certain at this point if he'd call a fire truck if he saw her house ablaze.

SINCE SHE'D LIVED alone and worked crazy hours in her former life, Taylor hadn't realized how much she depended on easy access to the advice of friends. On the one hand, she was glad that no one was close enough to see where she was living. Compared with the beautiful simplicity of her former apartment, this place was…the words *an abomination* occurred to her, but she reminded herself to be grateful. On the other, she couldn't get together with Carolyn or Paul or any of her peers over dinner or drinks and hash out the best course of action.

In this case, however, the best of course of action appeared to have been laid out for her by one annoyingly uncooperative guy. She was leaving the free-rent situation, so there would be no building of the nest egg. She'd be living paycheck to paycheck, which was something she'd never done before, and it frightened her.

She shouldn't have sunk so much money into attempting to pay off student loans ahead of schedule. She should have saved more, but she'd stupidly felt bulletproof.

Cole was right. She hadn't encountered

many failures in her life, and she'd had a sense of false security until the layoff.

Bottom line, she was going to have to scrape by on half the salary she was used to, while living in a city she didn't want to be in. Even accounting for the difference in the amount of rent paid, she was going to be one disaster away from withdrawing money from her IRA and invoking stiff penalties.

Taylor spent the rest of the morning devising a careful budget, crossing off items she could live without, calculating state taxes and federal withholdings, possible insurance premiums, factoring in a strict 10 percent savings margin. At the end of the month, she'd be about three dollars to the good, but it was better than her current situation.

She might still be trapped in Montana, but she would be standing on her own two freaking feet.

She showered, put on a superfine wool dress—the simple lines of which belied the amount of money she had paid—checked her shoes for scuffs, and stuffed what she needed into her small handbag. She also buffed up her leather carryall that served as a briefcase to carry extra materials to the meeting. A slim watch, silver earrings, a little makeup and she was good to go.

Taylor checked her reflection, shaking her head at the sad tan walls and the sheet pinned over the window that showed behind her. Maybe it was good that Cole so adamantly refused to let her stay for six months. She needed to get away from this dismal setting.

"I'm on my way, Max." The cat rolled over on his back and yawned—a sure sign that he was wishing her good luck. "Thanks, big guy. I'll bring you back some tuna."

COLE SLOWED AS he approached the driveway and swung wide to accommodate the gooseneck trailer. It was growing close to dusk, and Taylor's lights were on. Soon, if all went well, he'd drive home and the bunkhouse would be dark. He'd walk around his farm and not wonder if he was being watched. He wouldn't have people getting him out of the shower at seven in the morning. In other words, he would be living the life he'd intended—a gloriously solitary life where he solved no one's problems but his own.

He backed the trailer up to the gate of the newly restored corral and opened the gate so that it came to rest against the side of the trailer. He secured it, then unlatched the trailer door. As he started pulling open the door to form a narrow chute into the corral, the heel of his boot caught a piece of half-buried wire protruding from the ground. An instant later the yearling heifer, sensing freedom, hit the door hard, hitting him in the face and knocking him backward as she bounded out into the corral. Cole's knee twisted sideways as he went down, and he fought to break his fall by jutting out his hands instead of shoulder rolling as his football coach had taught him. And he felt the nasty snap in his wrist as his weight hit solid ground.

He scrambled to his feet, but not in time to put the trailer gate back into position to contain the animals in the corral. He twisted sideways as the heifer blasted past him, out of the corral and into the driveway, the calves close behind her.

They disappeared around the house, and Cole took a slow, limping step. Pain shot through his knee—a familiar feeling since it wasn't the first time he'd sprained it—and his wrist...he had a bad feeling that his wrist was toast. That was when he realized that he was bleeding.

Shit. Years and years of ranching and he'd

been done in by a heifer and three leppy calves—which couldn't be allowed to escape out onto the county road. Bad for them, worse for drivers.

Cole started toward the bunkhouse as fast as he could go, holding his injured wrist against his abs and squeezing his eyes shut against the pain in his knee, cursing with each step.

"Taylor!" he shouted as he got closer to the bunkhouse.

He waited, panting a little, then continued around the side of the house to her door. He started pounding. "Tay-*lor*!"

She jerked the door open just as he was about to pound again. "I need your help."

"You think you can insult me and then expect me to run to your aid—" Her words stopped abruptly and a look of horror formed. He reached up to his forehead and discovered where the blood was coming from.

"This is serious," he muttered.

"Who did this to you?"

He ignored the question. "I need you to run to the end of the driveway and close the big gate. Now."

She sucked in a breath, and just when he thought she was going to argue, she brushed past him and literally started running. He limped toward the middle of the driveway, trying to see if the cattle were still on the far side of the house. Once the gate was closed, Taylor jogged back to him. Before she could demand answers, he said, "And the gate to the field. That one needs to be closed, too."

She gave him a pained look and went on her way. Cole shut his eyes, barely able to believe the way this was all going down. But at least Taylor was cooperating. He'd half expected some kind of a stubborn standoff, but no. She'd closed gates without demanding explanations—which gave him time to try to think of one that would allow him to save face.

It didn't exist. He'd seen the half-buried wire days ago and had fully planned to dig it up, but since it was smooth and not barbed, he'd put it off.

His fault.

Taylor once again started jogging back toward him, then she dodged sideways, stifling a small scream as the heifer trotted around the house toward her. She stopped running, pressing her hand to her chest as calves trotted after the heifer.

"I see you got your calves."

Cole let out a breath, gently cradling his injured wrist. "I got them. They got me."

"What happened?"

"Long story." She folded her arms over her chest. Cole looked past her for a moment, then met her gaze. "I tripped opening the gate."

She sucked in her cheeks as she considered his very simple and very truthful explanation. "I guess there's a certain danger factor involved in living alone on a farm."

"That's why I carry a phone."

"Didn't do you much good tonight, did it?"

Because it was on the seat of the truck instead of in his pocket.

"What if I hadn't been here to close the gates?" she asked, jerking her chin toward the cattle now taking a turn around the barn.

"I would have managed."

"You hope." She dropped her hands. "How badly are you hurt?"

"I don't know." It wasn't something he wanted to discuss with her.

"Emergency room?"

He made a sputtering noise. "I don't think so. I sprained my knee. It's not the first time."

"You might need stitches."

"I'll decide when I clean up the cut."

"With your broken wrist." She glanced meaningfully at his injured hand.

"It's also a sprain." He knew full well that it

was probably broken—he'd heard the snap—
but until that was proven, he was going with
best-case scenario. "I can clean one-handed."

"Sucks, doesn't it?"

"Being hurt?"

"Needing help from others…especially
when you've been so adamant about not helping others."

He opened his mouth, then snapped it shut
again. This was not a conversation they needed
to have now. Or ever. "I owe you," he said.

"Yeah. You do. What are you going to do
about your animals?"

At the moment he was going to be thankful that Jancey had given the calves a goodbye
feeding so he didn't have to deal with bottles
until the morning.

"I'll see about luring the heifer into the pen
with some feed. The calves will follow. Even
if I can't get the heifer immediately, the calves
are bottle babies. They'll be easier to put back
in the corral."

"Bottle babies?" Another pointed look at
his wrist and then she gave a small shrug and
turned around, heading back to the bunkhouse,
thus driving home the point that his life would
be a lot easier if they worked together. It would
also be a lot less solitary.

But tonight, for the first time, it didn't seem like a total imposition to have Taylor there. She'd been a lifesaver, as hard as that was to acknowledge. He lifted his chin toward the sky and saw the first stars starting to shine through the twilight. Like she said, this situation sucked.

TAYLOR DEBATED WITH herself all the way back to the bunkhouse. Help with the cattle, or let Cole wallow in the mess he'd made? When she glanced over her shoulder, he was still standing where she'd left him, making her wonder if he could move. He caught her staring at him and started limping toward his house in a determined way.

He'd blown a knee and was going to need help, and she'd bet dollars to doughnuts that he wouldn't ask until he was on the brink of desperation. No—he wouldn't ask until he was truly desperate, as he'd been when he'd needed her to close the gates.

But what if she offered to help—in exchange for something she needed and he didn't want to give her?

Taylor abruptly turned and walked back toward him, easily catching up with him. He was in full guy mode when she stopped a few feet in front of him, bringing him to a standstill. He actually looked relieved to not be moving, though he practically snarled as he asked, "What?"

"You need to try to sound more defensive. You're not quite at maximum level yet." His jaw muscles tightened, but she didn't give him a chance to respond. "I'm going to help you into the house." She slid in under his shoulder on the side, wrapping her arm around his back. "For purely selfish reasons, of course. This way I don't have to keep checking to see if you made it home." She glanced up at him, reminding herself of the times she'd done this when her track teammates had been hurt. Nothing personal.

But none of her track teammates' bodies had felt like this. They'd been whipcord thin and wiry. For all his lean appearance, Cole was solid muscle. And he smelled good. He let out a breath as she eased her shoulder up under his, making her wonder if he was feeling the exact same thing as she was. Because she might drive him crazy, but she'd seen the way he'd reacted the few times they were close.

And now they were way too close.

"I can make it," he said on a growl. "Like I said, this isn't the first time."

"Ready?" she asked as if he hadn't spoken, cursing the husky note in her voice. She couldn't help it. The guy pissed her off, but at a primal level, he also turned her on.

Stop being turned on...

As if hormones listened to logic.

"Taylor..."

"Here we go." Taylor gritted her teeth and focused on getting Cole to the house rather than jumping him, curling her fingers into his hard side as he leaned on her. He was heavy, and she could only imagine how long it would have taken him to get to the front door under his own steam. He did his best to keep his weight off her as they slowly climbed the three porch steps, but he wasn't all that successful. Both were breathing heavily by the time they limped into the kitchen. Cole immediately sat himself in a chair, and Taylor pushed the hair back from her damp forehead.

"You're a mess," she said.

"Thanks." Cole closed his eyes. To shut her out or to deal with the pain? No telling. Taylor moved past him to the paper towel holder, which she happened to have made herself in day camp during one of her short summer visits. Her mother never wanted her to spend much time on the farm, having concluded that her daughter would hate it as much as she did. So she arranged camps for summer. She also arranged for Karl to pay for them.

Taylor dampened the towels and handed them to Cole, who pushed the folded wad up against his bleeding forehead. He pulled it away, grimaced, then pressed it back into place. Taylor waited until he pulled it away again before saying, "I don't think you'll need stitches."

"Small blessings," he muttered.

"Blessings all the same."

He gave her a look she couldn't interpret. "If you don't need help with anything else—"

"I'm good."

"Great." She went over to her grandfather's small kitchen desk and wrote her cell number on the pad there. "Give me a call if you get yourself into trouble." He scowled at her, but she left it at that. Having once had a broken arm herself, she had no idea how he was going to get out of his clothing, or back into it in the morning, but it wasn't her problem.

She cast one last look around the cheery kitchen, recalled the excellent times she'd had there with Karl as a kid—the times when she wasn't carted off to this camp or that—then with a small twist of her mouth let herself out the back door.

A cheery kitchen and a big bathtub. Cole had everything she wanted.

He also had a sprained or broken arm, a blown knee and wild bovines on the loose. And he was probably stuck in his clothing.

Taylor let out a small snort. He might end up needing her more than he expected, and she was not above taking advantage of the fact… while firmly ignoring the little voice that said maybe she also kind of liked being around him.

CHAPTER EIGHT

COLE WOKE UP with a raging headache—possibly from sleeping upright in Karl's recliner, but more likely because he smacked his head when the heifer flattened him yesterday. He set the now-warm gel packs on the floor beside the chair and dropped the recliner footrest as gently as he could, but the action of the chair swinging forward sent teeth-clenching pain shooting through his swollen knee, as well as his wrist—which was now double its normal size.

He struggled out of the chair, inhaling deeply as he gritted his teeth to stifle a groan.

How in the hell was he going to feed those calves when he could barely move?

He hobbled to the bathroom, telling himself that rodeo riders went through pain like this all the time. And after downing a dose of anti-inflammatory meds along with his coffee, he started to feel better. Until he moved again.

Son of a bitch.

He was still in yesterday's clothes, and he clapped his hat on his head, glad that the head wound was superficial. He limped out the door to move the truck and trailer so that he could get the heifer and calves into the pen. At the end of the walk, he changed directions and crossed the driveway to the bunkhouse. He needed help, and he may as well ask and get it over with.

Cursing under his breath, he knocked on the door, and a second later Taylor answered, wearing her running shorts and a hooded sweatshirt. Her forehead was damp and her shoes muddy.

"I need help," he said simply.

Her expression didn't change. "I need to stay here for six months at minimal rent."

He stared at her. Where was the woman who'd helped him into his house last night? Or rather bullied him into his house last night. "You'd hit me when I'm down?"

"I prefer calling it striking while the iron is hot." She grimaced as she took in his appearance.

He knew he looked like hell. Unshaven, rumpled clothing. It reflected how he felt and how close he was to his last nerve. He could call his sister for help. He could call Jordan.

But both would have a lengthy drive ahead of them to get to the farm, and it was possible that he'd need help for several days. His knee would be less painful within the week. The wrist...

"Six months." Why not? If he didn't agree, he had a feeling she'd come up with another work-around.

"From my date of employment."

He gave her a purposely dubious frown. "You're sure you'll be employed?"

"I had a second interview yesterday. It went well."

She spoke with quiet confidence, which made him believe that she wasn't trying to convince herself. It really had gone well.

Maybe he needed to look at this like a prison term. The sooner he started, the sooner it would be over. "Six months from today." Her expression clouded, but before she could speak, he said, "I thought you were getting this job."

"I am."

"Then it's not a problem."

She shifted her weight. "Six months from the date I fill out my W-2."

"For that I need a lot of help." She wasn't the only one who could strike while the iron was hot. And he had to admit to enjoying the way her forehead scrunched up as she debated his meaning.

"What are you proposing?"

"When you're not job hunting, you're working around the place. And after you land a job, you give me some time before and/or after work."

She eyed him warily. "I…"

"Think of it as helping out your grandfather. His place will be much nicer when he moves back."

"Dirty pool."

"Kind of like extorting me when I'm in a tough spot?"

"Very much," she deadpanned.

One corner of his mouth tilted up. Okay. He liked honesty. "Can you drive a stick?"

She cocked an eyebrow. The Z. Yes, she could drive a stick.

"I need the truck and trailer moved." At the moment, he didn't know how his knee would behave with the clutch and didn't feel like screwing around.

"Let me change."

Cole took a limping step backward and tested the pain level of his wrist while she changed. On a scale of one to ten, he was a solid eight. He could handle it, if nothing touched or jarred his arm. The chances of farming without using his wrist were nil, so he would go to urgent care and have someone look at it as soon as he got the cattle corralled and the calves fed.

"Where do you want the trailer?"

"The usual spot by the barn."

"I said I could drive a stick. I didn't say I could back up a trailer."

"Over by the tree, then."

Anywhere but where it was, blocking the gate to the corral. Taylor was already several yards ahead of him when he called, "The gate is tied to the trailer." *So please don't rip it off its hinges.*

"Good to know," she called back without looking at him.

He caught up with her just as she'd unhooked the rope securing the gate to the trailer and swung it back against the corral. "That tree there?" She pointed at the elm next to the machine shed.

"Yeah. Watch out for calves." They were hungry and already cautiously approaching to see if anyone had the bottles. The heifer was grazing in the backyard, and he could see that she'd had a fine old time walking all over Karl's rosebushes. He might have to replace them if they didn't snap back. No...his new farmhand could replace them.

He smiled grimly.

Taylor got into the truck and turned the key. The diesel engine gave a few coughing chugs, and Cole limped closer, waving for her to roll down the window. "It's an older diesel. You can't start it until the warning lights go off. And don't put it in gear until the needles on the gauges come to life."

She scowled at him. "Is there also a secret handshake?"

"No. Do those things and you're fine."

She nodded and left the window down. The next time she turned the key, the engine started. A few seconds later, she said, "The needle moved."

"You're good to go." He stood back as she put the truck into grandma gear and it bucked as she let out the clutch. Low-geared pickups were nothing like a nice little sports car. She didn't look his way as she moved the truck forward and stopped it under the elm. Once it was parked, she crossed the driveway, her hands pushing deep into her front pockets.

"Bad clutch," she said.

He shook his head. "Different gears."

"What now? The doctor?" She continued as if he hadn't spoken.

"Feed the calves."

"Where's the feed?"

"In the house. Milk replacer. I have to mix it up."

"And you feed it in a pan?"

"A bottle. You'll love it."

She gave him a cautious look. "I'm sure I will."

"You'll need a towel. They slobber and drip."

Taylor wrinkled her nose but didn't say a word. He jerked his head toward the house. "Come on. I'll show you."

TAYLOR MADE A supreme effort to keep her eyes from straying over to where Cole walked— or rather limped—beside her. Guys shouldn't look sexier after sleeping in their clothes. It wasn't right.

They shouldn't threaten people with calf slobber either.

Or work detail, in retaliation for a perfectly reasonable request. The only thing hurt by her staying on for six months was his sense of isolation and privacy.

If he wanted to play things this way, fine.

She could handle it if he could. No—she could handle it even if he *couldn't*.

She gave in to weakness and shot a quick glance his way. His mouth was tight, his lips close to white. The guy was hurting.

He was also lucky to have someone there. Lucky last night. Lucky this morning. He probably could have called a friend or relative to help, but if that had been an easy option, she wouldn't now be looking at a six-month reprieve.

"You know," she said as they approached the house, "I'm not staying here to torture you." He frowned at her, which barely changed his tight, pained expression. "All right, you got me. Now that I know you better, I am."

"Ha, ha," he muttered.

"That wasn't a joke," she said straight-faced. He shot her another sideways look, but she ignored it. "It's a matter of getting back on my feet as soon as possible."

"Yeah, I get it," he said in a way that told her he got it but didn't like it.

"I never thought something like this would happen to me." She wasn't certain why she continued to hammer on the matter. Maybe to distract him from his obvious pain. Or maybe because, now that they'd struck their deal, she wanted him to understand that she wasn't wild about the situation either but was doing what she could to survive.

"Why not, Taylor? What would make you immune?"

"Hard work and planning. I worked my ass off for Stratford. More sixty-to-eighty-hour weeks than I care to think about. I got awards. Raises. Bonuses."

"Maybe you became too high priced to keep on."

A possibility she'd considered more than once. "They got their money's worth."

He slowly climbed the steps, holding his arm against his chest, and Taylor eased past him to open the door.

"I'm not helpless," he muttered.

"And not good at receiving the help you ask for either."

"Hey—at least I asked."

"Only because you had no other option."

"Which you had no qualms about taking advantage of."

She smiled sweetly. "I gotta be me."

He limped into the kitchen and on into the mudroom. "That's the replacer," he said, pointing to a bag.

He gave her instructions to mix, and once

Taylor had three quart-size bottles filled and the nipples in place, Cole placed them in a metal bucket and they once again started for the door.

"How are you going to catch these guys? It isn't like you can chase them."

"But you can."

Her eyes widened as she held up her palms in a defensive gesture. "The calves don't concern me, but that big one is a renegade."

"You can carry a stick."

"Comforting," she muttered. Because he wasn't kidding.

Together they crossed to the barn, where Cole had her put alfalfa and grain into the feeders. Following instructions, Taylor went around the house to the backyard, where the heifer was grazing, and raised her arms to shoo her toward the driveway. The black cow eyed her balefully, then kinked her tail and started trotting toward where Cole stood blocking the driveway. Taylor hoped the cow wasn't going to run over him again, because his limping gait made a tortoise look like a speed demon. He waved his hat, and the cow shied sideways and headed straight for the metal panels Taylor had set up between the corral and the machine shop. Taylor closed in, and the cow, spotting the feed, headed straight into the corral. The calves followed, and she closed the gate, breathing hard—more from nerves than from exertion—as she locked it.

"Now what?"

"Now you experience the wonder of milk slobber." Taylor screwed up her face and Cole continued, "You're the one who chose to sell your soul for a few months of free rent."

"Free?" She'd offered to pay minimal rent. It seemed only fair, and damn it, she was trying to be fair. She wasn't above capitalizing on his situation, but she was going to do what was right now that she had.

"But I'm going to work your ass off."

"I think we might have to get some of this in writing."

"I have stuff in writing with your grandfather and it didn't save me from you."

She smirked at him and reached for the bottle. "I need instructions."

"Try not to get mobbed."

"Thanks." He handed her a bottle, and Taylor eased in through the gate, locking it behind her with one hand. The killer heifer barely acknowledged her presence, but the calves, which were nosing through the hay, recognized the bottle. She straddled the first one as Cole instructed, then held up its chin from behind, and it immediately latched on to the nipple. As promised, milk rolled down her hand and arm as the calf slurped, but the gross factor was counterbalanced by the cute factor.

"This isn't bad," she said, glancing up at Cole.

"Just time-consuming."

"And a little sticky."

After they were all fed, Taylor was ready for a second shower. She had milk replacer up to her armpits and cow poop on her shoes due to a misstep. "I want to negotiate for use of your washing machine."

He gave her a pained look that had nothing to do with his injuries.

"It isn't like I'll use it and forget to leave the house." Although she wouldn't mind doing that. The wind had blown the previous evening, and the bunkhouse was drafty.

"Let's get that in writing, too."

If it wasn't for the grimace on his face, she would have thought he was playing with her. But he was grimacing. And hurting.

"Are you going to see someone about your wrist?"

"Yeah."

"Let me drive you."

The "all right" didn't come easily, but Cole got it out and Taylor said, "I need to change again and wash up, then I'm ready whenever you are."

"Probably the sooner the better. There might be a crowd, and I don't want to kill the whole day."

"Yes. Because you can do so much in the shape you're in."

"I have someone to do my stuff for me now."

She sneered at him because he seemed to expect it. "Are you going to change?" Not that he didn't look good rumpled.

"I think the medical personnel will understand why I don't."

As did she. "Just making sure you don't need help before we go," she said, hoping against hope that he didn't call her bluff. Because she would help him…but that might not be the wisest move on her part. Interesting, yes. Wise? No.

"And baiting me in the process?"

"A little. Habit." She smiled tightly. "Give me fifteen minutes."

Fifteen minutes became twenty, but since Cole expected to wait at least half an hour, he was impressed. It wasn't that he thought that Taylor was going to waste time primping, but he figured it would take her a while to clean her shoes. Instead, she left her running shoes outside and wore ballet flats with jeans that hugged her legs in a way that made him want to peel them off. And he didn't feel bad about that, because it was more of a reaction than a plan. She looked good in her jeans, and he *was* a guy. One who hadn't peeled off anyone's jeans in quite a while. Obviously, he wouldn't be peeling *these* jeans, but he could think about it in a hypothetical way.

They took Taylor's SUV, and once Cole was signed in to the urgent care facility, she left him and went grocery shopping. He had her cell number, but from the looks of the crowded waiting room, he didn't think he'd need it. Two and a half hours, several X-rays, a knee brace and a wrist splint later, he was good to go. The only thing he'd been spared was an MRI, but only because he had to travel to get it done.

Taylor was waiting in the outer office when he came out of the treatment area, staring down at her lap. When he limped closer, she looked up at him, her expression instantly blanked out. The force field was in place. Something was wrong.

Why?

She got to her feet, shouldering her purse in one smooth move. "All wrapped up and ready to go, I see." Oh, yeah. Brisk voice, no-nonsense manner. Something had happened. But he played along.

He held up his wrist. "Sprained, not broken." Although sprains could take as long to heal as breaks, he was relieved not to have a cast knocking around.

"The knee?"

"I'm not getting an expensive test to tell me what I already know. It's also sprained."

"They can't do something for that?"

"Not a hell of a lot. I have to live with it." Just as he had before.

They drove most of the way home in silence, but not the same kind of silence that had settled between them on the trip to urgent care. This was a brittle silence, one that begged to be broken.

Taylor turned onto the county road leading to the farm, and Cole decided enough was enough. He shifted in his seat and was about to ask what the deal was when Taylor spoke.

"I didn't get the job."

Well, that sucked. Cole stared at her profile, wondering what the hell had gone wrong.

She'd been confident about the second interview. "Did they give a reason?"

She shook her head. "Nothing beyond the usual being-very-sorry kind of thing."

"That bites." She was never leaving the farm.

"Yes." She lifted her chin. "The search continues." She cleared her throat. "I hate telling Grandpa."

"Don't."

"That got me into trouble last time." She glanced at him. "You had something to say on the matter, if I recall."

Yeah, he did, but he hadn't thought about the reason she hadn't called Karl. "You didn't call him because you were embarrassed? About losing your job, I mean."

"I'd never failed so massively before."

"Did *you* fail? Like…do something wrong that got you fired?" Because he was curious if he'd gotten the entire story.

"I didn't do anything wrong," she snapped. "Other than putting in more hours than most people on staff. But it still felt like failure." The corner of her mouth turned down. "No… actually, it felt like getting screwed—and not the good kind."

She pulled into the farm driveway and parked

beside the bunkhouse, turned off the ignition and pulled the key out. She was reaching for the door handle when Cole asked the burning question. "Realistically, what are your chances of being employed here, in this area?"

"Well, I thought they'd be better here than in Seattle."

"And because this is where you can afford to live while you look?"

Her jaw shifted. "You know that's the case."

"You're in finance, right?"

"Yes."

"Yet you're in financial trouble."

Her expression iced over. "Do you ever get tired of judging me?"

"What the hell happened, Taylor?"

"Student loans. Tons of them. I didn't save as much as I should have, because I felt safe and was concentrating on trying to pay off loans—like the one from my grandfather. And I enjoyed my life in the city."

"Not to mention your car."

"That car is special."

He couldn't argue with that. Jordan's eyes had practically glazed over when he heard about it. "Selling it would probably keep you solvent for—"

"A few months. Then the money would be gone and the car would be gone."

"But you'd have a few more months of living expenses. Sometimes you have to sacrifice—"

"My dad left me that car." The words came grinding out, then Taylor jerked her gaze away, as if she hated showing him emotion that wasn't pure anger or snark. As if vulnerability was a bad thing. Maybe it was in her world. "I was fourteen when he passed away, and he left me that car. Before I could drive. He wanted me to have it."

"Okay," he said after a crackling stretch of silence. "I get it."

He let out a breath and leaned his head back, telling himself to get out of the vehicle. He didn't move.

"Do you have any idea what it's like to be kicked to the curb?"

"I've had my share of failures."

"I'm not talking failures. I'm talking rejection—from the very people you were trying to help." She let out a breath. "You don't have a clue."

She grabbed for the door handle, but before she got out, he put his good hand on her knee, and she froze. So did he. But he didn't move his hand. He didn't want her to leave yet…and he had to admit to liking the way her leg felt beneath his palm.

"Your attitude when you arrived…it wasn't exactly defeated."

"I'm here, Cole. Living in a shack. Doesn't that smack of defeat?"

He pulled his hand away. Now that they were in the heat of battle, there was no way she was leaving. "It smacked of you expecting to kick me out of the house and get a free ride while you sorted things out."

"That's exactly what I wanted." She didn't sound one bit sorry. "To tell you the truth, it's what I still want. I'm tired of the floor bumping under my feet and the wind whistling in through the window frame and having no bathtub, but you know what? I can deal."

"Because you have no choice?" he asked softly.

"That's the best reason to suck it up, don't you think?" She gave a small sniff. "What happens if I refuse to help you?"

"Then I guess I kick you off the property."

She let out a breath as she stared out the windshield at the bunkhouse. "That's what I thought."

Another silence fell, thick with tension. Finally, Cole gave in. "Of course, your grandfather will hate me because I'm messing with his princess."

"There is that." She didn't look at him. Her eyes slowly closed, and she inhaled again, as if centering herself. Or trying to come up with ways to do him bodily harm.

The thing was, right now, he needed her. It was a good thing she was on the farm. The irony of their situation did not escape him.

"You have your six months. More if you need it."

She sent him a sharp glance, waiting for the catch. "You'd do that for me?"

"I don't want to."

"How did you ever work on a guest ranch?"

"By not talking." He reached out with his good hand to cup his palm against her cheek. Touching her again felt right, as did lightly running his thumb over her bottom lip when her mouth parted. He felt her breath catch, felt it when she slowly exhaled a split second later.

"The pain meds are making you act out of character," she murmured.

"Not on pain meds."

"Take the excuse," she said lowly. Then she turned and reached for the door handle. Cole did the same, awkwardly climbing out of the SUV.

Taylor met him behind the SUV, her back

very straight, her chin lifted as she said, "If you work my ass off, I want more than a shack in compensation."

"What else could you possibly need?"

"Use of the washing machine so I don't have to go to the Laundromat. And when you have your poker nights, I want bathtub privileges."

"Not going to work, Evans."

She frowned at him. "What?"

"First it'll be the washer and the bathtub and then the entire house."

"Then I guess you'll have to be on your guard. Do we have a deal or not?"

He gave her a hard look. Waited for her to squirm. She didn't.

"Deal."

CHAPTER NINE

TAYLOR REFUSED TO allow herself to replay the conversation she'd had with Cole—not more than a couple of times anyway.

Did he feel sorry for her? After all, it had been a slam in the gut to expect the job, think that she was on her way out of the hole, then find out that she wasn't. Was that why he was compromising with her?

Or was it simply a matter of needing her help? If so, it would be for only a few days. Why sign on for six months or more?

Maybe he needed more help than she was aware of, but that didn't explain why he had touched her that second time. When he'd set his hand on her knee, it'd been to stop her from getting out of the SUV. It'd worked. She'd been so surprised that she probably couldn't have moved if she'd wanted to. But when he touched her face…her lip…that had been different. A tentative move in a direction that she was sure he hadn't considered taking up until that moment.

Her breath still went a little shallow when she thought about it.

Her instincts told her that a guy like Cole didn't make those kinds of moves lightly. So what did he want?

She'd bet money that he didn't know. She knew what he didn't want—her on his farm, which led her back into her circle of thought. Maybe he'd finally realized that she was free help. Hard to beat that.

That was the theory she was going with. Free help. Any good businessman would accept free help.

Taylor put her fingers back on the keyboard. She had no qualms about earning her keep, but what did she know about farmwork? During the times she'd spent here with her grandparents, she'd done chores, but they'd been fun chores—harvesting from the garden, maybe pulling weeds with her grandmother. Nothing that would come close to earning her keep. What on earth would he have her doing? What was she capable of doing? Digging, hoeing... she had no idea.

She glanced down at her pearly pink nails. This was going to destroy her hands.

And since when have you been such a priss?

Working would also help fill her days when she wasn't job hunting, and that was how she needed to look at the situation. Maybe working would also help her tamp down some of her residual anger. Give her something else to focus on. Even though what happened to her wasn't that unusual in the world of business, it still irked her. The guy they'd hired instead of her was already showcased on the bank website newsletter. So despite the assurances that US West Bank was all about growing people within the company, the bank had chosen a local guy with far less experience than her... one who planned to stay in the community. As would most rural institutions. They would grow local people from the ground up, because those people would stay.

So what now?

She put her fingers back on the keyboard to bring up a search engine.

A different career? A return to school? More student debt?

No to all.

She loved what she did for a living...she used to anyway. She was good at it. She loved the dynamics of her industry. Had there been moments when she'd wondered if it was all worth it? Very few. She refused to allow herself to think such things or deviate from her chosen course. Yes, all the hours were worth it when she had a job with prestige in a city she loved.

Now she had no job and was living in a farm building.

What if she spent the rest of her life on this farm? What if she never got another job in her field?

What if she'd been blackballed?

What if she was thinking crazy thoughts out of stress and anxiety? She settled her hands in her lap as she stared blankly at her monitor. Maybe *she* was the one who needed to pop a couple of pain pills. An escape from reality would be lovely.

Or maybe she needed to reshape her reality. During the first weeks after being laid off, she'd been centered on anger. She was still angry, but she was also hurt. Devastated. Her confidence wasn't entirely shattered, but it was shaken. She was questioning herself, wondering how this could have happened. Not once had her guidance counselors and mentors mentioned that hard work could lead to this. Or that hard work and advancement could make it difficult to get a lower-paying job.

She let out a sigh and got to her feet.

Maybe it was time to start focusing once again on what had happened between her and Cole this morning. At least that was a distraction.

AS A HORSEMAN, Cole knew the power of touch—with animals and with humans. But he hadn't expected the gut-level jolt triggered by the simple act of touching Taylor's face. Or the feeling of connection. And wanting.

It bothered him.

He'd formed an idea of who Taylor was. Of *what* she was—someone he didn't want to feel a connection with. Yet it had happened, and now he had to contend with it. The best way to do that was to focus on something other than touching and connecting and bullshit like that. So he would go to work and pretend nothing had happened. Because nothing else was going to happen.

Cole fully intended to put Taylor to work on the farm. He needed help. The knee he could deal with. He'd hurt it before and knew what to expect. The wrist was going to be a problem. It throbbed whenever he moved, which wasn't helping his low-grade headache. Nor was the sight of Taylor leaving the bunkhouse dressed

in jeans and a hoodie and crossing the driveway on her way to his house.

Time to go to work.

Time to shove aside idle thoughts about
what it would have felt like to put his mouth
where his thumb had been less than an hour
ago. He hadn't been laid in a month of Sun-
days, and that was clouding his judgment. His
body wanted what it couldn't have...well, his
body was just going to have to deal.

Taylor seemed surprised to see him standing
near the gate as she approached, and a guarded
look slid in over top of the thoughtful expression she'd worn as she'd walked toward the
house, her chin low, her gaze down.

Vulnerable wasn't a word he would have
used to describe her before this morning, but
when an overachiever was no longer able to
achieve, when everything the person knew
turned out to be wrong...it had to be a rough
adjustment.

Not that Taylor would purposely show weakness. Her chin lifted and she met his gaze
head-on...but he couldn't say she looked enthusiastic.

"What's on the farming agenda?"

Nope. Definitely not enthusiastic. Cole had

a grudging employee on his hands. Cool. All the better to give her back a little of her own.

"We're not farming." The seeds were in the ground, and until he had to deal with weed control and mowing along the ditches and roads, he didn't have a lot of farmwork to do.

Her eyebrows lifted in surprise. "Then how do you plan to work my ass off?"

"We're tackling the boneyard." The area where the scrap metal, wood and wire were collected had been long neglected, and part of his lease agreement with Karl had been to put the area into a semblance of order.

Her mouth opened, then closed again, telling him that he didn't need to explain the task any further. If he'd had any doubts about whether she understood what they were going to do, it was answered by the distasteful curl of her lips. She asked, "How are 'we' going to do that, when half of 'us' are injured?"

"The knee's already feeling better." As long as he was wearing his brace and iced the joint every few hours.

"How about the wrist?"

"I'll manage."

"Fine," she said darkly. "Just don't hurt your-self again, because I'm not above demanding eight months of free living."

"And I'm not above forgetting I ever made a deal."

She wrinkled her nose at him. He guessed she had no idea that it came off as cute rather than the sneer she was probably shooting for. "What's the goal for today?"

"To tackle the boneyard?" He thought he'd made that clear.

"No," she said with a slight roll of her eyes. "What is the specific goal?"

"I thought we'd start by dragging out the T-posts and stacking them, and then maybe go after the scrap wood."

"Are we only organizing? Or are we also sorting and discarding?"

"Sorting and discarding." He waited to see whether they needed to write a formal plan of action, delineating objectives before embarking on the cleanup, but Taylor seemed satisfied with a verbal.

"You're not really up for this, are you?" And was he horrible for rather enjoying her discomfort?

"A deal is a deal," she said stiffly. She looked down at her pretty painted nails. "I need gloves."

He reached into his pocket and pulled out his extra pair and handed them to her.

"Thank you."

They walked around the barn to where Karl had stacked debris for the past thirty years on top of the debris he'd inherited from his father.

"You know what a T-post looks like?"

"A 'T'?"

"Just checking," he said. "After insulting you with the Angus cow incident—"

"I did an oral report on cattle in the fifth grade. I have good recall."

"No report on fence posts?"

"Unfortunately, no."

He dug into the jumble of fence posts and grabbed a bent T-post. After fighting it for a few seconds, he managed to free it from its buddies and hold it up. "It's these ones with the spade on the end. If you find a bent one, we'll chuck it into the back of the truck." Which he did, one-handed. "If it's straight, we'll stack them here."

"Got it." She stepped onto the junk at the edge of the debris, and her foot slipped. Cole reached out and caught her arm with his good hand, steadying her. "You good?"

"Yeah."

"Up to date on tetanus?"

"If I say no, I guess that means you can't work my ass off." She shot him a hopeful glance.

"And then you'll have to move."

She gave a mock sigh. "Totally up to date."

She reached down for a T-post tangled in wire and a mishmash of other bent posts. It didn't move. She let go to choose another, which also refused to budge. "You?"

"Likewise." Handling as much rusty wire as he did while fixing fences, he couldn't afford not to be up to date.

Taylor propped her hands on her hips and surveyed the tangled mess with a deep frown.

This was going to take all day if Taylor kept grabbing posts and letting go of them. "Look, if you find a post that's—"

Taylor made a dismissive gesture, then reached down, grabbed the end of a post and pulled. When it didn't give, she started shaking it up and down and then twisting it sideways until finally she yanked it free, almost falling over backward in the process.

"Way to work out your aggressions," Cole muttered.

She ignored him and tossed the post toward the bed of the truck as he had. It hit the side with a clang and landed on the gravel. Cole gave her a look.

"Sorry," she muttered. "I'll do better next time."

"Or maybe you think if you beat up my truck that you'll get put on another detail?"

"Show me the dent," she said.

Okay. She had a point. The truck was so dented from years of work that it would be almost impossible to find the new ding.

Cole tipped back his hat. "I'm getting the idea you really hate this."

"I hate busywork." She lifted her chin at him, clearly challenging him to deny that was what they were doing. "This yard has been here since I was a kid. No one has ever done anything but add to it. Why are we sorting it?"

"I promised your grandfather."

She gave him a disbelieving look. "So this isn't something you cooked up to make me miserable?"

"I didn't cook it up," he said, without addressing the "make her miserable" part. He didn't really want her to be miserable...but he didn't mind seeing her get her hands dirty. "If you don't want to work, you can move. You agreed to farm labor."

"I'm not going to move."

"Then I guess you have to adapt."

She gave him a long look that he couldn't even come close to reading. Then she gave a small nod. "Good idea."

"How's that?" Cole asked automatically.

She reached down for another post. Cole

stood back, not wanting an elbow to the lip, but this time she lifted and twisted and eventually worked it free of the pile without doing either of them any damage.

She held up the post. "Johnson."

Cole stared at her. "You're naming the posts?"

"I'm working out my aggressions, as you suggested. Johnson always made me ask for information I needed twice. Or three times. Power game." She heaved the post toward the pickup, where it landed square in the middle of the bed with a rattling bang. "Take that, Johnson."

"Good aim this time," Cole muttered. "Who's next?"

Taylor grabbed another post and didn't bother pulling, but instead twisted. And twisted some more. "Melanie. Didn't do her job. Talked about me behind my back. Still…" *yank* "with…" *twist* "…the company…" A few seconds later, Melanie joined Johnson.

Cole tipped his hat back. "Anyone else?"

Taylor propped her gloved hands on her hips and pursed her lips as she considered the roster in her head. "One more." She took hold of a gnarly rusted post, twisted, yanked, pulled, tripped and fell backward on her ass. She got back up, took another crack at the post, then eventually worked it free. Perspiration beaded on her forehead. "Erickson."

"Ex-boyfriend?"

"My supervisor, who encouraged me to believe I was irreplaceable and that I should continue to work eighty-hour weeks." She heaved the post. It hit the bed of the truck on end and ricocheted out, landing on the ground. She climbed off the pile and retrieved Erickson.

"He always was a slippery dude, but I thought he was on my side." She threw the post back into the truck.

"Do you maybe want to bend him a little?" Cole asked, gesturing to where the post now lay.

She met his eyes, wiping her glove over her forehead, leaving a rusty smear. "You have no idea," she said grimly.

He reached down and started working a post free with his good hand. "Did you like *anyone* you worked with?"

Taylor also started working on freeing a post, more gently this time. "Of course." She gave him a sidelong look. "Some people even liked me."

Cole let out a snort. "Imagine that."

"Watch it," she said pleasantly. "The next post might have your name on it."

"I'll take care."

"You better."

Cole pulled his post free and handed it to Taylor. "Pretend it's Johnson."

Her gaze held his as she took the post from him. *Are we playing?*

Maybe a little.

She heaved the post. It landed perfectly in the bed of the truck, and then she reached into the pile and chose her next victim. "I'm still not convinced this isn't busywork."

"Ask Karl."

"Oh, yeah. I'm going to call Grandpa to ask if you were supposed to clean up the boneyard. Then he'll ask why, and I'll have to come up with a watered-down version of what's going on."

"Why watered down?"

Her hair spilled over her shoulder as she turned toward him. "Because I don't like to upset him, and I think you're using that to your advantage."

"No, Taylor. I'm striking while the iron is hot." She smirked as he echoed her words. "You're the one who chose to land here."

"And I'm the one who agreed to this deal." She went to work on another post that slid free with relative ease because it was one of the few straight ones. She held it up, and he pointed to the place where they'd stack the salvageable posts. She laid it down and went to work on another.

"I'm a hard worker," she said as she methodically twisted and pulled a pretzel of a post, "but this isn't the kind of work I do." She shot him a look. "Don't you have any financial stuff you need advice on?"

"Uh…"

Her expression darkened as she caught the reason for his hesitation. "We addressed that."

"Yes." He carefully freed a post and laid it in the straight-post pile. "I don't blame you for trying to pay off student loans and feeling bulletproof."

"But you still think I'm entitled."

"If our positions were reversed…"

She let out a breath. "Things look different on the outside."

"What?"

She put her hand on her hip. "I guess I'm saying walk a mile in my shoes. Your perspective might change."

"I guess that goes both ways."

"I guess."

The conversation ended there and, oddly, the tension between them seemed to dissipate as they worked in an almost companionable silence. Almost. He was too damned aware of her noncompanionable assets for it to be fully companionable.

"Did you live alone in the city?"

She stopped pulling on a post and shot him a frown.

"Yes." The word came out cautiously, as if she were expecting a setup, but this time he was just curious.

"Then living alone in the bunkhouse isn't a big change."

"No. It *is* a big change. Being alone is the only part of my life that's the same."

Over the course of the next hour, they sorted through the worst part of the web of bent and tangled posts. He heard Taylor's stomach growl a couple of times, but when he asked if she wanted to stop for lunch, she shook her head. "I don't eat much when I'm stressed."

But she did work. Cole would give her that.

"You should eat something."

"Thanks, Mom, but I'd just as soon finish my hours and be free of this."

"*I* need to eat."

She shrugged. "Whatever." The post she was working on finally came free, and she tossed it into the truck bed. "I don't mind continuing."

"I mind."

She rubbed her shoulder. "Fine, but you should know that once I stop, I may never get going again."

"Maybe you can pretend the next posts are the assholes who robbed you."

He caught the flash of amusement in her eyes, there and gone. He wished it had stayed. There were layers to Taylor. A woman beneath the princess exterior whom he thought he could like. He just needed to find her.

What the hell was he thinking?

He didn't need to find a hidden side to Taylor. He needed to focus on the job at hand and his life ATL—After Taylor Leaves.

BY THE TIME the day was over, Taylor would have happily killed for a long, hot soak. She briefly thought about negotiating for use of the tub—Cole was showing signs of being reasonable—then decided that maybe she didn't want to be naked that close to him, even if there was a door between them.

The guy set her on edge. And every now and again a random hot thought would flash into her head. What did *he* look like naked? Pretty damned awesome.

So, no bath. Instead she stood under a shower

head that drizzled more than it sprayed, rolling her shoulders, soothing her sore muscles and feeling thankful that the hot water tank worked well. Small blessings.

Damn but she didn't want to go back to that filthy post pile and dig out pieces of metal and wood. The best thing would be to hire heavy equipment to come in and haul the whole mess to the dump. To hell with recycling. Chances were the posts they were saving would merely become the beginning of a new boneyard.

Useless busywork. Done because Cole could make her do it. Maybe her grandfather had asked him to clean up the yard...but she didn't think he expected anyone to sort through the whole damned mess. The waste in man-hours was ridiculous.

The next morning Taylor's body creaked as she got out of bed. She loaded the coffeemaker, which she'd been too tired to deal with the night before, and then lowered herself down onto the plank floor and reached for her toes. She put her chest to her knees, then straightened back up, rubbing her shoulders. Her hammies were fine, but her traps, delts and pecs were killing her. Maybe she shouldn't have let that gym membership lapse. She got to her feet, opened her laptop and looked up shoulder stretches. She did not open her job links or check her email. She couldn't face it today.

She'd hit the job hunt hard again soon. Her student loans weren't going away, but they also wouldn't ruin her if she was living rent-free. She could scrape by. In a day or two, she'd send emails to Paul and Carolyn, confessing about the job and renewing her request to keep their eyes open for her. Right now, she'd focus on stretching her aching upper body.

And she might think about that guy she'd worked side by side with.

The guy who was going all power trip on her just because he could.

That didn't take away from the fact that Cole was hot. Annoying, but hot. His face, his shoulders, his very fine ass. The way his eyes kind of crinkled when he let loose with a grudging smile. She reminded herself yet again that hot yet annoying men were nothing new in her world, but she didn't seem to be able to disregard the hotness factor as easily as she did with all the other Ken-doll guys. Maybe because Cole wasn't a Ken doll.

He was waiting for her when she'd finished her stretching and her coffee, and she had the feeling that he would have been pacing if his knee wasn't giving him issues.

"Anxious to get going?"

"Debating the next move."

"I thought we agreed on the scrap wood pile." Which should be doused in gasoline and burned rather than sorted by hand. Taylor rubbed her sore shoulder again.

"I was thinking of something more fun."

Fun?

Heat began to bloom in her lower abdomen—exactly where she didn't want it to bloom.

"Ever drive a tractor?"

Oh, thank goodness. She swallowed as she lifted her chin and tried to appear as if her thoughts had not headed straight for the gutter. "Yes. But it's been a while."

He cocked a dark eyebrow at her. "You're not being facetious, right?"

She scowled at him, stung that he thought she was kidding. "Grandpa taught me." But they weren't supposed to tell her mother, because Cecilia would have gone through the roof if she'd known her daughter was doing anything farm related. "I drove that tractor right over there." She pointed at the blue-and-gray tractor parked next to the barn.

"Let's see how well he did."

The answer was that he'd trained her well enough that she didn't embarrass herself. It took her a few seconds and some direction from Cole to remember exactly how to start the beast, but after that, muscle memory kicked in. Her clutch work was jerky, but it wasn't long before she drove in a smooth circle, then up the driveway and back. Cole signaled for her to reverse the tractor to an area where a jumble of fence posts had been buried under other, smaller debris. Cole limped over to the pile and looped a heavy chain around a post.

"Put it in gear and pull forward slowly. Emphasis on slowly."

"What if the chain gives?"

"That's where the slow part comes in."

Taylor put the tractor in gear and eased it forward. The pile shifted and then the wood post slid free.

Taylor looked over her shoulder once the post clattered onto the gravel driveway and arched an eyebrow at Cole in a decent imitation of his own mocking expression.

"Do you want to do a victory dance on the hood?" he asked drily.

"I might," she called over the noise of the engine. "Care to join me?"

"The way my luck has been going, I'll fall off and break a leg."

Now this was the way farmwork should be

done. Driving the tractor while Cole did the chain work—oh, yeah. A much better day. By noon, the semirotted posts were lying in the yard and the smaller debris was ready to be picked up with the bucket.

Cole set his hand on the fender of the tractor as Taylor scrambled out of the cab. "Your grandfather did a good job teaching you to run this beast."

The compliment probably shouldn't have made her want to smile, but it did. When a guy who didn't really like you all that much complimented you, it was heady stuff.

And the fact that he looked like Cole...well, that didn't hurt matters.

"I think in another life I was an equipment operator," Taylor said after she jumped to the ground. "I had so much fun learning to drive this thing. Had to keep it from my mom, though. She had big plans for me that didn't involve the farm."

"And you followed through."

"No. She wanted me to be a lawyer. I didn't like law. I liked numbers. My dad and my grandpa encouraged me...then only my grandpa."

He caught her meaning easily. "It's rough losing a parent. I lost both of mine."

He didn't say how or when, and Taylor didn't

pry. Instead, she said, "Sorry to hear that." She and her mother butted heads, but she hated to think of life without her.

"Yeah." He looked back at the tractor. "How old were you when you learned to drive this beast?"

"Probably thirteen?"

"You spent a lot of time here?"

"I was *supposed* to spend a couple of months every summer, but Mom hated me being here, so she always arranged a camp or something so that I wasn't here for more than a few weeks."

"Karl didn't care?"

"Karl paid for the camps. He wanted me happy. My dad's death…the divorce before that. I didn't see it at the time, but I think he played along with Mom so that I wouldn't be stressed. I loved the camps and never considered the possibility that they were some kind of a power play by my mom."

"She really hated the farm."

"She claimed it ate her soul," Taylor said matter-of-factly.

"That pretty much says it all."

"Yeah, it does."

"How did you feel about the farm?"

"I loved it when I was young, despite my mom constantly harping about how awful the place was. Grandpa wasn't much for livestock, but he kept a horse for me and he always had a lot of cats and dogs, so I had fun. If I wanted something badly enough, he bought it." She gave a reminiscent smile. "He drew the line at the potbelly pig, but in general…"

She looked up to see Cole smiling back at her. "Those pigs are cute when they're small."

"I thought the mother pig had a certain *je ne sais quoi*. We saw the litter at a 4-H show. I wanted to join 4-H, but I wasn't here long enough during the year."

"What project would you have taken?"

"Horse or pig. Maybe both." He laughed, and she said, "What? Not fitting in with your preconceived notions?"

"Guilty."

"In your defense, that was when I was young—about ten, I think—and farms still seemed cool to me. I changed as I got older." And her mother continued to warn her about the dangers of stagnating in a rural environment. She rested her chin on her hands as she stared out across Cole's fields. "I visited the farm less often and started to rely more on phone calls and then emails. Grandpa never did pick up texting."

"Pity."

"Yeah. I know." She let out a soft breath.

"One of the hard lessons of life is that there are things you can't go back and fix."

"What would you fix?"

"More face time with Grandpa."

"Would you have *had* time?"

She gave her head a slow shake. No way, what with the hours she'd put into high school, college and then her job. Could she have adjusted the amount of time? Not if she'd wanted to see the same results.

Yet now you're out of work...

Bump in the road. That was all. Happened to most professionals.

She glanced up to see Cole studying her and cleared her throat, feeling uncharacteristically self-conscious. "It's not possible to fix the past," she said. "So I'm trying to do better with the here and now."

"How?"

The question made all traces of self-consciousness evaporate. "Do you really want to know, or are you challenging me?"

"Really want to know."

She had a ready answer, because she'd spent a lot of time thinking about how to set things right and not make mistakes in the future. "I'm calling my grandfather more often. I've made a vow to myself not to go to radio silence when things aren't going right. I may not share the details, but I'll stay in contact."

He nodded, then looked up at the horizon, his gaze coming back to her when she asked, "How about you?"

"How about me what?"

"Any regrets that you need to make right?" His expression shuttered at the question. "Ah... so *your* life isn't fair game?" she asked softly.

"I'm not big into talking about my life," he said.

"Yet you feel free to question mine."

"You didn't have to answer."

"I'll remember that."

"I was just making conversation." He shifted his weight as he spoke, his body language telling her that wasn't the full truth. He was curious about her. Because he wanted to know more about her as a person? Or because he was trying to figure out her weak spots?

"Me, too." Taylor gave him a pert and totally insincere smile, earning herself a frown in return. Cole did frown a lot...

She leaned her back against the tractor. "Were you like this with your ranch guests?"

"Like what?"

"All frowning and disapproving?"

"I'm not disapproving."

"Bullshit. You totally are."

Now his mouth flattened, and Taylor had to admit to being fascinated with his mouth. She couldn't nail down why exactly. The shape was pretty damned perfect, but it was more about the way his lips moved, the expressions he formed.

And the potential for exploration...

Taylor crossed her arms over her chest, trying to ignore the warmth spreading there.

"If I come off as disapproving, I apologize."

She allowed herself a wry half smile. "And if I come off as entitled, I apologize."

Cole shook his head. "Taylor—you tried to strong-arm me out of my house."

Taylor pressed a hand to her chest. *"Moi?"*

"Yes. *Vous.*"

Taylor couldn't resist smiling a little. "Okay, so I'm a little pushy."

"A little?"

The words didn't sting. In fact, they made things better—or maybe it was the way his fascinating mouth curved as he said them. "I can't help how I was raised, but I can do something about it now. Losing my job has opened my eyes to a few things."

"Like what?" At her lifted eyebrow, he quickly added, "If you care to share."

"The stuff I said about keeping better contact with Grandpa." She pursed her lips, debating about how much she wanted to reveal. No matter what, it would be a hell of a lot more than he was willing to reveal. Cole was one closed-off guy. "I know now that no one is irreplaceable, so I'll approach my work differently. I'll have my résumé polished up and at the ready. And—" she eased her thumbs into her front pockets "—there will be more smelling of the roses."

"Didn't do a lot of that before?"

"Work was my roses. And it'll still be important to me…but not everything."

"It was everything before?"

"I'll be honest with you. It was too much of my life before. Yes, I'll probably bury myself again, but not with the same attitude."

"Maybe you shouldn't bury yourself at all."

"In my field, burying is part of the territory."

"Guess that's why I like farming."

Taylor looked around her, trying to imagine this being her livelihood. Days spent outdoors, driving in circles around a field, sorting junk piles, taking care of animals. To be honest, a day on the tractor had shifted her perspective a bit. She'd had fun and felt a sense of accomplishment. But she hadn't used her degrees,

and after working her ass off for five years
to get those degrees…well, not using them
seemed like a sorry waste.

She met Cole's gaze, started to speak, then
stopped. He had gorgeous eyes to go with his
gorgeous mouth, and right now she wanted to
drink in the way he was looking at her, cautiously, questioningly. There wasn't much
about the man that wasn't easy on the eyes.
What would he look like in Armani?

Spectacular.

But he didn't belong in Armani. He looked
ridiculously good in denim, so why go the
multithousand-dollar route?

"Taylor?"

Telltale color warmed her cheeks as she realized she'd been staring, but her gaze didn't
waver. "I was imagining you in a business
suit."

Dark eyebrows came together, perplexed.
"Why?"

"You know what I look like in your world.
Maybe I wondered how you would look in
mine."

"Extremely uncomfortable."

"Yeah. That was my conclusion, too."

"But you don't look all that uncomfortable
in mine."

"Yeah?" She didn't want to look too comfortable in his world, because she didn't belong there. "I guess I'll have to work on that."

She'd thought Cole would smile, but he didn't. Instead he jerked his head toward the house. "We've talked through a good part of our lunch break."

"Beauty of farming," Taylor replied. "You can set your own hours." And actually…she *could* see the beauty of that.

Score one point for farming.

CHAPTER TEN

"I'M NOT A farm girl."

Max opened his green eyes, gave her the kitty equivalent of a scowl from where he lay on his back in the middle of the bed, and then he closed his eyes again and let out a tired kitty sigh.

"Right." Taylor sat down on the bed and started untying her poor beat-up running shoes. Even her cat agreed. Not a farm girl. Although the tractor was a lot of fun.

She kicked off her shoes, then rubbed a hand over the back of her neck, which wasn't stiff at all. The day in the tractor might not have taken a toll physically, but she was tired—tired in a way she'd never been after a day at the office.

So, what was the difference?

Maybe it was that she didn't have the gnawing sense she hadn't done enough that day?

And her back wasn't aching. Taylor's back was her stress barometer. High stress equaled tight muscles, which meant she could sit for only so long, yet today she'd sat for the entire day without a twinge.

Okay…score two points for farmwork, but she didn't see the score getting much higher. The pay was low and the benefits were nonexistent… unless one counted watching a great-looking guy do his thing with chains and posts.

But that wouldn't pay a hospital claim.

"One has to work in a realm of reality," she said to Max, who didn't bother to respond, or even open his eyes. He'd never been much of a conversationalist. "It's not bad doing this stuff, but in reality, do I belong here? No. Does Cole want me here?"

She didn't bother to answer the obvious, but instead got to her feet and went to the old refrigerator to see what she could nuke for dinner.

Her choices were macaroni and cheese or macaroni and cheese.

She was going to have to go shopping soon. If she were in Seattle, she could have popped down the street for a slice of pizza. It would have filled her belly without breaking the bank. Then she could have gone home, put on some jazz, opened a bottle of wine…

Yes, she was a city girl.

With a tight back and a sore neck.

But no dirt on her hands and in her hair.

She pulled out the frozen container of cheese and pasta and peeled off the wrapper, then opened a bottle of wine. She didn't know if red was the best choice for budget fare, but it was what she had and, better yet, what she liked.

It also made her sleepy. She managed a quick shower, then lay down on her bed, intending to read. Instead she conked out.

She wasn't certain what brought her awake, but it was something other than the usual thumping and bumping from below. She sat up, causing the book she'd been reading to slip onto the floor, startling her.

Taylor closed her eyes as she waited for her heart to stop racing, then reached down to lay a hand on Max, who'd barely stirred. Whatever had awoken her hadn't disturbed him, meaning no marauding mice or rats had broken through her patch job—which also meant it was safe to put her feet down.

She crossed to the window and pushed aside the droopy curtain. The driveway, the yard, Cole's house—everything appeared as it should be. A bluish light came through Cole's closed curtains. He was still up, watching television? Of course he was. The glowing clock next to her bed read ten thirty.

She heard the sound again—a distant, hollow thudding, which Cole probably couldn't hear over the television. Whatever it was, it wasn't a normal farm sound, or wind in the pines.

Taylor dropped the curtain and made her way to the door, where she slid her feet into her running shoes and pulled her hooded sweatshirt off the hook. She slipped outside and quietly closed the door, then stopped and listened. The noises were coming from the calf pen— the thuds of running feet on soft dirt. She was about to head across the driveway to alert Cole to the situation when she heard the growl. Not a threatening wolf growl, but a higher-pitched yappy dog growl.

What the...?

The next growl was followed by a yip. Or rather a yap.

Taylor shifted course and headed directly to the calf pen. Unless coyotes now sounded like poodles, she felt confident she could handle whatever it was that was stampeding her calves.

"Whatever it was" turned out to be a streak of white darting in and out of the calves' legs, then shooting back under the fence before darting back in again.

"Hey!"

The small dog froze middash, then pivoted and zipped past Taylor, making a beeline for the grain shed, where it disappeared under the building through a small hole near the door.

"Great," Taylor muttered. She had a feeling that as soon as she went back to bed, the dog would start harassing the calves again. She bent down at the hole, wishing she had a flashlight.

"Hey, puppy. Come on. Come on…"

There was no sign of movement under the shed.

Taylor let out a breath and tried again. "Come on, sweetie. Come on out."

Behind her she heard Cole's door open and shut again. Excellent. Reinforcements. She sat back on her heels as Cole approached, the light in his hand bobbing with his limp.

"I kind of hate to ask…" he said as he approached.

"A dog was bothering the calves."

"White fluffy dog?"

"That's the one."

He let out a breath and pushed a hand through his hair. "Mrs. Clovendale's sister is visiting again. Did you see a black-and-white collie?"

"No."

"She's the brains of the outfit. Probably on her way home right now. They've been here a couple of times before, but I didn't have animals then. She always takes off when she sees me and the poodle hides." Cole awkwardly bent down, accommodating his bad knee. He leaned toward the opening. "Come on, Chucky."

A whimper sounded from the depths of the foundation.

"Chuck, Chuck, Chucky."

Taylor pressed her lips together as she felt a laugh start to bubble up. "Chuck, Chuck, Chucky?"

"It works," Cole muttered, shifting his knee to a new position that looked just as uncomfortable as the old.

Taylor said nothing and, sure enough, on the fourth Chuck-Chuck-Chucky, the little dog crawled out from under the building on his belly and looked up at Cole with soulful brown eyes. Cole scooped the dog up with his good hand, tried to push up to his feet with the other and almost fell over in the process. Taylor took hold of his arm to steady him as he regained his balance, swallowing drily as his hard muscles flexed beneath her palm. As soon as he was on his feet she let go.

"Thanks." He held out the dog. "You want to keep him until morning?"

"Are you kidding?" she asked, ruffling the silky curls behind the dog's ear. "Max will eat him."

"Probably so." He cradled the poodle against his chest.

"Although… I could probably keep him safe from Max if you didn't want a roommate tonight." He gave her a quizzical look, and she shrugged. "I like dogs."

"Me, too."

"Hey. Something in common."

"Yeah."

"Don't sound so thrilled." She reached for the poodle, and he relinquished his hold. The little dog pressed his warm little body into her. He was panting hard from his evening's work.

A grudging smile lifted the corners of Cole's mouth. "I'll call Mrs. Clovendale in the morning. Deliver Chucky back home when I make my grocery run."

"Maybe you'd better take him," Taylor said. "I don't want Max's feelings to be hurt."

"Sure. We can finish watching *The Caine Mutiny* together."

"I love that movie."

Cole gave her a sideways look. "I got it out of Karl's DVD collection."

"If you look in his VHS collection, you'll find it there, too. We watched it at least once a summer. I have no idea why I like it so much, but I do." And she halfway wished he would invite her to watch the movie with him, even though for reasons of sanity, she would say no.

They were almost to the bunkhouse when Cole stopped walking. "Name your five favorite classic movies of all time."

"Classic meaning...?"

"Before the year 2000."

Taylor lifted her chin, squeezed her eyes shut. "Tough one. Uh... Anything with Rodney Dangerfield. *Wizard of Oz. The Right Stuff. Goodfellas. The Caine Mutiny. The Thin Man.*" She opened her eyes. "Did I pass the test?"

"Not the math portion. That's six."

"Eighteen if you count all the Rodneys."

"Yet you're in finance. I think I'm starting to see the problem."

Taylor's lips twitched despite herself. "Careful, Mr. Bryan."

He smiled that devastating smile of his—the one she didn't see very often, and almost wished she wasn't seeing now. "Couldn't resist."

She cocked her chin sideways. "I was good at my job." It was important to her that he know that.

"I believe you." He sounded sincere.

"Why?"

"I read about the professional papers you wrote and the industry award." Taylor gave him a thoughtful look, which he met without one trace of apology. "Long evenings. I also research weed control."

"Ah." One corner of her mouth crooked up. "So I shouldn't read anything into the research?"

"I'm just curious about my tenant."

"Do you feel as if you've learned everything you need to know?"

"Now that I know about your predilection for Rodney Dangerfield movies, I think I'm good." His hand stroked over the poodle's back, and Taylor focused on the movement rather than meeting his eyes. A crackling tension was building between them—one that had nothing to do with online searches and comedy movies. It was Cole who broke the tension by reaching out for the poodle. "Thanks for watching out for the calves."

"Oh, I'll take on a marauding poodle any time of the day or night."

"Good to know. Consider yourself on call until Mrs. Clovendale's sister goes home again."

She liked Rodney Dangerfield.

That spelled trouble.

He'd asked about movies hoping she'd spout off the names of some foreign films, or say she never watched old movies anymore. No such luck. They both liked dogs. They both liked classic movies…and she did have okay taste in that area, although he'd never been a fan of *The Wizard of Oz.* Those flying monkeys still freaked him out.

They had a few things in common. She wasn't exactly what he thought she was. So what?

Cole leaned his head back against the sofa cushions and idly stroked the dog, who was now snoring on his lap. A half hour ago, he'd swapped out *The Caine Mutiny* for *Caddyshack,* which he watched on mute. He didn't need sound, because he'd seen it so many times.

And he could probably be sitting here with Taylor right now, enjoying the movie, which could lead to…trouble.

He didn't see any way around it. If he pursued things with Taylor, then he would be pitting his new livelihood against an awakening interest in a woman whom he didn't want to be interested in. A woman who, by her own admission, wanted to live in an urban environment. A woman who would complicate his life just when he was starting to get it sorted out. Did he want complications?

No.

But that didn't keep his thoughts on the straight and narrow.

He couldn't help but wonder if Taylor was cool and controlled in bed. Business Taylor? Or did she let go, as she did when heaving a T-post through the air? Farm Taylor.

Maybe a mixture of the two? Maybe she started out businesslike and then slowly lost control.

Or maybe she took control.

That would be good.

He sucked in a sharp breath. He really needed to get laid.

Or better yet, he needed to get a grip. She was hot. He was horny. But he wasn't sixteen. He could deal.

He needed to distance himself, get things back under control.

Yeah. While working shoulder to shoulder. No problem there. He reached for the remote, turning the sound back on in time to hear a gopher laugh like a dolphin.

The reason he'd searched online for her the second time, three nights ago, was because he was looking for reasons to squelch his burgeoning interest in her. The reason he'd confessed was because he hoped that she'd accuse him of stalking or something. She hadn't. Probably because she'd researched him pretty carefully herself.

So what now?

Distance.

The next day, after Chucky had been returned to his owner, who proclaimed him to be a very naughty boy, Cole left the tractor parked and he and Taylor went to work sorting wood and scrap metal. In silence for the most part. By noon, they'd made some serious inroads into the junk behind the barn. Some Cole planned to sell for scrap, sinking the money back into Karl's place. Most of it went to the dump, with Taylor driving the ton truck, since his knee still wasn't clutch friendly. It was getting better, though.

His wrist was another story, but he had to use the hand to work. When the doctor had told him not to do anything to jar it for at least a week, he'd nodded as if he intended to follow orders. He had his own way of dealing with injuries. If it hurt, he stopped doing it. If it didn't, or hurt only a little, he carried on.

He glanced over at Taylor as she turned onto the road leading to the landfill. Today's load was wood, so they took the fork to the left after entering the facility. She expertly backed up to the oversize receptacle, then beat Cole around the truck to the tailgate, which she opened by hitting it in just the right place with the heel of her hand to pop the latch.

She was better at this farm stuff than she wanted to be. Maybe it was her natural-born efficiency. Maybe she couldn't help wanting to be the best at whatever she did.

Again, sex came to mind, and again, he shoved the thought aside.

Taylor started tossing wood out of the truck with a vengeance, and Cole stepped forward to help.

"Do any of these have names?" he asked as a split plank sailed past him.

She hurled another broken plank through the air. "I could go through the mean girls in high school."

Cole pulled a splintered piece of lodge

pole free. "Where did you fit in the social hierarchy?"

Taylor stopped and brushed the back of her glove over her forehead. "Are you asking if I was a mean girl?"

"Were you?"

She straightened and drilled him with a hard look that made him feel slightly ashamed, even if he had good reason to ask. He was attempting to distance himself—or better yet, to have her distance herself from him. "I wasn't mean. I was confident. How about you?"

"Wildly popular." Right. Cowboy geeks were never wildly popular. He tossed a piece of wood underhanded.

Her gaze never wavered. "I'll bet you were. And that was an asshole question you asked me."

Cole didn't argue with her. It had been. "Just trying to get a handle."

"By asking if I was mean?"

He bent to pick up another piece of rotten board. "All I was asking is if you were one of the school elite."

"I don't think you were." The words were cool, a statement of fact he couldn't deny.

"Maybe we should drop this subject."

She hurled a piece of wood with rather impressive force, making him wonder if his name was on that one. "Yes. Maybe we should."

Taylor didn't talk as she drove back to the farm. She focused on the road with an intensity that told Cole that he might have his wish. She might back totally away from him, and all it had taken was his acting like an ass.

Did he regret it?

He told himself no. He needed to focus on his livelihood. And what if Karl was the old-fashioned sort who didn't like his tenant screwing around with his granddaughter?

Not likely, but there was always a possibility.

After returning to the farm, they broke for lunch, heading off to their respective abodes. Cole made himself a sandwich, leaning back against his counter to eat as he wondered how the afternoon would play out. Until he'd asked about her place in high school society, there'd been a sense of something simmering just below the surface, ready to break out.

Hopefully he'd taken care of that.

Taylor was already sorting through debris when he walked around the barn, pulling a glove onto his good hand. He dived in, pulling bent rebar out of a stack of pipe and metal rails. They worked for most of the afternoon with next to no conversation.

It was not a comfortable silence.

Taylor worked methodically, seemingly lost in thought, but the few times they'd reached for the same piece of debris, she'd pulled her hand back as if not wanting to chance touching him.

And since that was what he wanted, it made no sense that he was so stupidly aware of her. Taylor was a hard worker. She may not like farmwork, she may still believe that clearing the boneyard was busywork, but she was now committed to the task.

And maybe he'd made his point about working her ass off. Did he really want to spend time like this, working next to a woman he would be better off avoiding? There were things they could each do alone.

The stack of pipe shifted, and Taylor let out a yelp as the fingers of her glove got trapped. She yanked her hand free of her glove, which dangled from where it was caught between two pieces of rusting metal.

"Son of a—"

"Are you okay?"

Taylor frowned at him before working her glove free. "Fine." She rubbed her thumb over her forefinger, which must have gotten pinched, then slipped the glove back on and went to work again.

Cole moved farther away. Working next to her was driving him kind of crazy—because he wasn't being honest about this whole situation.

Maybe he needed to say, "Hey, what should we do about this mutual attraction that won't be good for either of us?" Then Taylor could come up with some parameters and goals and they could deal. Together.

Yeah, right.

His phone buzzed in his pocket, and he stepped down off the pile of debris he was sorting through to answer.

"Hey, Jance. What's up?" Nothing bad, he hoped, but Jancey didn't usually call to shoot the breeze.

"I just wanted to touch base."

"Yeah?" he asked gently, staring off over his fields as he held the phone to his ear, yet totally aware of the woman still working behind him.

"Yeah." She fell into silence, and he waited. "I was wondering…since you've left and stuff…do you feel differently about the ranch?"

"Where's this coming from?"

"Oh…I've just been thinking a lot. Now that I'm about to leave the place."

"I love the ranch. I don't think anything will change that." He paced away from the debris piles toward the barn. If he was going to have to talk his sister down, he wanted to do it in private.

"So you'd never sell. Right?"

He made a sputtering noise. "No." He'd never sell because Miranda would somehow end up with the entire place, and he wasn't going to let that happen. And because it was his and Jancey's birthright. Their family settled that land, and it would damn well stay in the family.

Jancey let out a small breath. "That's what I thought. I'm just feeling kind of unsettled, you know?"

"That's normal when you're about to leave home for the first time." He ran a hand over the back of his neck. "Do you want me to come out to the ranch for a while?"

"No. I'm good. I just… I guess I wanted to be reassured that after I left I wouldn't feel differently."

"You might, Jance. I won't lie. But I don't."

He could hear the smile in her voice as she said, "Thanks, Cole. I feel better."

"Good. Are you sure you don't want me to drive out?"

"No. Really. I'm doing great. How are my babies?"

Cole smiled. "Your babies are greedy eaters. They're gaining weight fast."

"Good to know. I'll try to get in to see them—and you—soon."

"You do that, kid. And call anytime you're feeling unsettled. Okay?"

"Okay."

He dropped his phone back into his pocket as he strode back toward the pile. Taylor didn't even glance his way as he went back to work. Maybe he did need to take a drive to the ranch soon. Going back invariably stressed him out, but he needed to keep tabs. Make sure that Miranda was minding her p's and q's.

"Why'd you leave your ranch job if you owned the ranch?"

The question came out of the blue, startling him after a day of silence. Cole carefully set the pipe he'd just extracted onto the salvage pile. "I quit because I didn't like my boss. And I only own part of the operation."

"Do you miss it?" Taylor put a hand on her hip, and Cole couldn't help but follow the movement before bringing his gaze back up to her face. She wore her business expression, which made him think that she fully intended to get answers. So much for distance.

"I don't miss what it became." He went back to sorting the pipe. Taylor didn't move. He didn't look at her.

"Is the subject off-limits?"

"Pretty much."

"Because you're private, or because it's me?"

"Private."

"Uh-huh."

"Nothing personal, Taylor."

"Right."

He gave a small snort. He wasn't lying. "I don't discuss the ranch."

"Maybe you should start."

"Because?"

"You bottle things up and they come out in weird ways."

"I'll take the chance." Because the thought of opening up to…well, anyone, really…made him freeze. Telling the truth about his family… he hated what the ranch had become and hated that he no longer felt welcome on his own property. Talking about it only twisted the knife a little more.

"It isn't like I can use the information against

you," she continued as she went back to battling the rebar. A moment later the pieces she'd been working on slid free and she put them in the junk stack.

"I don't like talking about it."

"In my world, you grow a thick skin."

"In my world, you hide your true thoughts." In the guest ranch world anyway.

"Mine, too."

He turned to meet her gaze. "What are your true thoughts right now?" It was almost as if he couldn't help but edge toward trouble with this woman.

"You want the blistering truth?" she asked.

"I can take it."

"I think you don't want to like me. I think you're working hard to push me away."

Cole stilled. His first impulse was to deny it. His second was to admire her instincts. His third was to back up fast. "I have nothing against you."

Her eyes narrowed and her lips curved into a humorless smile, telling him that she wasn't fooled. Not even a little. "But…"

"No *but*."

"Liar." She spoke softly, holding his gaze in a way that warned him not to underestimate her. "But I'll let it go in the name of future peaceful calf feedings and wonderful days sorting junk." Taylor took off her gloves and uncapped the water bottle sitting on the tailgate. "I'm done for the day. I have a Skype interview in an hour."

She started to walk away, and Cole realized that even though the sane thing would be to let her walk away, he wasn't done.

He took hold of her arm as she went past him, and she stopped, her gaze slowly coming up to meet his. "You're right," he said.

"I know." Her voice was low and husky. It made him think of sex, although he didn't think that was her intention. Didn't matter. It came off that way.

"Getting closer will complicate things."

"We wouldn't want that." She spoke softly as her gaze moved down to his lips and held. "But you don't have to be a jerk to me. Just...talk."

He pulled in a breath. Her muscles were taut beneath his grip, light as it was. She could have easily moved away, but she didn't. She finally pulled her gaze from his mouth, her expression shifting ever so slightly as she met his eyes, then reached up to touch his face as he'd touched hers in the SUV the day she'd taken him to the doctor. Her fingers moved over his cheekbone, trailed down his jaw, brushed lightly over his lips, making his nerves sing and his dick jump.

She leaned closer. "If we kiss—"

He didn't wait for her to finish the sentence, didn't wait for her to set goals or outline parameters. He made the *if* a reality, releasing her arm and sliding his hand around the back of her neck as he brought his mouth down to hers.

Taylor gasped against his lips, even though she'd known the kiss was coming—maybe because she felt the same surge of raw need that he did as their mouths melded together and their tongues met. And what should have been a test-the-waters kiss became a long, deep exploratory kiss. One that had the blood pounding in his veins and his hands skimming over her body before he pulled her more tightly against him. He raised his head briefly, then went back for more. Taylor met him halfway as reality blurred. Dynamite in his hands.

When he raised his head for the second time, Taylor's lips clung to his and her eyes remained closed, as if she were savoring, keeping the moment for as long as she could. When she opened her eyes, she stepped back, putting space between them that seemed more like a chasm than a few feet of gravel. A slight frown drew her brows together as she lightly pressed her fingers against her lips, as if checking for damage, which only made him want to kiss her again.

"Aren't you going to say that you didn't see that coming?" she asked in a low voice.

He shook his head. Kissing Taylor had been inevitable. Like it or not, even when he'd thought she was a princess through and through, he'd been drawn to her. At first, he'd assumed it was wanting what was off-limits. Now he knew what he felt toward her was more complex, harder to define. Troublesome.

"No. That was the reason I was trying to push you away."

"Well," she said, wiping her hands down the sides of her jeans, as if she'd just finished a tough job, "you should have worked harder at that."

"It was the thick skin you mentioned. Things seem to bounce off you."

"At least it appears that way," she said before clearing her throat. "I have to do my networking."

Of course she did. Kiss and move on.

But Cole didn't see this being a done deal. He

couldn't help but think that it was a good thing she was going…and that working with her was going to be a hell of a lot more interesting.

CHAPTER ELEVEN

TAYLOR HEADED BACK to the bunkhouse, taking care not to walk too fast. Not to look too affected.

Holy smoke, but that guy could kiss.

This is no big deal. Get your breath. How many times had she kissed a guy and they'd gone their separate ways, no harm, no foul?

Many.

How many times had she done it when she'd had to interact with the guy on a daily basis? None. She'd taken the maxim about not getting involved with coworkers seriously, so maybe that was why this felt different.

He isn't a coworker.

But still...

A one-time deal. That was all this was. Shake it off. If he thought it was more...well, she'd set him straight.

She let herself into the bunkhouse and settled at the computer, checked her email, researched possible contacts, noted that the market was tightening even more, damn her luck.

There was a text from Carolyn waiting on her phone—a selfie of her and her new beau with a glacier behind them. Carolyn looked happy, and Taylor smiled at the photo. Carolyn sought out relationships the same way that Taylor had avoided them. Depend on yourself, her mother had told her at least five or six times a week as she was growing up. Depend on yourself and you'll be happier and more secure than if you depend on others.

Cecilia had lived her life that way. She'd been in a relationship with her artist husband, Jess, for almost a decade, but it was on her terms. He was the one who adjusted when compromise was necessary. In Taylor's mind, it didn't seem like a healthy way to run a relationship, but they seemed happy, at least on the surface. Surely Jess had to be going a little crazy, always bending and giving?

When Taylor was in a relationship—and usually she was not—she did fine in the beginning, but when it came to adapting and changing, the fear factor kicked in. What if she changed, gave up what was important to her, and then the deal crumbled? Where would she be then?

What if she couldn't get back what she'd given up, or if she lost a piece of herself?

Getting through the divorce, and her father's death, and now being fired, she felt as if she'd lost enough of herself.

So where did that leave her with Cole?

Excellent question. The pooling of sensual warmth in her midsection at the thought of that crazy-hot kiss was probably not a good sign—especially when she couldn't say she didn't want more. Sure, it was threatening, but it was also heady, and she wasn't about to run or hide.

Taylor got to her feet and went to the small window over the sink, studied the house where Cole was now…what? Analyzing what had just happened? Or had he pushed it out of his mind?

If he could do that, he was tougher than she was.

And he wasn't.

Taylor pushed off the sink, rolling her shoulders, which had stiffened up. So she'd kissed him. Whatever.

And, with that, she was right back to where she'd been when she'd crossed the drive from the house to the bunkhouse. And that was exactly where she was going to stay.

No. Big. Deal.

She had an interview to prepare for, and she needed to tidy up and get her equilibrium back. Act as if a big bump hadn't appeared in the road in front of her.

AND THAT WAS one decent interview.

Taylor leaned back in the kitchen chair and stretched after the video call had ended. She'd done well, considering the fact that she'd still been off-kilter—*thank you, Cole*—when the call had connected. But she'd managed to get her hair and makeup done before the call, and had slipped into a dark suit jacket, so all in all she'd been prepared.

And if she got the job…maybe she and Cole could have a last hurrah. Pursue this matter between them.

Taylor pushed her chair back. Not wise. Not when he was living in her grandfather's place.

Half an hour later she heard the barn door roll open and looked out the window. Cole was feeding the calves without her. Because of the kiss, or because he knew she had an interview?

The latter. It had to be. He probably wanted to move on as much as she did. No sense making things more uncomfortable than they needed to be while they were stuck together.

The best thing to do would be to forget the kiss had ever happened.

When she met up with Cole at the barn a few minutes later, he seemed to be on board. There was nothing self-conscious in the way he greeted her or handed her the grain bucket. Together they walked to the calf pen, and if Taylor was more aware of him than usual, tuned into his every move, that was biology in action. Fortunately, she had a brain able to overcome the pitfalls of primal biological responses. She was in control of this situation, not her lady parts.

"How was the interview?"

"I think it went well. It's a company in Ellensburg, Washington. Close to home."

"Ah."

The calves mobbed them, and Cole helped create a space for her to feed first one calf, then the next, without getting knocked down by the hungry trio. When the last bottle was empty and all the calves were picking at hay in the feeder, Cole opened the gate and stood back for her to pass. She was barely through when he said, "So. That kiss."

Her startled gaze met his. "What about it?" She stepped back so that he could come through and lock the gate. "It happened. We don't need to dissect it."

An odd expression crossed his face. "Wait... the queen of analysis doesn't want to analyze?"

"Maybe that is the result of my analysis."

"You don't want input from your research assistant?" There was no humor in his voice.

"What could you possibly say that I don't already know, or haven't already concluded?"

He leaned his shoulder on the fence post next to him, studying her with those green eyes until she felt like shifting her weight, folding her arms. Moving. She didn't. But it wasn't easy. Why wasn't he instantly agreeing with her to move on?

Suddenly the situation, which she'd hoped to blow off, was once again edging into threatening territory, and she wasn't going to have that.

"I analyzed," she said finally. "And came to the conclusion that, yes, there's chemistry. But we would be foolish to act on it. Not when we're living as we are. You were right, we don't want to complicate our lives."

He considered her words and then gave a slow nod. "Fair enough."

"It makes sense. Besides—" she nudged a rock with her toe before looking back up at him "——I'm getting to the point where I don't want to do you bodily harm on general principles, and why mess with that?"

"I see your point."

She pushed her hands into her pockets. "Surely you see things the same way?" She hadn't intended for the pleading note in her voice to be there.

"I...don't want to screw up my lease," he admitted.

"Right." She felt a small measure of relief. "There is that potential."

He cocked his head. "Doesn't stop me from wanting to kiss you again."

Taylor's breath went shallow. The images that flooded her brain were unsettling. "I... don't think that would be wise."

"Because you're feeling it, too?"

She gave him an impatient look. "Would I have kissed you back if I hadn't 'felt it'?"

He hooked his thumbs in his pockets, drawing her eyes down to...there. She casually swept her gaze on over the gravel to her running shoes.

Dear heavens.

"So the next step is no step."

Taylor let out a relieved breath. "Yes. Exactly."

COLE WAS GOOD with the next step being no step. It wasn't as if he had a lot of choice. The lady had spoken, and it would make their lives less complicated if they continued as they were.

But *what* were they?

More than acquaintances, but not quite friends. Friends felt comfortable together. When he was with Taylor, he was on edge. But he liked her.

His mouth tightened as he headed for his tractor, and he reflected that things would be a lot easier if he didn't, but somehow the prickly princess had turned out to be a real person. One who called him on his bullshit. One who honestly did work her butt off when asked.

He'd read her wrong...or maybe she'd lightened up. Whatever the reason, this new Taylor was a double threat.

Double threats were never good.

A streak of white headed across the yard just as he got on the tractor, and with a low groan he climbed back off again. Chucky disappeared through the windbreak separating Karl's place from the Clovendales' pastures.

He pulled his phone from his pocket and called Mrs. Clovendale, who explained that her sister was no longer able to get around like she used to and Chucky was now a permanent resident of Clovendale Farms. But she'd certainly ask her husband to fix the hole that Chucky had escaped through.

Cole agreed that was a great idea and then dropped the phone back into his pocket. If his biggest concerns were a renegade poodle and Taylor, then his life was good.

Miranda was a potential concern, too, but she'd been quiet and as far as he knew hadn't messed with Jancey lately. And he decided he should be grateful for that.

Why was Miranda so quiet?

He started the tractor and headed out to the fields, wishing he could just let things go. He didn't trust Miranda. Taylor had probably worked with nutso people like his step-aunt. There had to be tons of egos and power maneuvers in the business world. When things smoothed out between them, when he didn't feel the urge to touch her every time she got close to him, maybe he'd ask for insights… without going into a whole lot of detail about his ranch.

It was not only demoralizing, it was embarrassing.

Which was probably how Taylor had felt

after losing her job when she'd made it the primary focus of her life.

But he wasn't going to think about Taylor. Or Miranda. He was going to focus on weed control and seeing about getting water to the corners of his fields. At least that was a part of his life he could control.

THE NEXT MORNING after the calf feeding, Cole told Taylor that he had work to do in the fields, then asked if she would mind clearing out the old tack room in the barn.

"I want to store seed in there, but it's loaded with old tools and stuff. Most of it needs to be hauled away."

"Sure." She'd discovered that the work she hadn't wanted to do made the days go by and kept her from obsessing over her job search. She missed dealing with numbers, plotting strategies and keeping her finger on the pulse of business operations, but found that she didn't mind physical labor. It left her with a sense of satisfaction and beat staring at her computer or the four bunkhouse walls.

"It's a dirty job, so if you want use of the tub—" he looked vaguely self-conscious "—just let me know."

Use of the tub? Words she'd never thought

she'd hear him say. Taylor frowned at him. "What brought this on?"

He rubbed his cheek. "Too many hours in the tractor."

"Excuse me?"

He dropped his hand. "I was being a jerk about things when you first got here. There's no reason you shouldn't have access to the tub if you want."

As if she could relax naked in hot water with him on the other side of the door.

"Thank you," she said slowly. "I, uh, might take you up on it. If I had the house to myself."

"I'm not moving into the bunkhouse."

"I wasn't talking permanently. I was only thinking that I'd have a better shot at relaxation if I was alone as opposed to hogging the bathroom." Because Karl's old house had only the one.

"Okay. The next time I have a night out, I'll let you know."

She allowed herself a smile. "I'm trying hard not to do a happy dance right now."

"Tomorrow is poker night. I'll be gone for a while." He opened the barn door and set the grain bucket inside, then reached out to take the bottle bucket from Taylor.

"You have a poker night?"

"Karl's friends. I'm taking his place. In return, they take my money." He gave her a mock-innocent look. "Something wrong with that?"

"No…just that it seems to be at odds with your hermit persona."

He rolled the barn door shut again with his good hand. "For the record, I'm not a hermit. I just like to choose when I spend time with people. For the past four years I haven't been able to do that. I've not only had to spend time with them, I've had to pretend I'm happy doing it."

"What exactly did you do?"

"I saddled horses, answered questions, refrained from rolling my eyes at the dumb ones." He gave her a pointed look. "And for the record, there *are* dumb questions. I liked most of the guests, but…mostly I just wanted to disappear onto my part of the ranch and raise cows and hay."

"Why didn't you?"

"The technicalities of a handshake agreement."

Taylor frowned.

"I'll explain it sometime."

"Yeah?"

He stopped walking at the place where they would part ways. "Yeah."

That was...surprising. She wasn't certain she believed him, but the odd thing was that she *wanted* to believe him. "What's stopping you from explaining right now?"

His gaze met hers. "I don't know. Lack of whiskey, maybe?"

"That bad?"

He gave a short laugh. "No. It's just...family business and I'm not a great sharer."

Taylor slipped her thumbs into her back pockets and rocked back on her heels. "When I first met you, I had you pegged as working in the hospitality field."

He looked almost insulted. "No kidding."

"You were smooth and I could tell you'd worked with people. I would have guessed that you were a really good sharer. But as I get to know you better, you get rougher around the edges." She cocked her head. "How does that work?"

"Public me. Real me."

"You're good at hiding 'real you.'"

"Years of practice."

"But you weren't 'public you' with me for very long."

"I found you threatening at first. On a number of fronts."

Taylor lifted her eyebrows. "I find you threatening, too."

"Yeah?" He easily followed the shift in the subject of conversation. "Still?"

"Things like this don't dissipate overnight." *This* being an attraction that could easily veer out of control. "It's not that I'm not interested... but damn it, Cole, the timing is all wrong."

"And you're all about schedules."

"At this juncture of my life, I'm all about caution and control. You're screwing with both of those."

TAYLOR HAD TO give Cole points for not messing with her caution and control over the next two days. In fact, she barely saw him. When she got up on Tuesday morning, ready to hit the boneyard, he was out in the field on his tractor. She found a note tacked to her door that read "No work today or tomorrow."

It felt like a snow day. No farmwork, no temptation. Did it get any better than that?

Taylor parked herself in front of her computer and spent the morning drinking coffee and networking, sending out résumés and touching base with her contacts. Applying for everything she could possibly apply for. When she was done, she went for a run, stopping to admire the new calves playing in the fields across the road from her grandfather's farm.

The next day she did the same, and when she was done with her run, she went to what was left of her grandmother's vegetable garden and started thinking about what it would take to put it right again. Cole might be a farmer, but he hadn't touched the garden. Maybe she should?

Taylor abruptly turned and headed back to the bunkhouse. What was she thinking? Gardens? She had a black thumb, and gardening had never been her thing…but she had enjoyed picking peas and digging carrots—even when she'd become too cool for the farm. There was no reason that she shouldn't enjoy gardening again—except for the fact that she had no idea how long she was going to be there.

It would take less than six months to plant and harvest…

Great. Just what she needed. A farmer voice whispering in her ear.

To counteract it, Taylor sent a few more emails, accepted an offer for a phone interview the following week, then sent a text to Carolyn. She'd just set down her phone when a knock on the door brought her to her feet.

When she opened the door, Cole was standing a few feet away, covered in powdery dirt. "What happened?"

He looked down at his dusty jeans and T-shirt, then gave a few half-hearted slaps that raised the dust a little. "Chucky got out again. Chased the tractor, tried to go down an old badger hole. I had to lie on my stomach to get him out."

"And he's…"

"Back home. Mrs. Clovendale saw he was gone and came out across the field."

"Sorry to have missed that."

"Oh, yeah. Chucky's a lot of fun. I just wanted to remind you that it's poker night."

Taylor couldn't stop the smile that spread across her face. "I know."

"You should have at least two hours of privacy. The old guys let me and Dylan win for a while to kind of stretch things out before annihilating us."

"Could you maybe call before you come back?"

"I could do that."

"Sometimes I fall asleep in the tub."

He frowned at her. "No way."

She smiled dreamily. "I do love my baths."

Cole blew out a breath and gave her a smile that said, "O-k-a-a-y…" before adding, "I'll be gone in about an hour."

"Thanks, Cole." And she meant that from the bottom of her heart.

Exactly one hour later, before the dust had settled behind Cole's truck, Taylor started the tub running. While it filled, she went to the kitchen, opened the wine she'd brought and poured a healthy amount into a tumbler. The thieves had made off with her wineglasses, but somehow drinking wine out of a milk glass while soaking in an old pink bathtub seemed appropriate. Her life wasn't the same as it once was. Eventually she'd be home again, fighting deadlines and drinking wine out of crystal stemware, but in the meantime, a glass her grandmother had pulled out of a detergent box forty or fifty years ago worked.

The water was dangerously high by the time Taylor slipped out of her clothes and eased into the tub. It lapped at the edge but didn't spill over. She slid deeper, closing her eyes as the excess water gurgled into the overflow. The wine and the book could wait. Right now she was just going to—

A bang on the door brought her upright.

Another bang and she stood up, water sheeting off her and splashing onto the floor as she grabbed her towel. She heard the kitchen door open and cursed under her breath. So much for warning phone calls…

"Hello?"

Taylor froze.

That was not Cole. Far from it. The voice was feminine.

"Cole?"

Cole had a woman in his life. That solved the problem of what to do about the kiss. Taylor hitched the towel up a little higher. She'd never been the other woman. Hell, she wasn't the other woman now. She cracked open the door. "Hi?"

The footsteps that had passed by the bathroom stopped dead and then came back toward her. "Who are you?"

Taylor closed the door again—just in case this woman was the volatile kind. "I live next door. I don't have a tub. Cole let me use his while he's gone." *And it's really my grandfather's tub.*

"There is no next door."

"The bunkhouse. I live in the bunkhouse."

"No one lives in the bunkhouse. I'd know." *Guess again, honey.*

"Look," the woman continued, "if you're hooking up with my brother, I don't—"

Taylor opened the door. "Your brother?"

The woman, who was younger than Taylor had assumed, looked so much like Cole it was spooky. Definitely telling the truth about the relationship.

Taylor wrapped her towel a little tighter. "I'm Karl Evans's granddaughter, Taylor."

Cole's sister gave her a skeptical look. "If you're living here, then why didn't my brother tell me?"

"Because he's the most closemouthed individual I know?"

The sister gave a considering nod. "You might be right." She glanced down the hall, then back at Taylor. "This is kind of embarrassing."

"Was Cole expecting you?" The girl's mouth tightened, and that was when Taylor noted the blotchiness around her beautiful eyes. She'd either been crying or trying hard not to cry.

"No." She gave a small shrug. "I'm Jancey, by the way."

"Nice name."

"Norwegian uncle. Only his name was pronounced Yancey. I'm glad they went with 'J.'"

"Ah."

The girl glanced down at her very worn Western boots as if debating a course of action. "I kind of expected Cole to be here."

"He'll be back tonight. You could call him."

She shook her head. "Not a phone matter."

Taylor shivered. The house was cold. "I need to get dressed. Give me a second?" Because she didn't want this girl, who was obviously upset, to disappear into the night.

"Sure. Maybe I'll raid the fridge."

"Good plan."

Taylor pulled the door closed, dropped the towel and reached into the still deliciously warm water to pull the plug. *Goodbye, first bath in forever...*

She dressed in a hurry, grabbed the wine bottle, the glass and her book, and headed out into the kitchen, where Jancey was sitting at the empty table with no food in sight.

"Is the fridge empty?"

"I guess I'm really not hungry." She folded her arms across her midsection. "I didn't know Karl had a granddaughter. I've only been here a couple times. I came with Cole when they made the farming deal."

"I used to spend summers—well, parts of summers—here. My dad grew up here." *Brought my mother here and ruined her life.* Anyway, that was how Cecilia told the story.

"Why are you back?"

"I got laid off and couldn't find a job where

I lived. I needed a place to stay while I look for another job."

"And Cole let you stay here?"

Taylor barely kept from giving a derisive snort. "We…came to an agreement."

"Cole came here to get away from things."

"So I gather."

Jancey looked past Taylor to the darkened window behind her. "I might be staying here, too."

"The more the merrier," Taylor said lamely. Whatever the girl's reason for moving in, Taylor didn't think it was a happy one.

"Yeah." Jancey attempted a smile, but it fell flat.

"If I cooked something, would you eat it?"

The girl raised her eyes. "You don't have to do that."

"Except that I'm starving and the stove in the bunkhouse is really old and doesn't work very well."

"You should get a microwave."

"I had one, but it got stolen. And I don't think the wiring could take it."

"I'm surprised you're living there. You must have fixed it up."

"Patched a hole in the floor." Taylor went to the cupboard to see what Cole had on hand.

As she'd hoped, he had spaghetti and sauce. In her experience, pasta made everything better.

She put water on to boil, adding oil and salt. Everything was exactly where it had been when she'd stayed with her grandfather years ago. Cole had made no changes or additions to the kitchen, and Karl had barely taken anything with him.

"Are you in school?" Taylor asked as she opened the spaghetti sauce.

"I start college in the fall. I graduated high school almost a year ago and decided to work for a year so that I didn't have to borrow as much money."

"Great plan," Taylor said. "I'm still haunted by loans." And would be for some time to come.

"It was a great plan. Now…not so much."

She spoke in a way that didn't invite questions, so Taylor focused on cooking. "I wish I had hamburger to make a meat sauce."

"I like plain old red sauce. Our cook does a great Bolognese, but I don't need meat with my pasta."

"You have a cook?"

"The ranch does."

"You work on the guest ranch?"

Jancey's expression closed off, and Taylor turned back to the stove. *All righty, then.* "Shouldn't be too long." She almost wished aloud for bread but didn't want to remind Jancey of the cook again.

The phone rang, and Jancey answered. "I wanted to talk to you," she said after hello. "I'd rather wait until you get here. Okay. See you soon."

She hung up then smiled a little. "My brother says that you should get out of the tub."

"Will do." Taylor leaned back against the counter, feeling oddly nervous now that she knew Cole was on his way home. "What do you plan to study?"

"I thought about majoring in ag econ, like Cole, but my heart is set on veterinary science."

"Cole's degree is in...aggiecon?" Whatever that was. Taylor was surprised to hear that Cole had a degree at all, which drove home the point that she'd been as judgmental about him as he'd been about her.

"Agricultural economics."

Ag. Econ. Ah. "That wasn't a course of study at my university," Taylor said with a smile.

"He was working on an MBA, too, before he left the ranch. Online."

"No kidding."

"Cole's a smart guy."

Taylor considered why he'd kept working at the guest ranch he hated, but she had a feeling that the answer was sitting in front of her.

Once the pasta was ready, Taylor strained it and dumped it into a pan on the stove. She added the pasta sauce and a little Parmesan cheese, warming everything through before getting a plate and a plastic container out of the cupboard. "You don't care if I take mine with me, do you? I have some stuff to catch up on."

"Are you kidding? I'm thrilled you stayed long enough to cook for me." Her expression softened. "Thanks. I kind of needed a pick-me-up."

Taylor loaded the wine and damp towel into the tote she'd brought. "Trust me. I totally get it." She headed for the door just as the lights swung into the driveway. She didn't want to look as if she were running, but for reasons she didn't quite have a handle on, she didn't want to be there when Cole got home.

COLE'S STOMACH WAS in a knot by the time he parked next to the house. Taylor was just leaving as he pulled into the drive. She raised a hand and scurried toward the bunkhouse. Well, at least Jancey'd had some company while she waited for him.

He pushed open the kitchen door and stepped into the heavenly scent of fresh spaghetti sauce.

"You cooked?"

Jancey snorted. "Right."

"Taylor cooked."

"She felt sorry for me."

"Dare I ask why?"

"From the way she was looking at me, I'd say she'd guessed I'd been crying." And was about to start again, which disturbed him, since Jancey wasn't by nature a teary person.

He pulled out a chair and sat on the other side of the table. "What happened?"

"She who shall not be named."

"That goes without saying. What did she do?" Because he was going to hurt her if she hurt his sister.

She drew in a shaky breath then exhaled. "She threatened me."

Instant blood pressure spike. "Threatened you how?"

"She invited me to this private lunch, and we had this...dainty food...and she tried to make me feel all special. Then she said that she knew I was going to have some difficulty paying for college and that she could help me from getting too deeply into debt."

Cole pressed his fingers to his forehead. Miranda made people feel special only when she needed something. Her minions felt special all the time, which was why they were loyal to her.

"She asked me to sell my part of the ranch to her. She told me that since I was eighteen, I could do as I wanted, according to the trust, and that you weren't that interested in keeping the ranch—if you were, then you wouldn't be farming fifty miles away."

"You know that's not true." He hoped.

She cleared her throat. "She said you were only hanging on to your share to make her angry and if I asked you, you'd tell me to hang on for the same reason. She said it was selfish of you, when the money could help me through college."

"I'm hanging on because it's ours."

Jancey gave a jerky nod as she worried the amethyst ring she wore.

"That's not really a threat, Jancey. She tried to scam you—"

His sister's eyes came up. "She said that if I didn't sell, that she'd talk to people at my college. Tell them...stuff, I guess. I thought she was blowing smoke, and then I got a call from my high school counselor. College admissions called her because they were concerned I'd had someone else write my entrance essay. They sent it to her. Asked her whether it reflected my abilities."

Cole stared at her, stunned. "I thought this just happened."

Jancey shook her head. "It happened a couple weeks ago."

"And you didn't tell me."

"I…thought I could handle it. Right up…" Her voice cracked. "Right up until I got the call from Mrs. Chavez."

"Your counselor."

"Yeah."

Cole leaned back in his chair, carefully unclenching his fists. She should have told him sooner, but he needed to deal with it now. He scraped his chair back and Jancey reached out to touch his hand.

"Don't go to the ranch."

"Why?"

"Because I'm afraid of what she'll do."

Cole gave a choked laugh. It was more of a question of what he would do. Mess with him, fine. Mess with his baby sister…

Cole did his best to look reassuring as he

said, "There's nothing she can do, Jancey. She wants you to think she can."

"Look what she did to Jordan."

"Tried to do. There's a difference." She'd done her best to take control of his hideaway ranch, but ultimately, Jordan had prevailed.

"She *did* do it to me," his sister said darkly.

True. And she wasn't getting away with it.

TAYLOR CLOSED HER LAPTOP, taking care not to slam it down, and got to her feet. Three, count 'em, *three*, rejections. Two of them were for jobs that she didn't want, but the third rejection stung, having come after that lengthy, hope-inspiring late-afternoon Skype interview. She'd wanted that job. She stopped in front of the mirror and glared at herself.

"Three? Really?"

Max raised his head as she spun around, then laid it back on his paws, keeping his green gaze on her as she took a turn around the room, trying to get control of both her disappointment and her fears for the future.

"You may end up mousing for a living," she told the cat, "because I think we may be stuck here forever." Which clearly wasn't an option, but after receiving three rejections— *bam, bam, bam*—the doubts started rolling in.

She didn't *want* to live here forever. She had things to do, professional dragons to slay.

She had a goal list, for Pete's sake, and "stay on the farm forever" wasn't a line item there.

She started to shrug out of her shirt when she stopped moving. Was that...?

Oh, yeah. She could hear the now-familiar sounds of the calves stampeding around their pen and glanced at the clock. A little after ten, just as it'd been the first time Chucky had come to call. Was the Curly Terror back?

If so, at least she knew the magic words to get him out from under the grain shed. Unlike the last time that she encountered the poodle-in-the-night, Taylor didn't feel the least bit cautious as she headed out the door. She was glad to have something else to focus on.

She strode across the gravel toward the barn with a no-nonsense stride. The calves were milling nervously around in their pen, but she didn't see any flashes of white. She didn't see anything threatening in the bluish light cast by the light attached to the barn, but there was a movement in the shadows.

Taylor stopped dead. What if, instead of a poodle, it was a coyote or a wolf this time? Hanging in the shadows, waiting for the right moment to spring—

"Are you okay?"

Taylor gave a small shriek as the voice came out of nowhere, then pressed a hand to her chest as she recognized Cole's voice. Beneath her palm, her heart hammered.

"You scared the crap out of me." She took a couple of deep breaths, willing her heart to slow down. "I thought Chucky was back."

"Sorry about that. I startled the calves when I came out of the machine shop, so I thought I'd hang until they settled."

She let out one last breath, then reached down to zip her sweatshirt, doing her best to regain her equilibrium during the simple act. Once zipped, she asked, "How was poker?"

"I lost." It was a simple statement of fact. "Thanks for taking care of my sister. Feeding her, I mean."

"She's cute," Taylor said, taking a few steps closer. "And she seemed upset. I didn't want to leave her alone."

"I appreciate that." He fell silent as Taylor came to a stop a few feet away from him. The wind gently lifted her hair, and she pulled a hand out of her pocket to brush it away from her face.

"Do you want to be alone?" There had to be

a reason he was out here when his little sister was in the house.

He breathed deeply, then raised his gaze to the dark horizon past the house. "No," he said simply.

Amazing how one small word could mean so much.

"Me either."

He turned his head. "Why's that?"

"I got three rejection emails tonight. What happened to you?"

"A bully messed with my sister."

"You're kidding." She felt a sudden welling of protectiveness toward a girl she didn't even know. Jancey seemed like an okay kid. "Who?"

"Our step-aunt. The one who has control of our ranch."

"The handshake deal."

"Followed by a lot of paperwork."

Taylor looked down at the clumped-up dirt in the dimly lit pen. The calves had settled, and the night was quiet. She focused on Cole, who was still staring out across the dark fields. "What did she do?"

Cole shook his head.

Taylor moved forward to rest her forearms on the rail next to him, keeping her gaze on him. "Do you know why I'm the perfect person to talk to?"

He glanced over at her. "Why?"

"Sometimes an outsider sees things in a different way. And I don't know anyone to gossip to. Win."

He let out a short breath. "There's pretty much only one way to see this." He dropped his gaze and shook his head. When he looked up again, he met her eyes in a way that made her insides tumble. "But I will confess to having thought about getting your take on this."

"Why didn't you?" Neither had moved, but it felt as if he were closer.

"Just wasn't there yet."

"You know," she said softly, "I'm pretty sure I'd rather have three job rejections than find out someone had messed with my sister. The rejections are about me. The bullying…"

"Makes me want to punch Miranda's face in."

"That's your step-aunt?"

"That's her. She messed with Jancey's college application. Did her some damage credibility-wise."

Taylor's mouth fell open. "Will you be able to straighten out the matter?"

"We hope."

Taylor thought about how devastated she would have been had someone messed with her applications. The journey to success started in high school and segued into college. That had been hammered into her for so long that, even now, it shocked her to think of someone messing with another person's educational future. "What exactly did she do to Jancey?"

"Suggested that her entry essay was written by someone else."

Taylor shook her head. "That's low. Very low."

"Welcome to Miranda World."

"Which college?"

"Danner."

Taylor was familiar with the school. Small but prestigious. Located near Boise. She'd worked with at least one person who'd graduated from there. "If there's anything I can do—"

Cole reached out and covered her hand with his. Shock at the unexpected contact was quickly followed by warmth, and Taylor found that she no longer had a whole lot to say. Cole squeezed her fingers, then slid his hand away. A silent bit of communication from a guy who didn't share easily. He hadn't exactly spilled his secrets, but he was opening up to her, little by little. And even if things proved to be complicated, she wouldn't give back this moment.

He jerked his head toward his house. "Jancey's still up. Want to watch a Rodney movie?"

She blinked at him, surprised by the question, then smiled. "Yes. I would."

"I thought so." He pushed off the fence, and even though he didn't offer his hand again, they walked to the house, close enough that every now and again their shoulders bumped, and Taylor realized that she felt more at peace, more centered than she'd felt in a long, long time.

The only problem was that it was happening in a place where she didn't belong.

JANCEY WAS NOT much of a chaperone. They'd barely gotten twenty minutes into the movie when she fell asleep curled up in Karl's big chair with her fist tucked under her chin. She looked so vulnerable and emotionally spent that Cole's anger welled.

He must have been telegraphing because Taylor leaned into him during a particularly raucous part of the movie. "I know it's tough," she murmured. "Better to hurt yourself than see someone you love hurting."

He was so damned glad she didn't say something along the lines of "it'll be all right." It may well be, but they didn't know for sure.

"This is how Miranda works. She gets people so stirred up that they make stupid mistakes while she stays cool and collected. She feeds off this stuff."

"Lovely woman."

"Jancey's tough," he said. His little sister stirred in her sleep at the sound of her name, then settled again. "But…"

His voice trailed off as Taylor took his hand, very much as he'd taken hers earlier, and laced her fingers with his. It could have been the gesture of a good friend…or something else.

He was too wound up to properly evaluate, so instead he went with his gut, shifted on the sofa and brought his hand up to touch her face, lightly cupping her cheek. She held his gaze, raised her eyebrows, her lips curving into a soft I'm-game-if-you-are smile.

Hell, why not?

His lips met hers in a butterfly kiss. Barely a touch, but electric all the same. Her mouth opened, inviting him in. He accepted as he pushed his hand into her silky hair, twisting the strands gently as the kiss deepened.

Had his sister not been there, he would have pressed Taylor back onto the sofa and gotten serious about this. An explosion on the television screen yanked them back to the here and now, and he shot a look over at Jancey to see if she was still asleep. Thankfully she was. Taylor pulled back a little.

"You're distracting me from Rodney," she whispered.

"Who?"

She let out a soft laugh, her warm breath feathering over his lips. Her fingers splayed wide over the side of his face, the connection between them feeling so real. So good.

"I hate to miss the end of the movie, but perhaps I should go?"

Cole let out a breath. He didn't want her to go. And wasn't that just nuts?

"Yeah. Maybe so." He took her lips again in a kiss that promised more. Much more. Later.

Surely there'd be a later?

With Taylor, with their odd situation, there was no telling.

WHEN TAYLOR HEADED out to feed the calves the following morning, Jancey was already there, cooing and loving the little animals as she fed them.

"I take it these were your babies?" Taylor said as she approached.

"They *are*." There were still signs of stress in the girl's face, but she looked better than she had the night before, making Taylor wonder how Cole looked this morning. He'd been smoldering while they'd watched the movie. Before she'd distracted him, that is. Distracted him, distracted herself.

It was crazy how right it had felt.

Jancey finished the last calf and dropped the bottle in the bucket. "The heifer that tried to take out my brother is mine, too. I'm selling her, and he was supposed to deliver."

"Yeah. That didn't work out so well."

"Got to check your ground before working. He knows that." She climbed out of the pen. "I have to clean up. Job hunting today."

"Good luck." Taylor did her best to keep the irony out of her voice.

"Thanks. I guess I should be grateful that Miranda made me wait tables last summer."

Taylor smiled as if she didn't know who Miranda was, then headed back to the bunkhouse to do the networking she didn't feel like doing. Seattle seemed very far away today.

An hour later, a movement outside the window caught Taylor's attention, and she looked up in time to catch sight of Jancey getting into her car. Cole followed, leaning down to say a few words through the open window, then he headed for the machine shop after his sister drove away.

Taylor grabbed her jacket and let herself out of the bunkhouse. When she walked into the machine shed, Cole was standing in front of the long workbench staring at nothing in particular. He turned, scowling.

"Nice stay-away face." Taylor leaned a shoulder against the door.

"Not intended for you." He rubbed his hands over his cheeks and then dropped them again. "Still working through stuff."

She couldn't help but wonder if some of that stuff involved her...and how she felt about that. But for now, she wasn't thinking, plotting or planning. She was doing.

"How would you feel about taking a drive with me today?"

"To...?"

"The ranch."

Taylor pushed off from the door and moved a couple of steps closer. Jancey had been bullied by their step-aunt, and now Cole was going to the ranch. How could she say no? She wanted to see this ranch and meet Miranda. She wanted to make certain Cole didn't do anything he'd be sorry for later. The guy was starting to matter to her in ways she'd never dreamed of.

She gave an overly casual shrug. "When do you want to leave?"

CHAPTER TWELVE

COLE'S FAMILY RANCH was something out of a picture book. Set at the edge of a wide meadow where a herd of Angus grazed, it wasn't much bigger than Karl's farm but had so much more visual appeal. The house and barn were both sided with rustic boards, which had weathered to a beautiful golden brown. A jackleg fence stretched along one side of the meadow, and the corrals and pens were constructed of poles instead of wire. The place looked rustic yet manicured.

"The siding is fake," Cole said before she could utter a word. "Well, the barn's real, but Miranda wanted the house to have more impact, so she paid to have the vinyl siding taken off and replaced with the cedar boards. Then she wanted us to pay for it, but I fought her on it." He stopped at the gate. "That was our first rift after my uncle died."

He got out to open the gate, even though

Taylor had volunteered, hooking it back against the fence with a chain before driving through.

Cole had gone over the situation with his ranch as he drove, keeping his gaze locked on the road. He'd explained how Miranda had married his uncle several years ago and initially charmed everyone. The Bryan brothers—Cole's father and uncle—had been steadily losing money on their ranches and had agreed that a guest ranch was worth a shot, especially since Miranda had offered to take the helm. Things went well in the beginning, but once his uncle died, the situation had changed. Miranda had changed. True colors began to show.

Cole's expression had grown increasingly tight as they'd neared the ranch, and now, as he parked next to the house, she was wondering if he was in danger of cracking a tooth. She touched his arm.

His gaze jerked over to her, and then he made an effort to relax his features. "Sorry. Lots of crazy emotions tied up in this place."

Taylor was beginning to toy with the idea of kissing him before his blood pressure redlined. Instead she got out of the truck. A kid in his late teens came out of the barn as Taylor closed her door, and Cole motioned for her to join him. They walked over to meet the boy at the ATV he'd left near the pasture fence.

"How's it going, Matt?"

"Jancey's staying with you, right?"

"Yeah."

"I tried to text her, but she didn't answer."

"She's fine."

The kid nodded, looking relieved. He glanced behind him as if expecting someone to be there listening, then said, "The queen is pissed that she just took off without telling anyone."

"She's going to have to get over it."

Matt threw a leg over the ATV. "Tell Jancey hi and that it wouldn't kill her to text back."

"She's off her game right now, but I'll tell her."

The kid started the engine, then with a wave, headed back across the pasture.

"Miranda sends him to do the chores. Since she uses the place, she wants it public ready at all times."

"She uses the entire place?"

"Not the house. The house is ours. Well, the entire place is ours, but she has the rights to use it tied up."

"Renegotiate."

"It's a fifty-fifty ownership deal. She won't budge and neither will we."

"Unless you have something she wants and can bargain."

Cole turned to her, his expression serious. "I have nothing that Miranda wants other than this property. That leaves us in a bad place."

"So it seems."

"Come on. I'll show you the house and you can see why it isn't used for guests."

The house was totally old-fashioned inside, with small rooms. The kitchen was large, though. There were heat grates in the floors of the upstairs rooms to allow the heat from the kitchen to permeate the rest of the house.

"They made the rooms small so that they could close off the ones not in use during the winter and not heat them."

"I can understand that, but wow, if you knocked out some walls—"

Cole shot her a look that stopped her dead. "Then Miranda would probably come up with a loophole to use the house."

"Could she?"

"Probably not, but she'd drive me crazy in the process."

"You need out of this agreement."

He turned toward her. "You think?"

"Have you consulted an attorney?" A question she'd put off asking until she had more facts.

He put a gentle palm on each side of Taylor's face, making her nerves start doing a crazy dance, and instead of answering, focused on her as if she were the answer. Things were heating up between them, and she wasn't doing one damned thing to stop them.

"Cole?"

"Miranda has an attorney on retainer."

"That doesn't mean…"

"The land is mine and Jancey's. It's not going anywhere. When I get ahead, I'll hire a lawyer."

"But what if she finds a loophole to gain possession," Taylor asked. "Eminent domain, or *pedis possessio*?"

He gave a short laugh. "I think she would have already done that if she could, because that's exactly how my cousin got his ranch out of her clutches."

"Bottom line, you can't make a living on your own property?"

"I can, but I can't. Jancey and I get a percentage of the take from the guest ranch, but it's not as much as you might think. If there's an open position on the ranch, Jancey or I

could choose to take the job and draw a paycheck in addition to the percentage—which is
what we did in the past. I worked there for...
hell, since I was sixteen. Went back to work
after college, thinking that it was my job to
help the family business. Then my uncle died
and it all went to hell.

"I can live here on my ranch. However, if I
work the ranch, the money I make goes into
the general coffers and I pull a percentage of
that, as does Miranda."

"Her finger's in every pie."

"The result of an agreement between
brothers—one of whom was madly in love
with her."

Cole gestured toward the door with his chin.
"I'll show you the rest."

He toured her through the barns, which had
been expertly staged. He shook his head at the
gleaming leather harnesses hung on one wall.

"Looks good," Taylor murmured.

"Want to know how long it's been since
there's been a draft horse on the place?" He
stopped at the wide door at the far end of the
barn and stared out over the fields. Everything about him was stiff and defensive. Taylor was familiar with the posture, having held
it a few times herself as she dealt with prob-

lems at work…but those problems had never been personal.

She shifted her weight, and he slowly turned toward her, tearing his gaze away from his land. One corner of his mouth tightened. "You know why I brought you with me, right?"

"To keep you from doing something that might get you arrested?"

The corners of his mouth quirked into a faint smile. "Just so we're on the same page." He settled his hands on her shoulders, staring down at her seriously. "But I never asked if you were on board for a meeting with the queen."

"Totally." She couldn't wait to meet the woman.

"I thought about bringing my cousin Jordan, but he and Miranda…well, let's just say that until recently, I was able to play the game with her. He never was."

"Blood on the walls?"

"It'd be close to that."

She set her hands on his biceps, felt them tighten under her palms, but neither of them moved closer.

He went on. "I don't know which Miranda you'll see—probably the pathologically nice one to begin with, but since I'm not going to play her game…well, I just want you to watch.

See if you see what I do." He gave a small snort. "And then help me come up with a way to defeat her."

"She sounds like a supervillain."

"No." He brushed his fingers down her face and leaned down to give her a soft kiss before stepping back. The kiss was as heady as the hot one had been. Maybe more so. "She's just an evil narcissist."

Taylor smiled a little. "Same difference. I've encountered a few of them in my professional life."

"Another reason you're here." He swept his gaze around the barn, shook his head and then motioned toward the truck parked just outside. "Let's do this thing."

"Sure." She reached out and took his hand. He squeezed her fingers and kept hold of them until he opened the truck door for her.

Taylor settled inside. *Where is this going?* her little voice murmured as Cole got into the truck.

Into territory she'd never been in before.

She straightened her shoulders. Okay, so she was venturing into something new with a guy she was beginning to like a little too much. A guy who made her hormones happy.

A guy whose lifestyle didn't exactly mesh with her own.

Maybe it's time to stop thinking.

She didn't know if she could do that, but she could suspend activity until she got more information. Actually…she'd been doing pretty good at suspending activity lately. It wasn't a bad skill to hone.

Instead of following the road that Matt had taken, Cole drove out the main entrance, locked the gate after him, then followed the pavement to the guest ranch.

Like his ranch, this one was meticulously kept. The buildings were rustic, yet obviously new. And there were a lot of them.

"This is some place," Taylor said. A tastefully carved wooden sign on the cabin-like building to her right said Spa and Sauna.

"It used to look a lot like my ranch, once upon a time."

He took her hand as they walked up the steps to what was the main lodge. "My cousin grew up here. I don't think there's anything left that he recognizes."

A young woman in a white shirt approaching from the direction of the stairway smiled in welcome, but the smile disappeared when she saw Cole standing beside Taylor. One of the loyal minions, no doubt.

"I want to see Miranda."

"She's—"

"Right here," a carefully modulated voice sounded from the top of the stairs. A woman in her midfifties, dressed in dark-wash denim jeans, a plain white shirt and a zillion-dollar turquoise-and-silver necklace descended the staircase. As she caught sight of Taylor, her expression became one of gracious welcome. If Taylor hadn't been clued in, she would have totally bought it.

"Cole."

"Miranda."

"I'm Taylor." No sense waiting for introductions while these two faced off, one smiling graciously, the other stone-faced, both with hard, hard gazes pinned on the other.

"So nice to meet you." Miranda offered her hand and Taylor took it, noting that the woman wore no rings except for the gold band on her left hand, and that her nails were buffed but she didn't wear polish. Yet everything about her and her environment cried money. Purposeful? Probably.

She was attempting to look down-to-earth but elegant. It was working. With milky skin, pale green eyes and light auburn hair, simplicity suited her.

Taylor smiled and withdrew her hand, wishing she could have said she was Cole's attorney just to see the woman's reaction.

Miranda turned her attention to Cole. "Have you heard from Jancey?"

"She's staying with me," Cole said. "That's why I'm here."

Miranda wore an expression of extreme relief, then her features hardened. "Even though she's family, this isn't working, Cole. I can't have people disappearing like this. It's too nerve-racking."

"You didn't call to let me know she was missing."

"I didn't know if she was missing." The smile became strained. "She's eighteen. She might have been on an…overnight date."

The woman who'd greeted Taylor entered the room and passed behind them on her way to an office, but Miranda lifted her chin, the silent message was instantly received, and a second later they were alone again.

"You threatened my sister."

Miranda's eyes went wide. "I did no such thing."

"She told me everything. How you attempted to strong-arm her—"

Her chin went up before she interrupted him. "There is no crime in offering to buy something. Especially when Jancey can use the money."

"There is when you tell lies about her to college admissions."

Miranda's hand went to her chest. "I did no such thing."

"One of your little helpers, then. Which one is related to someone influential?"

An expression of outrage began to form. "I don't have to stand for this…"

"I know someone in Danner College admissions," Taylor said, which was almost but not quite true.

Miranda turned cold eyes toward her. Any hope that the woman would twitch instantly evaporated. "How lovely. It'll make it easier to check the facts, although I believe there are federal regulations that prevent such information from being released."

Cole glared. "If Jancey loses her slot at that school—"

Taylor took hold of Cole's uninjured wrist and wrapped her fingers firmly around it, both as a show of moral support and just in case he felt driven to do something he'd regret later.

"We'll open an investigation," she said quietly. "I don't believe anonymous tips are covered under federal regulations. There is a law against slander, however."

"You're both being ridiculously dramatic," Miranda snapped. "Jancey quit because she can't handle living here without you. She ran home to big brother and told him a tale about me threatening her." She lifted her chin, gave a small sniff. "If there's nothing else?"

"Threaten my sister again—do anything to my sister again—and you will regret it."

An expression closer to a smirk than a smile formed on the woman's face. "Jancey is my niece. I would never threaten her."

Cole drew in a breath. "I may well start spending more time on the ranch. My ranch."

"Be warned, then, that this summer we'll be doing a lot more with the working part of the ranch. Those packages are becoming very popular."

Cole simply smiled, and Taylor had to give him points for not breaking. "We'll see."

He took Taylor's hand in his and started back for the door.

"It's in the agreement, Cole. There's nothing you can do about it," Miranda called pleasantly after him. Cole's grip tightened on Taylor's hand, but other than that, he didn't react.

THE DRIVE BACK was silent.

Taylor stared out the windshield, processing what she'd just witnessed, making Cole wonder if she'd gotten a true enough glimpse of the real Miranda to understand what he was up against. She'd jumped in a time or two, but he didn't know if that had been because she was showing support or because she truly got what a liar Miranda was.

Whatever her take, at least her presence had kept him from blowing up—a tactic that never worked with Miranda. As people got angrier, she got icier. It was her go-to defense, and a difficult one to deal with.

Finally, as he exited the highway at the Eagle Valley, Taylor took a deep breath and turned her head to look his way, an expression of concern in her blue eyes. But she didn't say anything. Maybe she was waiting for him to lead the charge.

He didn't want to talk. He didn't know what he could say. Either Taylor got it or she didn't.

When he parked the truck and turned off the ignition, neither of them moved. Then they reached for their door handles simultaneously, exchanging a look before they got out. Cole met Taylor at the rear of the truck.

"Thanks for coming along."

"Do you...want to talk?" Judging from her tone, she already knew his answer—if he'd wanted to talk, he would have initiated—but since she'd asked...

"Not now. Maybe later." Maybe never, but he was glad he'd brought her along.

"All right." She started toward the bunkhouse, but made only a couple of steps before she reversed course, came to stand directly in front of him, reached up to take his face between her hands and kissed him. Not a soft kiss like the one he'd given her in the barn, just because, but a let's-tackle-our-frustrations kiss. An I'm-going-to-eat-you-alive kiss.

Cole put his hands on her slim waist, telling himself he was going to end the kiss, but instead he gave her a small tug and pulled her body into his. "Are you doing this because you feel sorry for me?"

She shook her head, her hands still on his face. "No." And then her mouth was back on his, and he decided that he didn't care if she felt sorry for him or not. He wanted her any way that he could have her. He walked her backward a few steps, then when she almost lost her balance, he lifted his head and nodded toward the bunkhouse.

"Yes."

Cole was rapidly becoming a fan of monosyllabic responses. He kept an arm around her as they covered the short distance to the place that neither of them had wanted to move into— a place that suddenly seemed perfect.

They were barely in the door when Taylor started working on his shirt buttons. No analysis, no "Are you sure?" Now he had his answer about what she'd be like—she took charge. He was good with that.

No—he sucked air in over his teeth as she finished with his shirt and started undoing his belt—he was great with that. But he also wanted his turn.

He covered her hands with his, and her gaze came up to his. He brushed a kiss over her mouth, nipped at her lower lip, took hold of the bottom of her T-shirt and pulled it up over her head, tossing it onto the chair.

"Nice undies," he muttered as he took in the sheer mesh bra that left nothing to the imagination. If he'd known she wore stuff like this, well, this moment might have arrived sooner.

"You should have seen the things that got stolen," she said, gasping as he lowered his mouth to suck her warm flesh through the sheer fabric.

"Yeah?"

"I haven't been able to replace them." Her voice squeaked a little as he pushed the mesh aside to allow himself access to her nipples, and then her hands fisted in his hair as he gave each perfect breast the attention it deserved.

"Do you like that?" he asked, swirling her nipple with his tongue, then slowly pulling it into his mouth.

Her grip on his hair tightened. "Oh, yeah." He went to one knee, his hands skimming over her hips as his tongue trailed a path down her tight abs toward her jeans. He undid the button, lowered the zipper, and had started to work them over her hips when she said his name. He met her questioning gaze, and reality crashed through the haze in his brain. "I have to go to my place to get condoms."

"I have one."

"I think I love you."

Something flashed in her eyes before she turned and went for her purse and soon held up the packet. "This is my one and only."

"One's enough." For now.

"You're sure?" She put a hand on his chest and moved him backward until his knees hit the edge of her bed. One last push and he toppled backward, reaching out at the last minute to pull her down with him. She gave a squeak as he rolled over on top of her, effectively trapping her beneath him. Her face was flushed, her eyes dark with desire, and her mouth... oh, that mouth. There were dozens of places he wanted that mouth to be.

"Is your knee okay?" she asked.

His knee had been steadily healing, and yes, it was up to sex if that was what she was wondering. He gave her a quick nod. "The wrist is fine, too."

"So you're a hundred percent now."

"Maybe a little more."

Her chest rose and fell beneath him. He propped himself on his elbows and brushed back her hair, needing to see her face, needing to know that she was 100 percent on board. She languidly reached up to wrap her arms around his neck and pull his mouth down to hers.

And he was lost.

When he'd imagined making love to Taylor, he'd thought it would be more desperate, more of a get-it-done-before-we-come-to-our-senses experience. He'd been wrong. Instead they embarked on a long, slow exploration. Clothing was swept aside, sweet spots found. And when he finally pushed inside her, he wanted the ride to go on forever.

Life didn't work that way, nor did sex.

Especially sex with a woman who'd brought him to the brink so many times before he'd slid into her. Taylor came before he did—just barely—and as she arched into him, her breath catching, holding, he lost control, thrusting deeply one last time.

Then he laid his head onto her shoulder and exhaled deeply as she stroked his damp hair, and wondered to himself if life could possibly get better than this.

"YOU SHOULD HAVE purloined the bigger bed." Cole lay on his back with Taylor draped over the top of him, because there simply wasn't enough room for the two of them to lie side by side on the twin mattress.

"I wanted the bigger one, but my delivery guy messed up."

He snorted. "You wanted the whole house."

"That, too." She smiled against his chest and stretched, loving the feel of his hair-roughened body against her skin. "But now that Jancey's here, maybe it's best that I never got my wish." She shifted so that she could see his face. "I don't know how you worked for that Miranda person for more than a heartbeat without hurting her."

"Wasn't easy," Cole said. "But Jancey needed to finish school. Also, and this might be hard to believe, but she wasn't that bad until her husband died. Then she changed. It was as if suddenly she could do whatever she wanted without fear of repercussions."

"Repercussions? Like divorce?"

"Possibly, although my uncle thought she was perfect until the day he died. Lucky for him, I guess. He never saw her emotionally torture his son, my cousin Jordan."

"I guess we can be glad for that." She half turned in her seat. "What are you going to do?"

"Persevere. Raise hay. Let Jancey live with me until she goes to college."

"What about the ranch?"

She felt his muscles tighten beneath her. Hot-button topic. "I'll work that out as I go."

He brought his hand up to stroke her hair, but his body was still tense.

"How do you guys handle the business end of things? The purchases for the ranch, that kind of stuff?"

"All larger purchases require two signatures."

"Payroll?"

"Set up through the bank. Automatic after Miranda plugs in the numbers." He looked down at her, his hand stilling with his fingers still grazing her temple. "Why?"

"Just looking for ways to take the bitch down."

He smiled a little. "I like the way you think."

"Do you go over the monthly statements?"

"I do, but I can't say I go over them all that closely. I just look at the amounts, see if anything seems out of whack. So far, no."

"Maybe I can go over them." She smiled suddenly. "Better yet, let my friend Carolyn do it."

"Carolyn is…"

"A kick-ass accountant. If she can't do it, then surely she'll know a forensic accountant."

"Who will no doubt charge as much as a lawyer."

"Mmm." She settled her cheek back against his chest.

"My accountant does keep a close eye on the books. I trust him."

"That's not the point," she said, shifting again to meet his gaze. "The point is to send a message to Miranda that you're no longer letting her control everything. And, damn, what if she's been playing fast and loose with the funds?"

"My wildest dream come true…but I don't

think she is." Taylor's shoulders slumped a little. "However, I like your idea. How much would your friend charge for an audit?"

"She'll give you family rates, I'm sure."

He took hold of her shoulders and pulled her higher onto his chest, so that he could reach her lips, give her a long, slow kiss. "Let's discuss business later."

She nipped his lower lip, then kissed the spot. "About this…"

"Biting?"

"Uh…no."

He understood her meaning. "Live for the day, Taylor. Not everything needs to be planned out. Let's just…go with this. For a while. Then we can make a plan."

"I'm only going to be here for so long," she pointed out.

"Which is a great reason to enjoy each other while we can."

CHAPTER THIRTEEN

TAYLOR WOKE AS Cole shifted in her narrow bed, and she lifted her head off his chest. "My legs are numb," he said as he first bent then straightened the leg she wasn't lying on.

"Max is on the chair," she murmured.

"It's not the two-ton cat. It's the narrow bed."

"Hmm." Taylor stretched out a little more. "Whose fault is that?"

"Yeah, yeah, yeah. I'm fixing the problem later today."

Taylor lifted her head again. "What about Jancey?"

"Jancey is an adult." Taylor lifted an eyebrow. By mutual agreement, they were keeping their relationship on the down low. Fewer complications that way. "And she's going to a job interview at ten." He smiled down at her, then gently eased her aside and swung his legs out of bed. He sat for a moment before getting to his feet and searching the floor for his jeans. He stilled as something bumped against the old floorboards, and in the semidarkness Taylor saw him shake his head.

"Just a bunny."

"One would hope."

He pulled on his jeans, then reached for his shirt draped over the chair where Max slept. He tugged a sleeve out from under the cat, who rolled over onto his back. Taylor sat up, pulling the sheets up to her chin as a guard against the crisp night air. Tiny as her bed was, she always missed him when he made the short trip across the driveway in the early-morning hours, keeping up appearances for his sister, who was probably well aware of what was going on.

Aware and probably doing the "la-la-la, I can't hear you" thing.

Even if she was, she seemed to be okay with Taylor, who was teaching her to cook in the evenings. They'd had only a couple of sessions, but the lessons had gone well. Cole stayed far away from the kitchen, and Jancey mentioned that he'd once set the kitchen on fire as a kid. Since that time, he'd avoided anything but the most basic food preparations.

"Good thing we had a cook at the ranch," Jancey had said the previous evening as Taylor showed her how to make a quick pasta sauce using fresh tomatoes and basil, "or he would have gone through life eating fried meat and bagged lettuce. Oh…and canned soup. That's also in his repertoire."

Now, Cole eased Max to the side so he could share the chair with the cat and pulled on his socks and boots. Taylor propped herself up on one elbow. "Are you sure you want to go to the trouble of moving a mattress?"

He paused before pulling his second boot all the way onto his foot. "Too much of a commitment?"

"Maybe?"

He got up from the chair and came over to bend down over the bed and kiss her. "We agreed to being in the moment, and when I'm in the moment, I want to be comfortable."

It made sense. No reason for her to feel edgy. She tried a smile. It felt genuine. She was simply not used to this kind of situation—one that defied neat classification.

She couldn't sleep after Cole let himself out into the crisp early morning air for the short trip to his much-bigger bed. She turned on the electric heater and wrapped up in her robe, then settled into the chair with her laptop. The job search had become less of a priority during the past week and a half—since the time she'd first slept with Cole—but she had an interview with a Bozeman accounting firm later that day and she wanted to brush up on a few more company facts and figures before she got ready.

She wanted this job. Her feeling of professional self-worth was taking a hit, while, ironically, her sense of personal self-worth was doing okay.

How could it not, with a guy like Cole sharing her bed? He wasn't a talker, but she knew she turned him on. Knew that he found their new relationship as satisfying as she did.

What she didn't know was how he planned to handle their future…any more than she did.

A very good reason to stay in the moment.

"YOU KNOW," JANCEY said as she set a cereal bowl onto the table where Cole was reading through the last batch of bank statements, "I don't care if Taylor stays here." Cole's gaze jerked up, and his sister gave him an ironic look. "I mean, really. Why all the subterfuge?"

Cole blew out a breath as he pushed the bank statement aside. Oh, yeah, this wasn't uncomfortable or anything. "I guess because I wouldn't be wild about you bringing a guy here."

Jancey filled her bowl as she considered his

words, then carefully closed the cereal box. "I get that, but you two are thirty. *Thirty.*"

"You'll be thirty before you know it." And Taylor was only twenty-eight.

"And when I am, I won't be sneaking around like a high school kid," she said before twisting the cap off the milk jug.

"Jancey?" She raised her gaze to his. "Tell you what. I'll focus on my personal life and you focus on getting a job. Okay?"

"Fine. Just close the door more quietly when you come in, okay? It always wakes me up."

He thought he had been closing it quietly.

"Hey," Jancey said after taking her first bite. "Do you know who owns that little white dog?"

Cole breathed a quick prayer of thanks at the change of conversation. "Mrs. Clovendale's sister. His name is Chucky, and he's an escape artist."

"I think he's cute. I caught him yesterday, but when I put him down, he took off. If I catch him again, I'll take him home."

For all the good it'll do. Cole smiled at his sister. "Are you ready for today?"

She'd snagged an interview for a position as a warehouse worker for a local distribution company. The pay was good, the benefits were good and she'd be able to save a lot more for her schooling than she would have been able to do working on the guest ranch.

"I am so ready. I researched the company, and I have some questions to ask them." She jabbed her spoon into the cornflakes with a loud crunch. "And they hire summer after summer, so if I get on with them, then I can move back here next summer."

"Sounds like a job you need to land."

"Oh, I will land it."

She reminded him of Taylor during her string of interviews that had gone nowhere, but these were different circumstances. Magnus Distributing hired summer workers to load and drive. They weren't expecting their hires to be there forever, as US West Bank had.

"I'll wish you luck now. I have to mow the edges of the field today. Weeds are popping up fast." And Taylor had an interview later that day in Bozeman.

Bozeman wouldn't be a bad place for her to land. A little more than a three-hour drive away, it might make Taylor feel more secure as she worked through the situation—give them both some autonomy and time to decide if they wanted to move forward with this thing that was growing between them. Whether Taylor liked it or not, it was growing.

It'd been a long time since Cole had felt this kind of connection with a woman, and the fact that it was Taylor blew him away. The princess had turned out to not be such a princess after all. She still had an air of privilege about her, but now, instead of putting his back up, it made him want to play with her, bring her down to earth. As she relaxed and as they worked, he saw more and more of the down-to-earth side of her. Saw it and liked it.

Wanted more of it.

If she returned to Seattle, what would happen to down-to-earth Taylor? Would she disappear as business Taylor took over again?

Or maybe once freed, she was there forever.

Maybe she wasn't so anxious to go back to Seattle anymore…

Cole pushed the thought aside and headed out the door to his tractor. When he passed the bunkhouse, he could hear the shower running. Taylor was getting ready for her interview, and he wasn't going to distract her, as tempting as that thought was. He'd wished her luck last night in the best way he knew how, and now it was all on her.

"I THINK I nailed it," Jancey said as she chopped onions for the beef stew that she and Taylor were making that night. When she'd reminded Cole a few nights ago that she was supposed to be earning her keep, he'd suggested she give Jancey cooking lessons, since his sister was determined to learn to cook and the results were closer to miss than hit. "The interview, I mean."

She scooped the onions into a pan, and they began to sizzle and pop. "You want to cook these slowly."

Jancey bit her lip and adjusted the burner. "Right." Once the onions stopped popping, she glanced over at Taylor. "How'd yours go?"

"Well." Her interview had gone well, but she hadn't been wild about the company or the committee that interviewed her. Still, she needed to get back into her own world. A place where she felt as if she belonged.

"But…"

"Not my kind of company."

Jancey stopped peeling a carrot. "What was wrong with it?"

"Hard to explain." Especially for someone so hard up for employment. "It felt wrong. I'd take a job there if offered, though."

"For a place you don't love?"

"It's a job," she said.

"That's where I am, too. I used to love working for the ranch. Then my uncle died and Miranda went all power mad."

It wasn't the first time she'd heard that story.

"She looked as if she'd be a difficult person to work for."

Jancey held the burger over the pan and glanced over her shoulder at Taylor, who nodded. The burger went in with the onions, and Jancey started stirring.

"Add the chili powder now while the burger browns. It creates more flavor."

"Mmm." Jancey's eyebrows lifted, and then she started measuring out the powder. "She's into messing with people's heads. If someone pisses her off, and trust me, that's not that hard to do, then she starts making life difficult."

"How so?"

"Well, take my calves, for instance. I always raise the leppies. It's been my job since I was twelve, unless there are too many for me to handle. But since we don't have that many cows anymore, that hasn't happened lately. Anyway, she made certain that I was miles away from where I needed to be at feeding time. I started paying Matt to feed them, and when she caught on, she started doing the same with him."

"That sounds…"

"Psycho? Totally. Matt and I used to talk about it—when we were miles from the ranch. Miranda has spies."

Before meeting the woman, Taylor would have thought Jancey was exaggerating. Spies in business, yes. Spies in a family-run guest ranch… What would have seemed far-fetched now seemed entirely possible.

"It's a good thing you got out of there." Safe thing to say. Taylor didn't want to get too deeply into Cole's business, but she felt protective of him and his sister—both of whom should probably be living on their ranch right now. Cole enjoyed his farming, but as he'd told her late the night before, he could also farm on his ranch if Miranda hadn't nixed that. She'd said that plowed-up fields, small though they were, were not conducive to the guest experience.

"I hated leaving home, but…" Jancey pressed her lips together hard.

"It no longer felt like home."

"She took that from me. I guess that, even more than the thing she pulled with the college, makes me kind of hate her." She gave a small sniff and started stirring the onions with a vengeance. "And I don't want to hate anyone."

THEY ATE EARLIER than usual that day. Jancey had paced the kitchen as dinner cooked, staying close to the phone, which remained stubbornly silent. Finally, at 4:45 p.m., she announced that the stew was done. Cole could hear the disappointment in her voice, but managed to quell the urge to tell her that no news was good news. Trite sayings never helped, so instead, he ate two bowls of stew.

"I did it all," she said, when he complimented her on the meal. "Cooking is a lot like chemistry lab, only you don't have to measure so carefully. And you want to watch how hot the burner is."

He was guilty of the same hot-burner crime. Impatience ran in the family.

Silence fell between them and then Jancey let out a sigh. Cole reached out to squeeze her shoulder.

"You know, it's sometimes worse if you get an answer right away."

"I know. But I'd hoped to get a job nailed down fast…to show Miranda, if nothing else." She smiled a little and picked up her bowl.

"I'm doing dishes," Cole announced.

She gave him a "for real?" look and he nodded. "Thank you."

After Jancey left the kitchen, he started

loading the dishwasher, shooting looks out the kitchen window toward the bunkhouse as he worked. He saw the occasional shadow cross in front of the muslin curtains and wondered if he should slip over in broad daylight, since Jancey was on to them, or follow the usual routine of easing out the back door—and apparently not closing it quietly enough—around ten.

The debate ended when Jancey's phone rang at five thirty on the dot.

He heard her answer it in the other room before it had a chance to ring again, and, judging from the breathless quality of her hello, it had to be Magnus Distributing. He edged closer to the doorway, openly eavesdropping. He heard a smile in her voice as she said, "No, this isn't a bad time." And then there was a silence. Too long of a silence.

"I see." The broken quality of his sister's voice almost broke him. He took an instinctive step forward, then caught himself and stayed where he was. "I'm not certain why that would be," she said. "I see. Yes, I know there were many applicants." She cleared her throat, and his heart swelled as she said, "I would appreciate if you kept my application on file. Thank you."

A second later Jancey came out of the living room still holding her phone, looking as if she'd been blindsided.

"What happened?" he asked.

"Some kind of trouble with my references."

Cole tamped down the instant flare of anger, doing his best to keep his voice level as he said, "All of your references were from the ranch?"

"One was my guidance counselor."

"The other two?"

"Beth and Raul. I didn't think they'd tell Miranda."

"She may have found out some other way." Magnus did business with the ranch.

Jancey closed her eyes, and Cole could see that she was fighting to not cry in front of him. "What if…" Her voice cracked, and Cole reached out to pull her into his arms, rocking his little sister as she said, "She knows everyone. Lots of people like her. What if…"

What if she ruined every job Jancey applied for.

The sick thing was that she may well try, even if Jancey removed all the ranch references from her applications.

"She has sway, kiddo, but she's not all powerful."

Jancey stepped back, rubbing her eyes. "Someone should tell her that."

"I volunteer," he said darkly, and his sister gave a sputtering laugh. "Don't. She'll figure out a way to use it to her advantage."

There was a light knock on the door, and Jancey gave him a wry look. She was doing her best to put a brave face on a sucky situation. "Whoever could that be?"

He tweaked her nose, as he had when she was six, and then called, "Come on in." By the time he got back to the kitchen, Taylor was already inside.

She bounced a look between him and Jancey and said, "What happened?"

"I was screwed over by a superbitch," Jancey said as she headed for the fridge and pulled out a half-pint of ice cream. She took three bowls out of the cupboard and set them on the counter. Taylor crossed the kitchen, put the bowls back, opened the utensil drawer and pulled out a single spoon, which she handed to Jancey.

"If you're going to do it, do it right."

Jancey gave a choked laugh, and then Taylor led her to the table, waiting for her to sit before taking her own seat. "Tell me what happened."

Jancey set down the spoon beside the ice cream container and launched into a brief account of her phone call. Taylor listened, her expression going grim by the end.

"I'm afraid that she's going to keep doing this," Jancey finished.

Taylor nodded, then studied the table between them for a few long moments, and Cole found himself halfway holding his breath as he waited to hear her take on matters. "You can confront Miranda on this, which is, of course, what she wants. People like her feed on that kind of stuff."

"I wouldn't mind confronting her," Jancey muttered, peeling the top off the ice cream container.

"Or you ignore her. Continue job hunting in spite of her maneuverings." One corner of her mouth tilted up. "I'll bet money that Miranda hates being ignored."

"I kind of need references," Jancey said in a dark voice.

Taylor glanced up at Cole then back to Jancey. "I think you should call my grandfather and see what he suggests. Miranda's not the only person with connections in this town."

"Culver Ranch and Feed," Cole said.

They both turned and looked at him.

"Culver's was looking for a warehouse person when Taylor first showed up. They might have an opening." Cole decided against telling Taylor that Cal had thought she should go to work there.

Jancey's eyes widened. "I haven't dropped off an application there."

"Do it," Taylor said. "Tomorrow."

"I will." Jancey started to smile, but it stalled out. Taylor pushed the ice cream toward her.

"You have to have faith in yourself and your ability to overcome, because no matter how many plans you make, life seems to happen."

TAYLOR LEFT COLE and Jancey making plans as well as backup plans and walked across the drive to the bunkhouse that now seemed more like home than it really should have. As soon as she got inside and changed into her flannels and an oversize T-shirt, she dialed her grandfather.

He was doing well. Her aunt was doing well. He didn't know when he was coming back. Dillon was growing on him, but he did miss his old friends.

"I have a favor to ask," Taylor said.

"Yeah?"

She gave him a rundown of everything that had happened with Jancey and Miranda. "Do you think you could have a word with your friend who runs Culver Ranch and Feed?

Make sure that Miranda doesn't screw up this deal, too?"

"I can just about guarantee you that Jancey has a job."

"That would be good, Grandpa. She's a decent kid and just wants to make money for school."

"I remember her as being about four years old with the cutest blond curls all over her head."

Taylor laughed. "She's changed. And I'm certain she'd do a good job for Culver's."

"How's your job search coming?"

Taylor let out a sigh, and shifted so that her legs draped over the arm of the easy chair. "I interviewed in Bozeman today. I'm not certain how it went. I still want to go home."

"Home meaning Seattle."

"I like it here," she said simply. "Things are…working out. But no one wants to hire a city girl who they know is going to jet back off to Seattle the first chance she gets."

"Maybe you should work on coming off as more homespun."

Taylor laughed at her grandfather's choice of words. "I could. I'm driving the tractor again for Cole."

"Don't tell your mother," Karl said in a

mock-serious tone. "Speaking of which, has Cecilia been nagging you about living the rural life?"

"I think she knows that unless she makes room for me with her and Jess, that I'm here until I get hired."

"Not such a bad thing, is it?"

A soft tap sounded on the door. Taylor smiled to herself. "No, Grandpa. I can honestly say it's not all bad."

Cole let himself in as Taylor hung up. She stayed where she was, draped over the easy chair, smiling at him, feeling strangely at peace with herself and this…situation. It couldn't last. She wasn't going to live in a bunkhouse across the driveway from a hot rancher/farmer forever. But this was where she was, what she was doing, right now and she was good with it.

"Thanks for giving Jancey the pep talk. She's feeling a lot better."

"No problem. I called my grandfather."

"I kind of thought you would." He cocked his head but didn't move any closer, so she pushed herself to her feet and took a couple of lazy steps toward him, half smiling, holding his gaze. "I notice that I still have a small bed."

"Mmm." A faint smile curved his lips. "My sister said you can sleep over if you want."

Taylor's eyes widened. He wasn't kidding. "That seems…"

He reached out for her, took her by the shoulders and eased her against his hard body, wrapping his arms around her. "I like the way we do things now." He found her lips, kissed her gently. "Even if the bed is narrow."

"Me, too," Taylor murmured against his perfect mouth. "I like it a lot." She kissed him back, a long, lingering kiss, more relaxed than the way they used to kiss, but just as hot. "I don't want to change a thing."

A scuffling outside on the gravel brought their heads up, and then Jancey yelled, "Cole! A little help!"

Cole hurried for the door at the sound of his sister's oddly muffled voice, Taylor close on his heels. But when they got outside—no Jancey.

"Cole!" Her voice sounded distant, muffled.

Cole jerked his head. "Grain shed." They rounded the corner of the bunkhouse, and then Cole skidded to a stop so fast that Taylor ran into his back. Jancey's feet extended out from beneath the foundation where she'd apparently worked her way into Chucky's hidey-hole. She was squirming but not really moving forward or back.

"Are you stuck?" Cole demanded.

"I'm not taking the air."

Taylor put a hand up to her mouth to stifle a laugh. Things like this never happened in her family.

"I've got Chucky's collar."

"Let go," Cole said.

"No. He almost got—" she squirmed again "—hit by a car. He might have gotten bumped. I want to—" she coughed as if she'd just inhaled some dirt "—make sure he's okay."

Cole rolled his eyes heavenward, and Taylor pressed her lips together hard. It wasn't funny—not if the little dog had gotten bumped, but if he was okay…

Cole bent down and grabbed his sister's ankles. "You know this isn't going to feel good."

"Don't. Care."

Cole shrugged, then started to work Jancey out from under the building. As soon as she was far enough out that she could get her knees underneath her, she scrambled the rest of the way by herself, pulling the shaking bundle of white fur with her. She flopped over into a sitting position, holding the little dog to her filthy chest.

Cole reached out to take Chucky. "Let's get him in the house. Have a look."

"Yeah." Jancey got to her feet, brushed herself off a few times then glanced over at Taylor. "Are you okay?"

"I'm fine. You?"

Jancey lifted her shirt to inspect her stomach, which was red and scraped from where her shirt had ridden up while Cole dragged her backward through the sandy soil. "Nothing that won't heal." She jerked her head toward Cole, who was already halfway to the house. "He always pretends to be such a hardass. He isn't."

"I know."

"Just making sure."

Which left Taylor to wonder why as she and Jancey trotted to catch up with him. Once inside, Jancey sat on one of the kitchen chairs and held Chucky while Cole looked him over. The pup had indeed been bumped by the car. He had a skinned leg and a sore spot on his hip.

"Bruised, not broken," he told Jancey.

"That's what I thought. I don't think he needs a vet call. I'll treat the scrapes myself."

"Maybe you should hand him over to Mrs. Clovendale."

"Tomorrow, on my way to the interview. I'll

call her right now and let her know I'm taking care of him until then."

She put the little white dog down on the floor. He looked at her sadly, and she gently scooped him back up. "Poor little guy. Come on. We'll go fix that leg."

She carted the dog out of the room, and Cole and Taylor exchanged looks. Then the laugh that Taylor had been holding burst out. She clamped her hand over her mouth.

"It's okay," Cole said drily. "We allow laughter in this house."

"I'm sorry that the little guy got hit, but since he's okay…" Taylor pressed her hand to the side of her face. "Jancey getting stuck was pretty entertaining."

"Haven't seen a lot of stuff like that?" he asked in an amused voice.

"I was an only child and my mother was kind of prissy. I didn't get moments like this."

"If you want to crawl under the grain shed, I'll be happy to pull you out," Cole offered. "Make up for what you lost out on growing up."

She took a step closer, biting her lip as she looked up at him. "Or I could pull you out."

He smiled. "Or…we could wait until Jancey

and Chucky go to sleep and pick up where we left off…"

She went on tiptoe to take his face and pull his lips to hers. "I like that option best of all."

CHAPTER FOURTEEN

"Okay. That was stupid easy." Jancey waltzed through the kitchen door and put Chucky down on the linoleum. Cole's eyebrows came together as the poodle pranced around Jancey's feet, but his sister didn't seem to notice.

"I got the job!"

Cole jumped to his feet and wrapped his arms around his little sister. "Way to go, kid."

"Congratulations!" Taylor dropped the spoon she'd been using to stir gravy and gave the girl a big hug as soon as Cole let her go.

"Stupid easy, you say?" Cole's tone was ultra-serious, but amusement lit his eyes.

Jancey gave him a nudge with her elbow. "You know what I mean."

"I do, and congratulations." He cleared his throat and indicated the poodle with a quick tilt of his head. "And Chucky?"

Jancey's smile grew even wider. "He's mine! Mrs. Clovendale can't keep up with him, and apparently, her sister isn't up to keeping him."

"I don't know if anyone is up to keeping him."

"I am." Jancey went to the counter, where Taylor had laid out the pot roast, and picked up a plate. "I have a job and a dog. This is a great day."

"Super," Cole muttered. Now Taylor gave him a nudge, and he winked at her.

Jancey put her plate on the table and took a seat. Chucky jumped up onto the chair next to her, and Taylor was afraid that if she looked at Cole she'd start laughing. So she focused on Jancey.

"Tell us about what happened. Every detail." She took the chair across from Jancey and did her best to ignore Chucky who peered across the table with his soulful eyes.

"I start on Monday. I was really nervous about not having any references from the ranch, but Jolie—she's my new boss—told me that if I was your sister, that was enough for her." She stabbed her fork into the pot roast. "Take that, Miranda."

Jancey's joy was infectious, and Taylor found herself wishing that she could share a similar joy soon. Her gaze connected with Cole's yet again, guessing he knew exactly what she was thinking—especially when his hand found her thigh under the table a few seconds later.

"I have to get a bunch of stuff from the ranch tomorrow," Jancey said to Cole. "Can I use your truck?"

"The bed is filthy. You'd have to wash it out first."

"How about the SUV?" Taylor asked. "I can go with you. Help load."

Jancey considered. "If you don't mind, that'd be great."

"Works for me," Cole said, looking back at his plate. He gave Taylor's thigh a gentle squeeze before pulling his hand away. "I have an appointment with my accountant in Missoula tomorrow or I'd go with you."

"I don't need a bodyguard," Jancey said darkly.

"It wasn't you I was worried about."

Jancey laughed. Landing the job at Culver Ranch and Feed had done wonders for her temperament. Or maybe it was breaking free from the family ranch, no longer having to deal with the stress there.

"I'm going to use my first paycheck to buy a kennel for Chucky. Jolie will give me a discount on both the fencing and the boards I'm going to bury in the ground around it so that he can't dig out."

"And then you'll continue to save for college."

Jancey blinked at him. "Of course."

After the dishwasher was loaded, Cole walked Taylor to the bunkhouse while Jancey tapped out messages on her phone. "Thank you for offering to drive her. I don't want her going to the ranch alone."

Taylor shifted her course toward the calves. The babies were growing fast, and she was almost as good at feeding them now as Jancey was. "Do you think there'll be trouble?"

He let out a snort. "I know there will be if Jancey goes to the main ranch and tells off Miranda."

"Ah. I'm supposed to keep that from happening?"

He smiled down at her. "If you did, I'd be grateful." He leaned his arms on the top rail of the calf pen. "Jancey has a lot of fight in her, and I think it would be best if she didn't tangle with Miranda right now."

"Let things cool for a bit."

"Yeah."

"So that you can do the tangling?" He didn't

answer, and Taylor bumped her shoulder up against his.

He turned and smiled down at her. "I plead the fifth."

"Yeah." She captured his face between her hands and kissed him. This thing they shared...she liked it. She was comfortable with it, and after dissecting the matter late last night when the wind was leaking through the loose windows and the critters under the bunkhouse were particularly active, she decided that it was because they understood one another. He knew her goals, she knew his. They were comfortable with sharing the time they had. A rare thing and special thing, one she would treasure as life went on and their paths eventually diverged.

SHE AND JANCEY left for the ranch at the same time Cole headed off to Missoula. She followed his truck down the highway until he entered the freeway and she continued on to the Bryan Ranch. When they got to the place, Jancey's friend Matt was there, throwing hay to the horses.

"He's taken over feeding for me," Jancey explained to Taylor. "He has fence duty, so he can work it into his schedule without going out of his way." She gave a small shrug. "I can pay him a little more than I thought I could, too, because I'll make more working at Culver's."

Jancey crossed the drive to speak with her friend while Taylor opened the SUV's hatch and laid the back seat down to make more cargo space. Then she hauled the empty boxes they'd brought onto the porch. The house was locked, so she sat in one of the weathered rocking chairs and surveyed Cole's beautiful property while she waited for Jancey to finish her conversation.

Once Matt got on his ATV to head back to the guest ranch, she and Jancey got into the house, and Jancey started dumping the contents of her dresser into black trash bags. The clothes hanging in the closet were doubled over and also stuffed into bags, hangers and all. She cleaned out the small bathroom, loading the boxes, and then stacked the books on the shelf by her bed into the last box.

"I think this is it for now." She propped her hands on her hips and looked around the room. "I'll get the rest later, if I need it."

Taylor gave her a sympathetic nod, then grabbed one of the heavy trash bags and headed for the SUV. They'd just finished loading when the sound of an engine brought their heads up.

"Shit."

A small open Jeep rounded the corner, an auburn-haired woman at the wheel. She pulled to a stop in front of the SUV, as if to block its exit. Fine. Taylor would back the vehicle onto the lawn if she had to.

Miranda got out and pulled off a pair of driving gloves as she walked toward them. "Moving out?"

"I am," Jancey said with an upward tilt of her chin. "I got a job. It pays more than the job you messed up for me, and I'm working for people who know exactly what kind of a person you are, because I told them."

Taylor sucked in a breath, but before she could intercede, Miranda asked, "What about your horses and cattle?"

"I've hired someone to feed them."

"Ah. Of course. Well." Miranda smiled a bone-chilling smile. "Good luck with the future, Jancey. I'm sure it'll be bright."

"No thanks to you." Jancey gave Miranda a cool look. "Have you heard the term 'cut off your nose to spite your face'?"

Taylor frowned at Jancey's use of a phrase that she hadn't heard since her grandmother had died. Miranda didn't seem to notice. She merely lifted her eyebrows in a silent invitation to continue.

"That's what I'm going to do. I'll tell anyone who will listen not to stay at this place. It might hurt me, but I hope it hurts you more. Social media is a wonderful thing, *Aunt* Miranda."

The woman's face turned to ice, and Taylor took hold of Jancey's arm, intent on getting her out of there before more damage was done.

"We're leaving," she said to Miranda. "Cole wanted me to tell you to stay out of his house. He means it."

She got Jancey into the SUV without any more salvos being fired.

"Mission *so* not accomplished." She gave Jancey a dark sidelong look. "What you just did was what I was supposed to prevent."

"Sorry," Jancey said, but it was obvious she was not.

"I understand why you did it." The woman had screwed with Jancey's life and Jancey very much wanted to do the same to her. "But maybe pouring gas on the matter isn't the best solution."

Jancey let out a huff of air. "There is no solution, so I settled for a moment of satisfaction."

Taylor slowed as she crossed the cattle

guard, then gave Jancey a quick glance. "Cut off your nose to spite your face?"

"We had to do an English paper on idioms," Jancey said on a sigh. "Damn it. That woman…"

Her voice trailed off, and Taylor hoped Jancey standing up to Miranda wouldn't cause *that woman* to seek yet another path of petty revenge.

Later that evening, when Cole got back from Missoula, they walked the perimeter of the smallest field and Taylor told him about the confrontation.

"No way to keep it from happening," she said in conclusion.

"Yeah. I get it." Cole pulled a long weed as they walked and tossed it aside. "I just wanted you to keep her from going to the main office and telling off Miranda. Nothing you could do about Miranda showing up." He gave a small snort. "Which she did just to upset Jancey."

"The woman is a classic bully," Taylor mused. "You can't reason with bullies."

"No kidding," Cole muttered.

"Have you ever considered selling the place?" The thought had worked its way into her head a number of times that day. Cole's expression darkened. "Okay. No."

He shook his head, his mouth flattening. "I won't sell. She won't win."

"Sometimes winning isn't all that great if it eats your soul in the process." He looked down at her and she said, "Borrowing my mother's dramatic term." She frowned up at him. "It's appropriate to the situation, though. That woman will suck the life out of you."

"Jordan won."

"How much did he suffer in the process?"

"He's happy now."

She turned and put her hands on his biceps, stopping him. "You belong on the land, but does it have to be that land?"

"My great-great-grandfather homesteaded that place. Miranda's great-great-grandfather did not. Why should she get what my family worked so hard for? Why should she be rewarded for psycho behavior?"

"Why should you suffer when you don't have to?"

Cole brought his hands up to thread through her hair. "Because I want my ranch. I don't want her or anyone else to have it."

"What if that's not possible?"

"What if you can't get a job you want in Seattle?"

"I will. It'll take time, but I will."

He gave her a smile that didn't quite reach his eyes. "That's my answer, too."

AFTER TWO WEEKS of nothing, Taylor received a small rush of interest. She booked three interviews, and two headhunters contacted her with promising leads in Portland and Sacramento—both areas where she'd feel comfortable living. She was an urban girl, born and bred.

An urban girl who got a kick out of driving farm equipment. The day before she'd swathed hay for Cole while he baled in an adjoining field. Jancey drove the retriever, and the three of them put in a full day's work before eating dinner together. Her stay at the farm, which had started as a desperate survival move, had become more of an idyll. A temporary idyll, because she was not going to winter in the bunkhouse. The job market was picking up, and several of the people who'd been laid off with her had landed new positions.

As to Cole…things were perfect because they weren't dealing with real-life stresses a real couple would face. There was no jockeying for position. No compromises. Their paths were clearly laid out. They had the moment, as Cole had put it.

Still, there was no getting around the fact that separating was going to sting.

So she didn't think about it.

And if she did, she told herself that perhaps they could continue long distance…but she didn't really believe that was a possibility. Distance made feelings fade. Different worlds exacerbated the process. They had the here and now, and she was enjoying every second of it.

That night, when they walked the property after dinner, she told Cole about her job leads, then wondered if she was imagining the tension in the silence that followed.

"That's good," he finally said, giving her fingers a squeeze.

"I'm feeling encouraged. Two of my fellow Stratfordites have gotten jobs over the past two weeks. Things are turning around."

"Good."

And then…nothing.

Taylor let the matter drop. She didn't want to ruin the time they had left together.

"Jancey's loving her job at Culver Ranch and Feed," Cole said as they headed back toward the house. "The old guys there have adopted her, and Jolie is giving her advice on how to battle Miranda. I'd appreciate it if you told her not to battle Miranda."

Taylor smiled a little. "I will." She and Jancey did well together. She'd miss Cole's little sister almost as much as she'd miss him.

"Speaking of doing battle, I'm going to the ranch this weekend—probably on Saturday. Want to come?"

"To keep you out of trouble?"

He gave her a look. "Or maybe because I want your company?"

She pulled in a breath and told herself there was no need to feel the small twinge of anxiety at his words. Or rather at her reaction to his words. Her heart shouldn't jump at things like that. "Sure."

"Good."

Taylor didn't sleep well that night and told herself it was because her critters were unusually quiet. She put on the coffee, dragged herself to the shower hoping hot water would revive her and had just got undressed when the phone rang.

Her heart jumped when she saw the number.

She cleared her throat, nervously pushing her hair back over one shoulder as she answered. "Hello, Paul."

"Evans. How are you?"

"All things considered, I'm doing well."

"Have you nailed something down yet?"

"Three interviews next week."

"Market's picking up."

"I noticed."

"So you may not be interested in this." From the way her stomach flipped, Taylor knew that she would be interested. "My assistant here at Whitcote is going on sabbatical. I have a six-month position that could well work into full time if things continue as they are. There's talk of staffing up this fall."

Seattle.

"No guarantees. I don't have the final say. It's a committee decision…but you're good, Taylor, and I'd love to have you on board."

"Do I interview in person?"

"Skype."

"When?"

"Is tomorrow too soon?"

"Not to appear easy, but interviewing within the next fifteen minutes wouldn't be too soon."

THE DRIVE TO the ranch was quiet, and even though he and Taylor were comfortable with their mutual silences, this was different. Bad different.

Taylor was distancing herself, getting ready for the move back to the city. He felt the chasm between them widening and didn't know what to do about it. Or if there was anything he could do. The bitch of it was that the farm—make that his life—was better when she was in it.

She wasn't staying.

They bumped over the cattle guard, then both sat up straighter at the sight of the two ATVs next to his corrals.

"Tweedle Dum and Tweedle Dummer," he said as he parked. He glanced over at Taylor. "Let's see what's happening." They walked together to where the two model employees, Wyatt and Ashley, stood shoulder to shoulder, pointing out across the fields.

"Big plans?" Cole asked.

"Spring branding," Wyatt said. Cole had never much liked the guy—primarily because (a) he was a pompous jerk, and (b) he was a kiss-ass. "We're going to make it an overnight event, with canvas tents to house the guests."

"Instead of making the long trek back to the ranch?" Which was all of a couple of miles.

"A different kind of experience," Wyatt assured him.

Cole hooked a thumb into the top edge of his belt. "Any other big happenings?"

"Cattle drives."

"Drives? As in plural?"

Ashley, Miranda's chief minion, piped in then. "The drives are very popular, so we're going to be doing several."

Cole frowned at her. "How…?"

"We'll drive them to the high pasture with one group of guests, then drive them back to the ranch with another."

"You're kidding."

"It only makes sense," Ashley said.

"Not if you're a cow. They'll lose weight if you push them all summer long."

"Miranda is sending the calves to a feed lot once they're weaned."

"What?"

"Also," Ashley said, "I'll email you the schedule of events here on the working ranch. It's very full this year, and you might want to plan your visits around them."

Visits? To his own place?

Taylor put a hand on his arm. He didn't look at her. He was about to speak when Ashley gave him a sympathetic smile. "You had to know when you left that things would change."

He pressed his lips together, glanced down at Taylor. "Let's take care of what we came here for."

She nodded, and they turned as one and headed for the house.

"Why did we come?" she asked after Cole unlocked the door and they went inside.

"Because I didn't hear from Miranda after Jancey's encounter, so I figured something was up. I hadn't expected to find out what the deal was so easily."

"Good that it worked out."

"Yes." He stepped to the window and studied the nimrods making plans for his land. Son of a bitch.

"How wise is it to hold on to this place, Cole?"

"What do you mean?"

She drew in a breath. "I mean," she said slowly, "that you could sell for a decent amount and buy something new. Something that doesn't come with built-in heartaches and a lot of issues to contend with."

He wasn't selling. The thought made his jaw go tight. Totally the wrong move.

Before he could say anything, Taylor continued. "And don't tell me that she'll win. She's winning now."

"Thanks."

"Cole." He shot her a look. "You know it's true. And sometimes, despite your best efforts, the sanest thing to do is to walk away instead of beating your head on a wall."

He turned toward Taylor. "Isn't that what you've been doing?"

Her cheeks flushed. "It might look that way, but job hunting is different. Eventually something shifts."

He decided to ask the question. Even though he was fairly certain of the answer, and just as certain that Taylor would eventually fill him in, he wanted to know now. Get his pain all at once. "Has something shifted for you?"

"Do you want to discuss this here?" She gestured as if to remind him of where they were and what his current source of stress was.

"Just got a kick to the nuts. May as well get another."

She let out a sigh. "I think I've landed a job in Seattle. I interviewed yesterday via Skype. It's with an old associate. It's temporary but may work into full time."

"Congratulations."

Her mouth tightened. "I hope you mean that."

"I do."

He looked back out the window. The dynamic duo were climbing onto their ATVs. He propped his palms on the windowsill and for one brief moment let his chin drop to his chest.

Things were stacking up faster than he could deal with them.

"Cole?"

"I'm good." He straightened back up, pulled in a deep breath. "I always knew you were leaving." She nodded. "It doesn't mean I have to like it."

"How on earth would we ever mesh our lives?"

Good question. "Compromise?"

Her shoulders stiffened. "How?"

"Hell if I know."

"I have a career to build, Cole."

"A career only gives you so much."

"But I need what it gives me."

"I know." He spoke softly. Admitting the truth wasn't easy. She wanted him, but she didn't necessarily need him. She needed her career. "I have to get some stuff, just in case the place accidentally catches fire during a lightning storm or something."

Taylor followed his meaning. "You think she'd do that?"

"At this point, I wouldn't put much of anything past her."

CHUCKY DANCED INTO the laundry room as Taylor started folding the clothes she'd pulled out of the dryer. Jancey followed him into the room, a laundry basket on one hip.

"Here, I'm done," Taylor said. "Small load."

"Cool."

Jancey opened the lid to the washer and dumped the entire basket in—whites, jeans, a red T-shirt. When she glanced up and saw Taylor's expression of horror, she gave a small shrug. "I know, but this is easier."

"Did someone do your laundry on the ranch?"

"No. That was all me." She gave Taylor a frowning look. "Cole won't tell me what went on at the ranch."

Then it wasn't her place to fill his sister in. "I'm not sure what happened."

Jancey frowned at her. "Did you sit in the truck or something?"

"I thought it was best to let Cole handle things."

The nonanswer worked. Jancey snorted and then poured soap directly into the washer, ignoring the dispenser tray. Taylor wouldn't have been surprised had she added a few glugs of straight bleach, but she closed the lid.

"I don't want Cole all stressed out. I shouldn't have threatened Miranda." She turned and leaned back against the washer, gripping it with both hands.

"Sometimes we just…act. Then we have to do damage control. Part of life. No one does it perfectly. The important thing is to learn from your mistakes." Taylor put a hand on Jancey's shoulder. "Are you putting stuff on your socials?"

"I haven't. Yet."

Chucky gave a small whimper, and Jancey scooped him up. "But if Miranda keeps messing with us, I will."

And maybe that was why Cole hadn't yet filled her in.

Taylor's phone rang, and she dug it out from her back pocket, her pulse rate jumping when she saw the name on the screen. She gave Jancey a quick nod. "I have to take this." She put the phone to her ear and said hello as she abandoned her laundry and headed out of the house so she could speak to Paul in private. She preferred to get her news, good or bad, alone.

"We knocked around the idea of a second interview," Paul said after a quick hello, "then decided we didn't have time. We need someone now, and you fit the bill. Welcome aboard."

She'd gotten the job.

Taylor pressed her lips together and some-how refrained from punching the sky. Her luck had finally turned. She made her way across the driveway to the bunkhouse as Paul gave her the details. Once he was done, and all of her questions were answered, she disconnected the call, set down the phone and let out a breath that felt as if it had come from the tips of her toes. Finally! Progress. It might be temporary, but she was moving forward after too long a period of professional stagnation.

Now she had about a hundred things to do before her Monday start time.

There was only one that she wasn't looking forward to. Telling Cole that she was leaving.

But it wasn't as if she could have stayed on the farm forever. They'd both known she was leaving when they'd started sleeping together. If things were different, if their lives and needs were more closely aligned, then her leaving might be a goodbye-for-now.

She saw no way around it being a goodbye-forever. And it was tearing her up. No matter how badly she might want this to be different.

She was urban. He was country. She was all about her career and so was he—nonmeshable careers.

This moment had been inevitable, and she'd

fully expected it to be bittersweet. She hadn't expected it to feel as if a hole was opening up in her heart. She crossed the room and pulled out her suitcase and the boxes she'd packed her dishes in. She didn't need to get everything together immediately, but she could dive in tonight as soon as she did the hard thing and crossed the driveway to tell Cole the news.

According to Paul, they needed her yesterday. Things had started to heat up for the firm, and they needed all hands putting in as many hours as possible. Which meant she had to pack and leave so much sooner than anticipated. She'd fully expected at least two weeks…time to wind things down, time for her and Cole to say a proper goodbye. Maybe even to make plans to meet again in the future—in some capacity.

She needed that time.

She wasn't going to get it.

And then there was Jancey. Taylor headed back across the drive to pick up her laundry. The washing machine swished away, but Jancey wasn't around. Nor was Cole.

She got back to the bunkhouse and set the laundry down next to the suitcase.

She was excited to be moving forward… but she couldn't say she felt happy about it.

She didn't need to dig too deeply to figure out why. She hadn't anticipated things happening so quickly, hadn't thought she'd have to tell Cole goodbye so soon.

She'd just gotten a job and wasn't feeling ecstatic—and that wasn't right. She abandoned her suitcase and picked up her phone from where she'd set it down on the table. She'd call Carolyn and her mother and her grandfather, tell them the good news before she started packing. Maybe hearing some congratulations would jolt her back to reality.

Because it simply wasn't possible to have everything.

COLE WAS IN the middle of putting something together for dinner when the phone rang. Jancey wasn't yet home, so he snagged the receiver on the second ring, hoping he wasn't going to hear that her truck had broken down.

"Cole."

The hairs seemed to rise on the back of his neck. "Miranda."

"I heard you ran into Wyatt and Ashley today."

"Yes." He knew from experience that the less said, the better.

"And that they filled you in on the summer plans for the working ranch."

He didn't give in to the temptation to tell her what he thought of her plans. "Yes."

"Good. What I'm calling about is the livestock you have on the property. The horses, to be exact."

"What about them?"

"Matt will not be feeding them. We've spoken and he agrees that feeding the horses is outside the scope of his duties."

"So maybe he can feed them on his own time. Or do you control that, too?"

"He doesn't want to feed them on his own time."

In other words, she'd threatened him. "Fine. I'll get someone else."

Who, he had no idea.

"Have them check into the main ranch when they arrive so that we know they're authorized."

Cole pressed a hand to his head. There was no reason for anyone visiting his place to do that, but that wouldn't slow Miranda down. "I will. Anything else?"

"No, Cole. That's all."

Cole hung up and planted a hand against the

wall. Took a deep breath. Okay. He'd bring his horses here to the farm.

And he'd show great restraint by doing it without putting his hands around Miranda's throat. A tidal wave of frustration smashed into him.

Was this the way he wanted to live his life?

He shoved the question aside and headed for the door. He wanted to talk to Taylor. Get her take. He knocked on her door, and it took her a few seconds to answer. When she did, he saw that her suitcase was open on the bed, and his gut tightened.

"You got the job." Another happy surprise.

"I did." She attempted a smile, but it flattened out almost immediately. "It's a temporary position, but looks as if it'll work into permanent by late fall."

"And you'll have to work like crazy to prove yourself."

"It's what I do."

"Where will you live?"

"Subletting the apartment of the person on leave."

"Ah. So…everything is falling into place."

"It is."

"How do you feel about that?" He leaned a shoulder against the doorjamb. "About leaving?"

"I…we knew this day was coming."

"Were you going to discuss this with me?"

"I was actually on my way over when you knocked." He knew her well enough to tell that she was being honest. "This isn't easy for me, Cole. You know it isn't. But…this situation. We always knew it was temporary. Right?"

"It started that way." He let out a breath, telling himself that this was the future they'd agreed upon. When Taylor got a job, she would move on. Embrace her old existence instead of the one she'd built here.

The phone buzzed in his pocket. Jancey's ring. He held Taylor's gaze as he answered. "Yeah?"

"Can you pick me up? My car just broke down. Halfway home. You can't miss me."

"Sure. See you in a few."

He dumped his phone back in his pocket. "I have to get Jancey. We can…talk later if we need to." Taylor nodded, as if she couldn't find her voice, and then he headed to his truck. Not that many hours ago, she would have gone with him to get Jancey. Now…

Yeah. Definitely the queen mother of all bad days.

TAYLOR HAD EXPECTED Cole to come back to see her after he'd towed Jancey's dead car home. He didn't, which was killing her. She wanted to tell him how precious their time together had been.

To maybe suggest that it didn't need to be over…maybe they could leave the door cracked?

She wanted to believe that was true.

But she didn't.

Too many years of talk intervened—talk of independence and careers and making one's own way. Talk of never settling for mediocre, and in her mother's view compromise meant not living up to potential. Of settling for less and slowly dying inside.

Taylor let herself out of the bunkhouse and stood for a moment watching her grandfather's house. Shadows moved past the curtains, and her heart squeezed. *You aren't meant to be here.*

She'd grown to like the farm. The affection she felt for the place had kind of snuck up on her. Cole played a major part in that affection, but there was more to it than that. She'd begun to reclaim her grandmother's garden—to see if she could change her black thumb into more of a greenish gray. She didn't need prize vegetables, but she wouldn't have minded seeing her seeds grow.

The door opened to the house and Cole stepped out onto the porch. She'd thought it was because he'd seen her saying goodbye to the place and was coming out to meet up with her, but the way his head came up when she started toward him told her no. He had not been about to seek her out.

Fine. She'd seek him out.

He came down the steps as she opened the gate and met her on the sidewalk.

"How's Jancey?" she asked.

"Fine. The car needs a new battery."

"How are you?"

"Almost bootless. Chucky ate one of my boots." He glanced over at the barn, presenting her his profile. She saw his jaw muscles tighten before he looked back at her. "I'm sorry for not being more congratulatory about your job. I know it's what you wanted. So—" he pushed his hands into his pockets "—congratulations."

"I wish our circumstances were different."

"Circumstances are what you make them."

Taylor tilted her head, wondering if she'd

imagined the note of censure in his voice. "What does that mean?"

"Exactly what I said. Sometimes it's worth compromising instead of following a carved-in-stone plan."

"You have a crop in the ground. A ranch to watch over. A sister who needs you."

"Meaning?"

"You're the one who would have the hardest time changing lifestyles if we ever…" She made a gesture instead of finishing her sentence. "I'm the one who'd have to give up everything."

"It doesn't have to be all or nothing."

"Given what we're working with, what else can it be? You saw how much luck I had getting a career off the ground here in Montana."

"You don't want to try?"

She pulled in a breath. "I'm afraid of embarking on something that has no hope of succeeding."

His expression, which had already bordered on cool, totally shuttered. "That's answer enough for me."

She felt a stab of desperation as he took a backward step. She'd hoped—really hoped—for one more night together.

It wasn't going to happen, and she felt as if a small part of her had just curled up and died.

"I'd like to part friends."

He nodded, keeping his hands in his jacket pockets as if he couldn't handle touching her now. "When are you leaving?"

"Tomorrow morning. I was going to ask Jancey to take care of Max until I get settled. I start work the day after tomorrow."

"I'll ask her."

"Thanks, Cole." Since she didn't know what else to do, she held out her hand. He shook his head. "Don't do that to me, Taylor."

"I don't know what *to* do," she said softly.

"Just say goodbye and leave it at that."

This was a situation she'd walked into willingly, and she couldn't cry foul now that it hurt to get herself back out of it. But damned if she was going to say goodbye and leave it at that. She stepped closer and took his face in her hands, rose up on her toes and kissed him.

"Goodbye, Cole. I will miss you."

She pulled in a shaky breath and walked back to the bunkhouse, wishing that he would follow her.

Knowing that he would not.

CHAPTER FIFTEEN

ONE WEEK LATER, Taylor was fully immersed in her element, living and breathing finance. She was part of a team, and, being the newbie temp, far from taking the lead as she'd done before. She had to build a reputation for being efficient, cooperative and creative, while at the same time not coming off as a threat to anyone else. What had been second nature to her now required thought. She was gun-shy, aware that going above and beyond didn't guarantee anything. In fact, some of the people who had hung back were still employed by Stratford.

Every company was different, though. They had their cultures and hierarchies and personalities to work around.

But she was working and back in her city.

And lonely as hell.

She didn't text or call Cole. It was for the best. They truly were star-crossed lovers and would continue to be so, unless one of them gave up their professional life to be near the other…and thereby gave up their independence.

Her mother had, of course, assumed that Taylor was as happy about leaving the farm as she had been. "This was a good experience, honey. Now you'll know for sure what you *don't* want if you happen to run into a good-looking country guy." Which was exactly what had happened with Cecilia and Taylor's father. "Like that's going to happen," Taylor murmured, hoping her mother missed the irony in her tone.

"Good-looking only goes so far when you are tiptoeing around cow poop. I loved your father, but…" Cecilia made a shuddering noise.

Since her grandfather never had cows, that was an exaggeration, but Taylor understood what she was getting at. And she also understood that she was different from her mom. She'd hated living in the bunkhouse, but she missed the farm.

Or did she just miss Cole?

Her heart still hurt when she thought about him, but she told herself it had been only a week. Then two weeks. Then three.

She threw herself into her work, had Carolyn and her guy over for budget dinners instead of going out every week. She was socking away all the money she possibly could. It was sobering to realize that she could have saved more being a loan officer and renting an apartment in the Eagle Valley than she could subletting and working for a decent salary here.

"You're a city girl," Carolyn told her when she explained that to her friend. "You pay more, but you get more. Can you walk down to the ocean or take a ferry or club hop in Montana? I don't think so. And your dating life had to be limited."

"It only takes one," Taylor said, just as Carolyn's wineglass touched her lips.

"You've never said anything like that before." She abruptly set down her glass. "You met someone."

"I did."

Carolyn gave her a frowning once-over. "You're still thinking about him."

"Yeah."

"Well, damn, girl. It's about time."

Taylor shook her head. "Our lifestyles and occupations are not compatible."

Carolyn took a healthy drink of wine, wiping her lips with the back of her fingers. "So you work something out."

"And one of us becomes resentful, and the beautiful thing becomes a source of bitterness."

Now Carolyn was staring at her as if she'd just met her. "Yeah. You're right. That will totally happen if one of you gives up something that they don't want to give up. But there is that thing called compromise."

Taylor pushed her hair back with both hands as her temples began to throb. That word again.

"Are you glad to be back in the city?"

"Totally." It was the life she knew and loved. The place she'd been raised. It was comfortable and safe and predictable, if one didn't count the possibility of layoffs. Plus the food was great.

"Were there good parts about Montana? I mean other than the guy who's driving you nuts."

Taylor sipped her wine thoughtfully, basically trying to lie to herself so that she could say no as if she meant it. "I enjoyed working outside. A whole lot more than I thought I would."

"Huh."

"I hated it at first," she said as if that was a viable defense.

"But not anymore?"

Taylor frowned. She hadn't expected this conversation to be all about her, but now that

Carolyn was primed, there would be no stopping her. "I wouldn't work outside for a living."

"What could you do there inside for a living?"

As if she hadn't asked herself that at least once a day lately—in a hypothetical sense, of course.

"Well," Taylor said ironically, "I think the fact that I looked for work there for over two months and couldn't land a job kind of answers that question."

"Consult. Do books. Get your CPA license." Carolyn placed her palm flat on the leather sofa with a soft smack. "Teach school."

Taylor made a face at her. "Are you trying to get rid of me?"

Carolyn leaned back against the sofa, stretching her arm out along the back. "I am not. But your job is temporary and you need a backup plan."

"Before I end up on the farm again?" The scary thing was that she couldn't go back to the farm. Not after the way she'd left. Her stomach started tightening into a sick knot.

"Taylor?" She glanced up at her friend. "You've changed."

"I was gone for two and a half months."

"Doesn't matter. I'm not saying it was the

guy. Maybe it was living out of the city. Maybe it was Montana."

Taylor leaned her head back to study the ceiling.

No. It was mostly the guy.

Although Montana had played a part…and in a way, she missed living there. Missed her life on the farm.

Her mother would have a cow if she knew.

COLE PUT UP his meadow hay four weeks after Taylor left, and he couldn't help but reflect that he'd have enjoyed it more if she'd been there to swath. Part of him wanted to contact her and ask how she was doing in her new job—like friends would do. More than once he'd picked up the phone, only to set it back down again. It was crazy to reopen a semihealed wound.

They weren't friends. Not yet. Not when he still felt so raw about her departure.

Karl had called a couple of times, almost as if he was checking on Cole, which led Cole to suspect that his relationship with Taylor hadn't stayed a secret. Karl wasn't returning from Dillon anytime soon, but Elise had started dating and Cole had a feeling that Karl would be back within the year. He'd have to move out of the house, find a place to live. He could live in the bunkhouse, but he didn't particularly want to kick around in the place where he and Taylor had shared so much.

He'd prefer to live on his ranch.

Instead, he'd moved his horses to Karl's place, allowing Miranda another victory. It was killing him.

He hated the feeling of inertia that permeated his life. He was doing well on the farm, but he missed Taylor, and the situation with his ranch was beyond his control. For the moment. He would come up with something.

He'd just washed off the field dust when his cell phone rang. Jancey. She was coming home from college on the weekends and filling in at the feed store. Unbeknownst to Miranda, she'd done Jancey a huge favor by sabotaging the job with Magnus Distribution. His sister loved the feed store. "Just wanted you to know I'm heading out. I should be there in an hour."

"Thanks, kid. See you then."

He hung up and headed for the shower. Instead of lounging around in his sweats, crunching numbers and trying to figure out how to get his ranch away from Miranda, he'd grill a steak for his sister and maybe whip some instant mashed potatoes. He was spending too much time plotting against the bitch. It really was starting to wear.

Taylor had told him to sell the ranch.

The thought killed him.

But trying to figure out a way to hold on to it and regain control was almost as brutal. He'd crossed Miranda, and she was going to make him pay. And pay. Any thoughts of a peaceful settlement had gone out the window when she'd tried to buy Jancey's part of the property without discussing the matter with him. She'd actually tried to pit sister against brother, which was sick, especially when they were the only members left of their immediate family.

But if he sold, after he got over the anguish of having let Miranda win once and for all... of having lost the family ranch to the woman who'd tried to ruin both him and Jancey...he could start fresh.

A fresh start sounded good. Really good.

Could he let go? Did letting Miranda win make him a coward?

The working-ranch part of the vacation packages was becoming more and more popular. The accountant's report, which put Miranda in the clear as far as her fiscal honesty went—damn it all—supported that. If he sold—to anyone but her, because there was no way he was doing that—she'd lose those packages, because she lost access to the property if it sold. There was no transfer of usage.

Cole stopped drying off and studied his reflection, a thoughtful frown drawing his eyebrows together. He lost. She lost.

When Jancey came home that evening, he broached the subject. "What if we sold the ranch?"

"To Miranda? No way." She picked up her steak knife and started sawing on the T-bone.

"Not to Miranda."

She put down the knife. "Then to who?"

"Anyone. Just to keep it out of Miranda's hands, and to keep her from having use of the property."

Jancey's mouth opened. Closed again. Then she shook her head. "I don't want to sell."

"It would hurt Miranda's pocketbook."

"For a while." She set down her fork and gave Cole a pleading look. "The land is all we have that's from our family. It's our heritage."

"Which makes us miserable."

"No. *She* makes us miserable." She cocked her head at him. "Is this so that you can go after Taylor?"

"Go after?"

"She's not coming back." Before Cole could

reply, Jancey went on. "She says it's important to be independent. Then you can control your life."

"Which is how she ended up here on the farm, living in a ramshackle building."

Jancey nodded. "Good point."

"I care for Taylor," he said simply. It was ridiculous to pretend he didn't. Not when he had this many sleepless nights under his belt.

"But not enough to go after her?"

"I think I have to wait until she's ready to find a middle ground."

"How long do you think that will take?" Jancey asked softly.

"That's the million-dollar question."

And he was half-afraid of the answer. Had the city reclaimed her? Was she once again working megahour weeks and not taking care of herself? Worse yet, had she met a guy? A city guy? One she had a lot in common with?

Those were the questions that kept him up at night. The questions that had him very, very close to giving up his harvest and heading to Seattle to see if he could claim what he knew in his soul was his.

IT WAS FUNNY how the life Taylor had so carefully crafted prior to getting laid off from

Stratford now felt oddly empty. The aftermath of Cole.

She loved Seattle, was glad to be back… but it didn't feel the same. And she almost felt angry about it—as if she'd made a pact with herself, then fallen short of fulfilling it. She was back. She was supposed to love it. She wasn't supposed to wonder if Cole had turned the bunkhouse into a grain bin as he'd once threatened. Or if the rabbits under the floorboards had litters of little rabbits. Or if Chucky had eaten Cole's other boot.

She shouldn't be wondering how Jancey was enjoying college. Or missing the girl as much as she did.

Life went on.

And on.

A guy at her firm was hitting on her. He was attractive and personable and when she'd looked him up, she couldn't find anything about him that wasn't admirable. But just like her life in Seattle, something was missing.

He wasn't Cole.

She didn't know why she finally settled on her sofa and dialed her mother's number, other than the fact that they hadn't talked since she'd first returned to Seattle. Maybe she needed to hear someone tell her again how lucky she was to escape that rural hell.

The phone rang twice and then Jess answered in his almost too-quiet voice.

"Hi, Jess. Taylor. Is my mom there?"

"She's marketing."

"Oh. Well, tell her…" The words trailed off as she realized she didn't know exactly what she wanted to tell her other than that she'd called. "Jess?"

"Yeah?"

"Can I ask you a personal question? You don't have to answer."

"Sure."

"How much did you give up to be with my mom?"

"I don't quite follow. I really didn't have anything."

"Not material things…how much of yourself? Your goals and the plans you'd made for your future."

"I gave up nothing."

Taylor waited a beat, and when the phone remained silent, she said, "Are you living the life you would have lived without her?"

"No. This is different."

Different. Not worse. Different.

"I changed my goals when I met your mom.

They're still *my* goals." He spoke in a musing way, making Taylor think that he'd never truly analyzed the situation, but instead had adapted as things in his life changed.

"Mom always told me to be independent. I guess that made me think that in your relationship…" *You were the loser*. "Uh, never mind. Too personal. I apologize."

"Don't apologize, Taylor. We make the decisions together. Sometimes she goes commando on me, but I wear her down. I'm the water. She's the rock."

A true artist's answer.

"I made assumptions."

"Don't we all. You haven't been around us enough to know how things are between us. They're good. I'm happy. If I wasn't, I would have walked long ago."

"I can't believe we're having this conversation," Taylor said.

"Which means you must have needed to have it."

She snorted softly. "Maybe so."

Only instead of making her situation clearer, Jess's revelation muddied it further. And then to make things worse, she did a terrible thing— she started looking for jobs in Montana again. Just…looking.

She wasn't that serious…or at least that was what she told herself. Cole hadn't contacted her since she'd left—not that she'd contacted him, but she'd had the last word when she kissed him. The ball was in his court. And he hadn't done anything with it. That was why the job search wasn't that serious.

But she was curious. Were there options out there? Could she get different training? There were pluses to living in a more rural environment, after all, or there wouldn't be so many people relocating to the state. There were definite financial pluses. The cost of living in the city was eating her alive.

The culmination of her craziness came when Carolyn dropped by and noticed the Montana job search she'd left up on the screen before answering the door.

"This is serious," Carolyn said.

"Just curious." Which was why she could feel herself blush a guilty pink.

"Uh-huh." Carolyn picked up the laptop and carried it to the sofa while Taylor got the wine, cursing herself for not shutting the lid. "Most of these don't pay that well."

"I can rent an apartment for less than a zillion dollars a month." Not that she was going to.

"Do you want to go back?"

"I just have to keep my options open in case the temp job doesn't pan out. I'm looking for jobs here, too."

"You know that if this job ends that you and Max can move in with me."

Taylor's eyebrows rose as she tried to imagine the two of them, plus one giant cat, maneuvering around Carolyn's tiny studio. "I, uh…"

Carolyn grinned at her. "I'm moving in four months when my lease expires. I already have the new place nailed down. It took a lot of orchestration and luck, but I will soon have a lot more room."

"Congratulations! Now you'll have room for all your shoes."

"I didn't say that," Carolyn said with a sniff. "But I'm serious about the offer. I'd thought about inviting Bradley to move in, and he's kind of hinted at it, but…" Carolyn made a fluttering gesture with one hand.

"You're not feeling it?"

Carolyn shook her head. "I'm feeling it, but for once in my life I'm not rushing it."

"Good to know that I have a safety net." Really good. But not enough to still the anxiety that simmered away just under the surface.

Carolyn adjusted the laptop so that they could

both see it. "Now, let's see what's out there for you—or someone very much like you."

They shared a bottle of wine as they filled out an application for a school district budget manager, and for the answers that had started out being silly, they'd gone back and changed to serious.

"Are you going to send it?" Carolyn asked as she topped off their glasses.

Taylor held up her finger, gave it a theatrical twirl, then stabbed the apply button. "Yes."

Carolyn smiled. "Let's see what else is out there. You never know…maybe there's something for me in the great outdoors."

"Uh, have you ever been outdoors?"

"The cruise to Alaska. We stood on deck many times." Carolyn made a face at her, then continued scrolling through the sites on her tablet.

"You know that if I get called for an interview, I won't take it."

"Of course not," Carolyn said. "We're just doing this for fun."

"Good." Taylor took a long drink of wine. "I just wanted to make certain we're on the same page."

Carolyn slanted a sideways look at her. "Although…"

Taylor let out a sigh. "He hasn't called or texted. It's done."

Carolyn pushed the hair back from her forehead. "And you feel…?"

"Like I made the only choice I could have made. The only logical choice. The choice I told him I would make before we started sleeping together. I was totally up front and he was good with it."

"What happened?" Carolyn's expression shifted as she connected the dots. "Oh, no… you didn't tell him that stuff about compromise?"

Taylor closed her eyes and pulled in a breath. "I believed that stuff about compromise."

"And now?"

"If it was true, I wouldn't feel this miserable right now."

TAYLOR WENT OUT for a run late Friday afternoon after getting off work, and when she got back, a message was waiting for her on her phone. Not her mother, as she'd expected, but Jancey. A simple "Call me."

Taylor's heart started to thump as she hit the redial. Had something happened to Cole? To Chucky? Jancey answered instantly.

"Taylor. Thanks for getting back to me." The

girl sounded stressed, but not Cole's-in-the-hospital stressed.

"Not a problem. Is everything okay?" As in, did her heart need to be beating this rapidly?

"Cole's talking about selling the ranch."

Taylor almost dropped the phone. "No."

"I know. I think he's doing it to be with you."

"Um…" Taylor sank down to the sofa as guilt washed over her. She'd told him to sell and now he was going to do it? "I'm not certain what to say." Total understatement.

"There's got to be another way, Taylor. I don't want to lose the ranch."

Taylor cleared her throat, then leaned forward to rest one elbow on her knee and prop her forehead with her hand as she stared down at the floor. "What reason did he give for wanting to sell?"

"He said that it'll keep Miranda from being able to use the land for the working ranch packages. I guess she's making a lot of money from those, and this would stop her."

"That means you guys are making money, too."

"I guess."

"He said he wanted to sell." Taylor was still having trouble wrapping her mind around that.

"Can you talk to him? Please, Taylor. Let

him know that it isn't the ranch keeping you guys apart."

"I'll, uh, see what I can do."

"I would really appreciate it." Jancey's voice cracked, making Taylor's heart squeeze. The girl loved her ranch.

Taylor ended the call and slumped backward without asking how Max was doing. Cole was talking about selling the ranch. Whatever the reason was, it was his business. Totally his business…except that she'd suggested it to him, and now Jancey was beside herself.

Regardless of what Jancey thought, she couldn't just shove her nose back into Cole's business. She'd lost that right. She *would* call once she felt ready—it wasn't as if he'd sell the ranch overnight—and maybe together they could come up with a way to help Jancey deal with whatever decision he made.

Jancey is never going to be okay with the decision. It'll be a regret she harbors forever… and maybe Cole will feel the same.

Not her fault, but she had a finger in this.

Call. Get it over with. Do what you promised and move on.

She started to search for Cole's number, then put the phone down again.

She wasn't ready to hear his voice. Wasn't ready to be dismissed.

She had unknowingly lost a big part of herself when she'd walked away. Returned to what she thought she'd wanted—the city and the lifestyle that, by all rights, should have made her feel exactly the way it had before she'd taken refuge on her grandfather's farm.

You love Cole and it's tearing you apart.

Oh, yeah. No argument there.

Taylor paced to the window. The view wasn't as beautiful as the one from her former apartment building, where her name had already moved two spots up the list, but it should have brought on a similar feeling of contentment. Instead she had the oddest feeling that she no longer belonged. Her city was rejecting her.

So where did that leave her?

With a very short weekend to do what she had to do.

CHAPTER SIXTEEN

IT WAS WELL after midnight when the crunch of gravel under tires woke Cole. He got out of bed and pushed back the curtain, wondering who the hell was driving into the place that late at night. His jaw dropped when he caught sight of the Z pulling to a stop next to the bunkhouse.

The door opened and Taylor stepped out, looking like something out of a dream.

What the hell?

He jammed his legs into his jeans and was out of his room and halfway down the hall before he went back and got a shirt. Taylor was letting herself into the bunkhouse when he opened the kitchen door.

"Taylor?" His voice sounded overly loud in the quiet night.

She started and then turned toward the house. Toward him. He snapped a couple of more fasteners on his shirt as she approached.

"What are you doing here?"

"I was planning to spend the night in the

bunkhouse if you haven't turned it into a grain bin. There's a softball tournament in the Eagle Valley. No rooms in town."

He walked toward her, keeping his gaze on her, half wondering if maybe this was all some kind of a hallucination. A walking dream. Maybe he'd wanted her back so badly that he was imagining this.

"No. *Why* are you here?"

She rolled her neck. "Do you want to know how many times I asked myself that question as I drove?" She met his gaze as if those few words explained everything—a seven-hour drive, no warning, her purpose in being there. "We need to talk. I wanted to do it in person. I have to be back by tomorrow night."

His heart beat a hard rhythm against his ribs. "What are we going to talk about?"

"Selling the ranch."

Wild hopes dissipated as he realized what the deal was. "Jancey's been in contact?"

"Yes."

"Taylor…"

"If you're going to send me packing, do it in the morning, when I can drive more safely. I really hadn't expected to not be able to get a room. That motel is a thorn in my side. Robberies. No vacancies."

"I'm not sending you packing."

She came up the steps to stand beside him, looking exhausted and so damned beautiful. "Not yet anyway?"

He opened his mouth to say, "Not ever," but closed it again. It wasn't time. He needed more information before he gave away too much. Although, what would it matter? It wasn't as if he could be tied in knots any tighter. And the way Taylor was looking at him, so open and unguarded… Maybe it was because of exhaustion.

Or maybe it was something more.

She gave him a faint smile. Tentative. Beautiful. "I feel good being back."

The simple words rocked him. He stared at her, realized he was frowning and did his best to clear his forehead. Then he held out his hand. Slowly Taylor lifted hers and settled her fingers in his palm. It felt right. He closed his hand, and she squeezed his palm as if drawing strength.

"Come on inside." He led her into the house, and she let go of his hand to go sit at the kitchen table.

"Could you make me a cup of coffee?"

"You don't think it'll keep you up?"

"I'm hoping it'll keep me from passing out."

"Want to talk in the morning?"

"It is morning. I want to talk now."

She waited until he'd turned toward the sink to say, "I have an idea about the ranch."

"What's that?" As he scooped coffee into the filter, he fought the feeling that he was going to turn around and find her gone.

"I think we should try to sell the ranch to someone who will in turn sell it back to you."

He stopped pouring water into the coffee machine, wondering if he'd heard right. "Come again?"

She waited for him to finish pouring and sit down before saying, "If you sold to someone who sold it back to you before capital gains kicked in, that would negate Miranda's claim on use of the property, right?"

"It would. I just don't know anyone with that kind of money."

"I know someone."

He frowned at her.

"It wouldn't be free. You'd have to cover all the sales costs and buy it back for more than you sold it for, which is what would make it worth the guy's time and money, but you'd get it back without Miranda."

"How much more?"

"Maybe ten grand. Maybe a little more."

"Ten thousand dollars to rid the place of Miranda?"

She let out a short breath as the coffee started dripping noisily into the carafe. "Sounds pretty reasonable, doesn't it?" She reached for his hand, and he turned it over as they made contact so that they were palm to palm. Cole swallowed as he worked to process what she was telling him, along with the fact that she was there. Touching him. Connecting with him.

Acting as if she'd been as torn up about parting as he'd been.

"I'll come up with ten grand."

"I think we can swing this. The idea struck at about Ellensburg, and I spent a good part of the drive discussing the ins and outs with people I know." She smiled a little. "Late-night calls, but my associates keep late hours. It kept me awake."

"Wait." Cole's grip tightened on her fingers. "You started driving before you thought of this?"

"I did."

Cole felt himself go still. "Why?"

"I love you."

And there they were. The words he'd wanted

to hear. He let go of her fingers to lean toward her, sliding his hand behind her neck and easing her closer until her forehead rested against his. "I love you, too. Haven't been able to find a cure."

"That's what Jancey insinuated."

She met his lips, and before the kiss deepened, he pulled her from her chair, onto his lap, and she melted into him. His arms tightened, and he held on to the woman he'd truly thought he'd never hold again.

"You really have to be back tomorrow?" he whispered against her skin before kissing her forehead and then resting his cheek on top of her hair. Her scent filled his lungs. His world was complete.

"I do."

He tamped down the disappointment. She was here. She loved him.

She angled back, bringing a hand up to stroke the side of his face. "I want to talk about other things. Compromises, mainly."

"What about compromises?"

"I'm developing a different take on them. And…my city, my job…it isn't enough anymore. My goals have changed." She looped her hands around his neck, clasping them. "I think we can do this."

"Make a relationship?"

She smiled and brushed her lips against his, and he wanted to haul her off to bed. "We already have one of those. I was talking more about making a life."

He was about to answer when the sound of clicking toenails on linoleum brought his head up. Max sauntered into the room with Chucky close behind him, followed by a yawning Jancey, who stopped in her tracks when she caught sight of Taylor sitting on Cole's lap, her arms wrapped around his neck.

"Uh…" She closed her mouth, then smiled as if she'd just accomplished some major coup. "I heard voices. Thought you left the television on." The smile became a satisfied smirk. "Hey… you guys can say thank you, if you want."

Cole met Taylor's eyes before she slid off his lap onto the chair next to him. Max sidled closer, acting as if she'd never left. Taylor bent down and hefted the cat onto her lap. He butted his head against her chin and started purring as Jancey headed for the coffeepot, Chucky at her heels. "I'm pouring. Is everyone in?"

"Yes. I think we're all in," Cole said.

Jancey glanced over her shoulder. "And the ranch?"

Cole leaned back in his chair, feeling more

relaxed and happy than he'd felt in weeks. "I think we'll keep the ranch." And before she could say anything else, he took Taylor's hand in his and said simply, "Thank you."

EPILOGUE

"YOU GUYS TOOK good care of this place." Karl gave an approving nod as he stopped at the neatly organized and much-reduced boneyard.

"Least I could do," Cole said.

They continued on to the barn, where Cole showed Karl how he'd upgraded the old harness room for seed storage, making it as vermin-proof as possible, and then on to the bunkhouse, which he and Taylor had made cozy for those times that she wanted to visit her grandfather.

"I like this," Karl said, rocking back on his heels as his gaze swept over the place. "Elise can stay here, too, when she comes to visit with that beau of hers."

After his sister had come to grips with her grief and started putting her life back on track, she'd released Karl from his promise to live nearby and had even agreed to move onto the farm if she needed family to be close again. "Wish she'd agreed to that in the first place," Karl muttered, then catching sight of Taylor coming out of the house, he added, "or maybe not."

"I'm going with maybe not," Cole answered.

Had Karl not moved, then Cole wouldn't have met Taylor and they wouldn't be starting their new lives on the Bryan Ranch. His Bryan Ranch, with no ties to Miranda's hoity-toity operation. He and Taylor had torn down the sign reading Bryan Working Ranch and replaced it with one that showed the brand—the Quarter Circle Slash B—which he owned and Miranda had no right to.

She was still his neighbor, but all the legal t's were crossed and i's dotted. She was out of his life. And the improvements made to his ranch were all his.

Damn but he loved a happy ending.

"Are you sure you want to keep farming the place?" Karl asked as Taylor approached. "Lots of miles between the ranch and here."

"Taylor and I have a task calendar worked out. We'd like to try, at least for this year." He held out his hand as Taylor approached, and she slid her fingers into his.

"Talking calendars?" she asked.

Karl smiled at her. "Your favorite topic."

She laughed. "I made you a copy, so you'll

know where we are at all times and what we're doing—at least for farm season."

Having made the leap to rural life, Taylor had immersed herself. She did a lot of tractor work during the day, and three days a week, she did books for a farm accounting firm in anticipation of eventually hanging out her own shingle.

"The sandwiches are ready," Jancey called from the porch. "Chucky didn't get them this time."

"Be right there, sweetheart." Karl headed off across the driveway, while Cole and Taylor followed at a slower pace.

"I think this is all going to work out," he said, turning to face her. Taylor lifted her eyebrows and smiled. Then she reached up, took his face in her hands and answered him in the best way possible.

"Yes, babe. It's totally going to work."

* * * * *

Be sure to check out the other books in the
BRODYS OF LIGHTNING CREEK
Miniseries by Jeannie Watt!

TO TEMPT A COWGIRL
TO KISS A COWGIRL
TO COURT A COWGIRL
MOLLY'S MR. WRONG

All available now from
Harlequin Superromance.

And look for the next
BRODYS OF LIGHTNING CREEK *story*
from Jeannie Watt, coming in 2018!

Get 2 Free Books,
Plus 2 Free Gifts—
just for trying the Reader Service!

Get 2 Free Books,
Plus 2 Free Gifts—
just for trying the Reader Service!

YES! Please send me 2 FREE Harlequin Presents® novels and my 2 FREE gifts (gifts are worth about $10 retail). After receiving them, if I don't wish to receive any more books, I can return the shipping statement marked "cancel." If I don't cancel, I will receive 6 brand-new novels every month and be billed just $4.55 each for the regular-print edition or $5.55 each for the larger-print edition in the U.S., or $5.49 each for the regular-print edition or $5.99 each for the larger-print edition in Canada. That's a saving of at least 11% off the cover price! It's quite a bargain! Shipping and handling is just 50¢ per book in the U.S. and 75¢ per book in Canada.* I understand that accepting the 2 free books and gifts places me under no obligation to buy anything. I can always return a shipment and cancel at any time. The free books and gifts are mine to keep no matter what I decide.

Please check one: ☐ Harlequin Presents® Regular-Print   ☐ Harlequin Presents® Larger-Print
                               (106/306 HDN GLWL)   (176/376 HDN GLWL)

Name _____ (PLEASE PRINT) _____

Address _____ Apt. # _____

City _____ State/Prov. _____ Zip/Postal Code _____

Signature (if under 18, a parent or guardian must sign) _____

Mail to the **Reader Service:**
IN U.S.A.: P.O. Box 1341, Buffalo, NY 14240-8531
IN CANADA: P.O. Box 603, Fort Erie, Ontario L2A 5X3

Want to try two free books from another series?
Call 1-800-873-8635 or visit www.ReaderService.com.

* Terms and prices subject to change without notice. Prices do not include applicable taxes. Sales tax applicable in N.Y. Canadian residents will be charged applicable taxes. Offer not valid in Quebec. This offer is limited to one order per household. Books received may not be as shown. Not valid for current subscribers to Harlequin Presents books. All orders subject to approval. Credit or debit balances in a customer's account(s) may be offset by any other outstanding balance owed by or to the customer. Please allow 4 to 6 weeks for delivery. Offer available while quantities last.

Your Privacy—The Reader Service is committed to protecting your privacy. Our Privacy Policy is available online at www.ReaderService.com or upon request from the Reader Service.

We make a portion of our mailing list available to reputable third parties that offer products we believe may interest you. If you prefer that we not exchange your name with third parties, or if you wish to clarify or modify your communication preferences, please visit us at www.ReaderService.com/consumerschoice or write to us at Reader Service Preference Service, P.O. Box 9062, Buffalo, NY 14240-9062. Include your complete name and address.

HP17R2

Get 2 Free Books,
Plus 2 Free Gifts—
just for trying the Reader Service!

Get 2 Free Books,
Plus 2 Free Gifts—
just for trying the *Reader Service!*

HARLEQUIN
INTRIGUE

READERSERVICE.COM

Manage your account online!

- Review your order history
- Manage your payments
- Update your address

We've designed the Reader Service website just for you.

Enjoy all the features!

- Discover new series available to you, and read excerpts from any series.
- Respond to mailings and special monthly offers.
- Browse the Bonus Bucks catalog and online-only exculsives.
- Share your feedback.

Visit us at:

ReaderService.com

RS16R